T0205114

**Also available from Delores Fossen
and Canary Street Press**

To see the complete list of titles available from Delores Fossen,
please visit deloresfossen.com.

DELORES FOSSEN

COWBOYING UP

CANARY STREET PRESS

CANARY
STREET
PRESS™

Recycling programs
for this product may
not exist in your area.

ISBN-13: 978-1-335-14695-3

Cowboying Up

Canary Street Press
22 Adelaide St. West, 41st Floor
Toronto, Ontario M5H 4E3, Canada
CanaryStPress.com

Printed in U.S.A.

COWBOYING UP

CHAPTER ONE

LIEUTENANT COLONEL CAL DONNELLY had flown dangerous missions in his F-22 Raptor. Missions where his
own life and the lives of others had been on the line.
Missions that hadn't cranked up as much adrenaline
and concern as this visit was causing.

Ironic, since this visit wasn't to some hot zone where
he could be shot down by enemy fire but rather to an office on Main Street in his hometown of Emerald Creek,
Texas.

Cal pulled into the parking lot of the town's Old
West–style saloon, Saddle and Sip, and he stopped the
rental truck he'd picked up at the airport. Since it was
barely ten in the morning, he had the lot to himself,
which suited him just fine. He didn't want anyone to
see him as he definitely wasn't in the mood for any
meet and greets.

It was usually nice to feel welcomed back home when
he was on leave, but he wanted to delay those welcomes—
and other *things*—until he'd gotten his footing.

Whenever the heck that might be.

Cal dreaded the gut-punching one-month anniversary that he'd have to face tomorrow. He cursed Dear
John letters, especially living, breathing ones when he
was the messenger and deliverer of such a letter. And

he especially cursed sneaking off to the creek and falling off a broken tree limb there when he'd been eight.

Without that fall, Cal wouldn't have smacked his head on a protruding limestone rock, plummeted into the water and nearly drowned. Then, his best friend, Noah Granger, wouldn't have had to save him.

Cal was thankful for the saving. Thankful to Noah for dragging his semiconscious body out of the water, but at age eight, the act had become a life-pact. An agreement that Cal would always owe Noah, well, pretty much anything Noah wanted. That was dramatic stuff for kids who hadn't yet learned how to add fractions or write compound sentences, but they'd both embraced it as the only way to mark such an event.

Over the years, that life-pact had meant favors. Lots and lots of them. With Noah being the favor requester and Cal being the favor provider. It had shaped their friendship, bonded them, and very often had made Noah a pain in the ass.

Like now, for instance.

At a time when Cal's mind was already weighed down even more than pulling nine Gs in his F-22, here he was going to deliver that Dear John in person to Charlotte Wilson, a woman who deserved better. She at least deserved to hear it not from him but from the source.

That source being Noah.

But Noah was thousands of miles away, heading to another deployment, and had decided he couldn't squeeze in a leave home to spill the bad news to Charlotte. That he was ending their on-again, off-again relationship that'd started in eighth grade.

Since Noah, Charlotte and Cal were all now thirty-six, that on-ing and off-ing had been happening for twenty-three years. Still, Charlotte hadn't moved on in all that time, so that told Cal she was all for the relationship continuing.

Yeah, this visit was a ballbuster, all right.

Cal checked his surroundings in the parking lot, and when he didn't see anyone nearby, he got out of the truck. He'd purposely not worn his uniform, something that worked better than a flashing, pointing neon sign to draw attention to him. Instead, he'd opted for jeans, boots and a Stetson, which hopefully would allow him to blend into this cowboy town where that clothing combo was standard wear.

Once, during some evasion training maneuvers, Cal had had to practice running and sneaking around, and he put that training to use now. Ducking in and out of alleys, he threaded his way to his destination on the south end of Main Street.

Despite the fairly early hour and the fact that it was only early April and not even summer yet, it was blisteringly hot. That was the norm for this part of Texas that really only had two seasons. Eleven months of heat and maybe a month of cooler temps. Clearly, the cooler temps weren't prevailing today because he'd worked up a sweat by the time he spotted the law office.

Such that it was.

It was a converted Victorian cottage that had to be the worst shade of yellow in the history of that particular color. Not sunshine, not mustard, not lemon. More like baby puke. The office was the polar opposite of the law firm of Carson, Elder and Carson housed in the shiny silver granite building just up the street. Heck, Charlotte's law office didn't even have a fancy lawyerly name. The old shingle sign above the bay window just said *Attorney*.

There was a blue Ford Fusion and a rust-scabbed Chevy truck parked right outside the office, and Cal hoped that meant Charlotte didn't have a client. When he'd texted her an hour earlier from the airport to say he needed to see her, she'd said she would be in her office and that she didn't have any appointments. He was hoping that was still true because he didn't want to delay this Dear John. Best to deliver it, help Charlotte cope in any way he could and then move on to his next chore.

Going home.

That'd be ballbuster two of the morning.

Since there were several people on the opposite side of the street, Cal quickly glanced inside the large bay window of the law office, and he immediately spotted his target. Charlotte. Not at one of the two desks in the open floor plan but rather standing in the small foyer with her back to him.

She wasn't alone. There was an elderly man across from her, and even though it'd been a while since Cal had seen him, this was Emerald Creek with little to no degrees of separation. The guy was Clark Gable Becker, who bore absolutely no resemblance to his namesake. He was more of a Scrooge, a crotchety rancher who owned the property to the west of Cal's family ranch, Saddlebrook.

At the sound of the bell jingling over the door that Cal opened, Charlotte whirled around to face him, her long dark brown hair swishing with the movement, and her blue eyes going wide. Not exactly wide with surprise, but Cal couldn't figure out the meaning behind the look she was giving him.

"Cal," she greeted, her tone overly enthusiastic and breathy, and she hurried to him.

Not that she had to hurry far. Only a few steps. Then, she threw her arms around him, pulling him to her.

Definitely some overenthusiasm.

Charlotte and he had always been friendly toward each other, friendly in a sort of way of her being his best friend's woman, but Cal had never remembered her greeting him like this. Maybe because she sensed he was there to deliver the bad news about the breakup? Maybe.

But it seemed more than that. Charlotte looked at him as if he were the answer to her prayers.

"Cal," she repeated in a rather loud voice. Then she put her mouth directly against his ear and whispered, "Pretend you're my fiancé. *Please.*"

Of all the things Cal had thought she might say, that wasn't one of them. "Huh?" he managed.

"Please," she muttered again. She kept her arms around him but pulled back enough to meet him eye to eye. "And forgive me for this."

She kissed him. A full-on-the-mouth kiss. The kind of scorching, welcome-home kiss a person might indeed give a fiancé. She tasted like tea and gingerbread. Smelled like Ivory soap and sex.

Well, maybe not actual sex.

But a certain part of him went straight in that bad direction.

Even though this kiss was obviously some kind of

pretense, Cal felt the heat from her mouth on his. Didn't want to. But he felt it anyway. And that's why he was buzzing a little when she finally pulled back.

Looping her arm around his waist, she turned back to face Mr. Becker. "This is my fiancé I was just telling you about," Charlotte gushed, and the gushing was apparently meant for the man.

Mr. Becker didn't have a no-possible-way reaction, something that plenty of people would have had. Many folks knew that Charlotte and Noah had been together forever, but Becker wasn't exactly the social, gossiping type. More like a mean-as-a-snake recluse who probably wouldn't have paid any attention to the romances in the town. Or anything else happening in town for that matter.

Becker squinted his watery left eye that was the color of pond scum. "You're one of those Donnelly boys," he grumbled to Cal.

The man hadn't exactly used a flattering tone for Cal's surname and siblings. Probably because of the squabbles that'd gone on between the man and Cal's dad, Derek, over the past four decades or so. Cal was betting the squabbles had continued even though his brothers, Egan and Blue, now had the reins of the ranch.

"I am," he verified. "I'm Cal, the second-oldest one."

"You're the one who's not around much," he muttered, and that seemed to inject a smidge of pleasantness in the man's sourpuss mood. "You're home on leave or something?"

Cal nearly divulged the *or something*, but that could possibly open up a conversation he wasn't ready to have.

Not before he spoke to his family first, anyway. So he settled for a nod.

Charlotte tightened her grip on his waist. "Cal's stationed at Eglin AFB, Florida, where he flies fighter jets. He's a superstar in the Air Force and on a fast track to become a general. He's a real hometown hero."

Cal silently did a lot of groaning at her recap of his career. The first part of that was true. The second had once been true. The third was a big-assed lie. He wasn't a hero. He was an asshole who'd put his career ahead of…everything.

Especially ahead of Harper.

At the thought of her name, her image popped into his head. Of course it did. Her image was always there, and once just the sight of her face had fired up every competitive fiber in his body. Now, it avalanched him into grief. Bone-deep, soul-crushing grief.

"Cal came home to help me finalize this deal with you," Charlotte added to Becker. That yanked Cal's attention back to her.

Deal?

Cal tried not to look too surprised especially since Becker had his eyes trained on him as if looking for some kind of proof that he was being scammed. Cal truly hoped it wasn't an actual scam, but clearly there was something that wasn't aboveboard here or Charlotte wouldn't have asked him to pretend he was her fiancé.

Becker made a sound that could have meant anything, and his steely gaze slid to Charlotte's left hand. "Engaged, but you didn't give your intended a ring," the man pointed out.

"We're going ring shopping soon," Charlotte was

quick to say. "Then, I'll post pictures of it all over social media."

Becker's mouth tightened even more, something Cal hadn't thought possible. If it went any tighter, he might crack some teeth. "Social media," he repeated, using that "unidentified fungus" tone. "That's for people with too much time on their hands. I don't even own a computer or one of those so-called phones people carry with them everywhere they go."

That info surprised exactly no one. Cal was reasonably sure the ranch had electricity and indoor plumbing, but those were probably the only modern luxuries that Becker allowed.

"So, is it a deal?" Charlotte asked Becker, snuggling up to Cal even closer, apparently to remind the man that she had a fiancé present.

The silence crawled by. And crawled. And crawled. "Maybe," Becker finally said. "I'll do some more thinking on it and will let you know in a day or two."

Charlotte made a soft groan of disappointment and seemed ready to launch into some kind of argument that would prompt Becker to make a decision here and now, not in a day or two. But the man didn't give her the chance. Becker stepped around them and headed out of the office.

This time her groan wasn't quite so soft, and she muttered some profanity under her breath. "The old coot keeps putting me off," she grumbled, but then looked up at Cal. "By the way, you're a lifesaver. If you hadn't arrived when you did, I'm pretty sure the geezer would have been about to tell me *no*. So thank you for doing this."

"For doing what exactly?" Cal had to ask.

She pulled in a long breath. "I'm trying to buy Becker's ranch, but he has this old-fashioned notion that a single woman shouldn't be owning a ranch or a farm because that's man's work." Charlotte rolled her eyes. "Yes, I could sue him for discrimination, but he'd sell the place to someone—anyone—else out of spite, and his place is perfect for me."

Cal was still confused. Not the part about Becker being a misogynistic jerk. He'd already known that. He was confused about the rest of it. "I didn't know you wanted to own a ranch."

"Oh, I don't," Charlotte was quick to say. "I want the house, barn and the land."

Gone were the groans of disappointment, and there was excitement on her face when she took hold of his hand and practically dragged him toward the desk in the corner.

"My office is in there," she said, tipping her head to one of the two other rooms, "but I prefer being out here." She unrolled a large piece of paper. "I didn't want Mr. Becker to see this because then he'd probably never sell me the ranch. My guess is this sort of thing is also man's work, in his eyes. Added to that, he probably believes the land is sacred or something and should only be used to raise cattle, even though he hasn't raised livestock of any kind in years."

Cal looked at the paper and realized it was some kind of architectural drawing, and while he hadn't been to Becker's ranch since he was a kid, he thought he recognized the layout. The large three-story house that Becker's ancestors had built over a hundred years ago and the equally large barn. In this design plan, both the barn and the house had updated exteriors, and the person who'd drawn this had added what appeared to be walking trails, sitting areas under trees and even a pond.

The name at the top of the drawing was *Port in a Storm*.

"What is this?" he had to ask.

Her eyes lit up. Heck, so did her whole face. "A sanctuary for veterans. Not just those with physical injuries but those just needing a place of respite. Or just a vacation. It'll be a Care B and B with a spa," she added, tapping the barn. "I've already got a physical therapist, a masseuse and a counselor on board in case their services are needed. A personal trainer, too, for those wanting to stay in or get back in shape."

Charlotte was talking so fast that it took Cal's mind a moment to catch up with all she was saying. And why she was saying it.

Or rather why she wanted to do this.

"This is about Noah's brother," Cal muttered.

"It is," she was quick to verify.

Sergeant Alden Granger had been on his first special ops deployment when he'd been injured in a bombing three years ago. He'd broken nearly every bone in his body and had required many surgeries to fix all that and reconstruct his face. That meant he'd been in and out of the hospital and various recovery centers all this time.

"Alden is within a month or less of being discharged from his current facility, and he doesn't want to move back home. Between you and me, he doesn't want to be a burden to his dad, but he told his father that he needed a place, even if only a room, that he could call his own."

Cal could understand that. He enjoyed staying at his family's ranch, but he had a cabin on the grounds in case his family got to be a bit too much.

"I'm guessing Alden didn't want to just get a place in town on his own?" Cal asked.

She shook her head. "He wanted the camaraderie of being around other vets. Plus, this will become a job for him. The plan is for Alden to eventually become a peer counselor and caretaker of the place," Charlotte explained. "His dad is fully on board with that."

Cal had to mentally pause again to absorb all of what she was saying. Of course, Alden and Noah's widower dad, Taggert, would want his wounded son nearby. Taggert was a good man who loved his kids and had to be hopeful that Alden could rebuild his life here.

"This project is about your Uncle Rob, too," Cal muttered. He slid his gaze from the plans to her.

She verified that with a nod, and Cal saw the swirl of emotions in her eyes. Her paternal uncle had been a pseudodad to Charlotte after her own father walked out on his family, and it'd crushed Charlotte, again, when Rob, a military veteran, had been injured in a car accident. He'd never recovered and, like Alden, had been moved from one facility to another—none of them stellar—before finally passing away from pneumonia. He'd been just thirty-six, the same age Charlotte was now.

"I don't need funding," Charlotte went on after she cleared her throat. "I've gotten a lot of investors already, including Taggert and my mother. Especially my mother, who thinks this will be a great addition to the town. There's also some staggering amounts of money from a couple of foundations, and I'm using the trust fund my grandmother left me. Because of the terms of her will, I'm just now getting it."

Noah had mentioned that trust fund. Sizable, Noah had claimed, and it obviously was if it would help pay for something like this.

"Instead of pretending I'm your fiancé, Becker might have sold you the place if Taggert asked him," Cal remarked.

She was quick to shake her head. "Taggert said there's bad blood between Becker and him. Something to do with Becker accusing Taggert of lowballing him on the sale of some cattle. Mind you, that was before either of us were born, but Taggert warned me that Becker could hold a grudge."

"He can," Cal had to agree.

"Apparently, Becker dislikes my mother as well. That has to do with her being the wrong political party."

Cal frowned. "Isn't she an Independent?"

"Yes, but Becker says that's a cop-out way of trying to please everybody and not pleasing anyone. I'm one of the few people in the county Becker isn't pissed at." She paused. "He will be, once he sells me the place and I create Port in a Storm. That's why it has to stay hush-hush until he agrees to sell. Thankfully, he needs the money since he's behind in the taxes."

Again, not a surprise since the ranch wasn't exactly operational. "Any idea where Becker will go?"

She shrugged, then frowned. "I'm not sure. And yes, part of me feels guilty for displacing a former rancher from his family land, but like I said, this place is perfect for Port in a Storm, and it'll put Alden close to his dad."

It would, but that led Cal to another thought. "Noah doesn't know anything about this."

"No." Charlotte smiled again. "He's going to be so excited. He's coming home this week, and I plan on telling him then."

Crap. It was time for him to do his messenger duties. But before he could get a word out, Charlotte continued.

"Of course, I hope by the time Noah gets here, Becker will have already sold me the place. Then we can celebrate...and deal with my mother."

That put Cal's messenger on hold. "Deal with Izzie? What's wrong with her?"

"Nothing. Well, nothing except a starry-eyed notion." She paused a heartbeat. "She and Taggert are dating, and I guess things have gotten serious. My mother is convinced Taggert's going to ask her to marry him."

Cal was sure he blinked. Charlotte's mom had been divorced for over twenty years, and this was the first Cal was hearing about Izzie dating Taggert, much less marrying him. Obviously, the gossip mill wasn't as efficient as it usually was because his Grammy Effie and the ranch's cook, Maybell, normally emailed him about such things.

"Anyway," she went on, "my mom wants to marry Taggert, and she wants to make it a double wedding with Noah and me."

Cal mentally repeated his *crap*, adding some much stronger profanity. "Are they engaged? Does Taggert want to marry your mother?" Because he was having a hard time seeing them as a couple. Izzie was more into fashion and status, and Taggert, well, wasn't. He was as cowboy as they came.

Charlotte shrugged. "Taggert and my mom got close when we were all working to get the investors for Port in a Storm."

Ah, that would do it. Taggert would be ever so thankful to anyone trying to help Alden. Still, if Taggert hadn't actually proposed, then it was possible a wedding between the two wasn't on the horizon.

Especially a double wedding that included Noah and Charlotte.

That was Cal's cue to spill what he'd come to spill, but again when he opened his mouth, Charlotte interrupted him.

"Again, keep all of this quiet for now," she reminded him. "Then, all can be blabbed from the rooftops, et cetera." She paused, not long enough for him to speak, though, and her eyes met his. "By the way, I'm so sorry about Harper."

That stopped him in his verbal tracks. Of course, he should have expected Harper's name to come up since, like him, Charlotte had known Harper her whole life. Again, no degrees of separation since Charlotte, Harper, Noah and he had started preschool together and had graduated from high school together. Charlotte's path had diverged after that when she'd stayed in Texas and attended law school. Harper, Noah and he had all gone into the military.

And that had set up the god-awful competition.

Always do more. Do better. Outbest each other. It'd been even more fierce between him and Harper since they were both fighter pilots. Or rather had been fighter pilots.

Harper had ended the competition in a really bad

way. She was alive, but her injuries were so serious that she might never recover from them.

"It's just awful what happened to her," Charlotte went on, and with their gazes still locked, she asked a question he was dreading. "Do you know why she did it?"

Cal had plenty of answers as to the *why*, but he couldn't manage to voice any of them. He settled for shaking his head.

Charlotte nodded, sighed and then touched her finger to his arm to rub gently. "Well, I'm sorry." She paused again, sucked in a quick breath. "So, you haven't said. Why did you want to see me?"

That was yet another question he'd been dreading, and there was even more dread now that Charlotte had brought up the m-word.

Marriage.

Cal didn't think he should sugarcoat this. So he opened his mouth and got ready to send Charlotte's life into a serious tailspin.

CHAPTER TWO

CHARLOTTE'S WORRY ROCKETED when she saw that look of dread on Cal's face. "No," she muttered. "Did something happen to Noah? Is he hurt?"

"No," Cal was quick to say. "It's nothing like that."

But he wasn't quick to say anything else. He looked at her as if she were a pressure cooker about to blow, and then he gently took hold of her shoulders. Maybe to be sure they had eye contact, but the contact was already there. What was missing was any explanation to go along with it. And mercy, did she need one because the worst-case scenarios were having a field day in her head.

"Tell me," she demanded when she could take no more.

He cleared his throat. "Noah wanted me to let you know that…he's breaking up with you."

Because what Cal had just said was so unexpected, it took her a moment to grasp it. And Charlotte practically sank to the floor in relief. "Noah's not hurt?" she questioned.

Cal shook his head. "He's fine. He just had to leave earlier than expected on the deployment."

Her legs wobbled more than a little, and she blew out a breath of relief that could have no doubt extinguished all the candles on Mr. Becker's birthday cake—if he were ever to have such an indulgence, that is.

"Good," she managed to say. "Because his father wouldn't be able to deal with another son getting hurt."

"Yes," Cal agreed. He kept staring at her. "Are you okay?"

He thought she was perhaps in shock or something. She wasn't. Nor was she especially surprised now that she'd gotten over what Cal had said. It had been a year since she'd even seen Noah, and while they kept up at least weekly emails, it hadn't been her pipe dream to have a double wedding with Noah's dad and her mom.

"I'm fine," she assured him.

Cal sighed. Not an ordinary sigh, either. It was the sound of a person who didn't believe what they were hearing. He was probably wondering how she could be fine when Noah had been her life for, well, her entire life.

Except he hadn't been.

That was a facade on both Noah's and her parts. Oh, they loved each other, but over the years, it had morphed into something that didn't lead to a double wedding. Or a heated rush to be with each other. Truth was, she'd gotten more out of that pretend kiss with Cal than she had with Noah in a long, long time.

She couldn't tell Cal all of that. She especially couldn't tell him all about the heat-from-the-kiss thing. No way did she want to share that reaction with him since he'd consider it totally inappropriate.

But telling him the rest would mean having a conversation that he might not be ready to hear.

After all, most people in Emerald Creek thought

Noah and she were *the* couple. Smitten since third grade. In love with her holding down the home front while he did the hero thing in the military.

"Charlotte," Cal said, and there was even more concern in his voice. "Are you sure you're okay?" Probably because she'd gone a little glassy-eyed over reliving the past. Best for her to get the conversation moving.

"I'm fine, really. How'd you get stuck being the messenger for this?" she asked, but then stopped, sighed. "This is about that life-pact thing because Noah saved you when you were eight?"

"Yes," he verified.

"Of course," she muttered. "I'll bet you've lost count of the crappy stuff you've had to do because of that." Charlotte didn't wait for further verification. "Like asking Missy, my best friend at the time, to go to the prom with you so we could double-date."

Missy had been a temporary friend, mainly because that had been the phase when Charlotte had been obsessed with Backstreet Boys, Justin Timberlake and makeup. Missy had managed to wrangle tickets to both Backstreet Boys and NSYNC, and she'd had kilo stashes of various face and eye gunk. Unfortunately, Missy liked to discuss boy bands and popular shades of lip gloss so Cal had likely had a very dull night on what should have been a fun rite of passage.

"There have been a few occasions where Noah's played the life-pact card," Cal admitted.

This time she huffed because she figured there'd been a whole lot more than a few. There were likely ones that were military-related that she hadn't even heard about yet.

"You know, both Harper and I were at the creek that day," Charlotte reminded him. "If Noah hadn't pulled you out, one of us would have. So yes, Noah did a good thing, but if he hadn't gotten to you first, your life-pact could have been with Harper or me."

Something changed in his expression, and she instantly knew what. It was the mention of Harper. Yeah, that would do it. There'd never been anything romantic between Harper and Cal so they weren't *the* couple. Instead, they were *the* competition, and Harper had said more than once she wouldn't have excelled as fast and as high in her career if it hadn't been for the rivalry she had with Cal.

A rivalry that had crashed and burned.

Charlotte opened her mouth to try to apologize, but she caught some movement out the window. Cal must have noticed her eyes flicker in the direction of the sidewalk across the street, because he turned and looked, too.

And he immediately cursed.

It wasn't the reaction she'd been expecting since the two people were his brother Blue and his soon-to-be sister-in-law, Marin Galloway, who had the cool job of being a horse whisperer at the Donnellys' sprawling ranch. Even though Blue was still recovering from injuries he'd gotten the previous autumn from a crash landing, he was still his usual friendly self. Ditto for Marin. And Charlotte hadn't caught a whiff of gossip that there'd been some kind of rift between Cal and anyone in his family or anyone who worked at the ranch.

That's why his reaction puzzled her.

Not only did Cal curse, but he also stepped back.

Fast. Moving away from the window and doing his level best to blend into the wall.

"Is, uh, everything okay?" she asked, dropping the plans back on her desk.

"No." He sighed, squeezed his eyes shut a moment and groaned. "Forget you heard me curse."

"Not a chance," Charlotte was quick to inform him. Cal was her friend, and if there was trouble, she wanted to know about it and try to help. "Is everything all right with your dad?"

It was a valid question, since less than a year earlier, his dad had had not one but two serious heart attacks. Serious enough to force him into early retirement. But Cal just shook his head and peered out, watching his brother and Marin stroll down Main Street.

"I just don't want to see them yet," Cal muttered.

That got her attention, too, because Cal fell into that "usual friendly self" category, too. For him to avoid his family meant something was wrong.

"Oh, God," Charlotte blurted, touching her fingers to her mouth that had started to tremble when she'd gotten a bad thought. A really bad one. "Is your sister okay? She didn't get hurt, did she?"

Again, it was a super valid question because his kid sister was an Air Force Combat Rescue Officer, a CRO. It was a highly dangerous job, often performed in equally dangerous locations. Charlotte knew all about that since it was also Noah's chosen career field.

"No. Remi's fine," he assured her.

Good. That was a huge relief. So that left his other brother, Egan. The oldest and the one who was now helping to run the ranch along with still being on active duty. Charlotte knew Egan as well as she did all the Donnellys. Knew Egan's wife, Alana, too, and was well aware that Alana was seven months pregnant. But Charlotte had spoken to Alana only an hour ago when they'd been discussing Alana providing her dietitian services to Port in a Storm, and Alana hadn't mentioned a word about anything being wrong.

"Is this about Harper?" she risked asking, and it was a Texas-sized risk. Any mention of the woman's name would no doubt give Cal a whole lot of jabs of grief.

Maybe even guilt.

She considered telling him that what had happened to Harper wasn't his fault. Charlotte knew Cal well enough to be certain of that. But just because a person wasn't at fault didn't mean they were blameless.

She had to only look at her own situation for proof of that.

Her father had disappeared from her life, and if that wasn't on her shoulders, then Charlotte didn't know who else bore guilt like that.

Great. Now she was getting images from the past that could yank her right under, into a dark pit, and Cal was no doubt right there with her. No way should she have asked about the very person who could land Cal right in that dark pit with her.

"Shit," Cal muttered.

For a moment Charlotte thought he was cursing because of her question. But then she followed his gaze and realized he was looking at the SUV that had gotten caught by the single traffic light on Main Street.

"That's Audrey," he added to his grumble.

Audrey, as in General Audrey Donnelly, his stepmother. Now, this was someone Charlotte didn't know well at all, even though the woman had been married to Cal's dad since Cal was ten years old. That lack of knowing her was because, unlike Cal and his siblings, Audrey rarely made it back to Emerald Creek. At least, that'd been the case before her husband had nearly died from the heart attacks. Charlotte had heard that Audrey was making more visits these days.

"Audrey must know," Cal said under his breath, and he tacked some more profanity onto that.

Know what? was the question that might have popped right out of her mouth, but Charlotte's phone dinged with a text from her mom. Since Izzie knew about her meeting with Becker, Charlotte figured she knew what this was about.

Did the grouch butt agree to the deal?

Sighing, she responded. Not yet. Maybe soon. Fingers crossed.

Izzie answered with a sad-face emoji and a follow-up that had Charlotte groaning. Can't wait for Noah to come home so we can do the double celebration.

"Crud," she grumbled, and that caused Cal to shift his attention back to her. She held up her phone to show him the text. "I'll have to let my mom know about the breakup."

Cal stared at her but didn't say anything for a couple of slowpokey moments. "How are you dealing with the breakup?"

She frowned. "I'll get back to you on that."

But Charlotte suspected she wouldn't be wallowing

in a puddle of sorrow—something that Cal probably thought she would be. Others would think that, too, once word spread.

"I'll be fine," she added when his forehead bunched up with worry. "Just do me a favor and don't mention it to anyone else." She paused. "Don't mention the not-being-my-fiancé, either, if you're anywhere around Mr. Becker." Charlotte glanced at the plans. "So much is riding on Port in a Storm. The sooner we can get it finished, the sooner Alden and Harper can come."

Cal had been glancing at Audrey's SUV as she finally got a green light and drove off, but he did a sort of double take when his attention flew back to Charlotte.

"Harper?" he asked.

Crap. Charlotte hadn't meant to dump that on him without warning. She definitely should have eased into the news. Well, if easing was even possible, that is.

"Yes," she said. "As soon as Port in a Storm is up and running, Harper will be coming home."

Clearly shaken by that news, Cal opened his mouth, closed it and seemed to lose every drop of his usual polished composure.

"Good," he muttered, heading for the door. He repeated his response as if trying to convince himself that was the truth, and he walked out.

CHAPTER THREE

CAL'S SENSE OF dread sure as hell hadn't lessened even though he had one thing checked off his list. He'd delivered the breakup news to Charlotte, and while he'd still need to make sure she was handling it all right, for now he had to do some handling of his own life.

Yeah, there definitely was that sense of dread.

Normally, the drive past the Saddlebrook pastures would fix any crap mood, but that was asking way too much of horses, cows and pretty spring grass. He'd hoped the sight of it would anchor him. No such luck. Anchoring apparently wasn't in the cards for him today, either.

Might never be.

A truly dismal thought that made him want to give himself a kick in his own ass. But that kind of kick required a hell of a lot more resolve than he was feeling at the moment.

He took the turn onto the ranch road, and the house came into view. *Home.* He'd been raised here, and it would always be special to him, but he knew that most people just saw the massive size of the place. White, two stories and with a wraparound porch, it was about sixty feet wide and had around ten thousand square feet inside. That meant it was bigger than some office buildings, and Cal wasn't exactly sure how many rooms it had. *Plenty* was always his dad's answer when he asked.

Since he was already in a pisser of a dark mood, he didn't get the usual images of him and his siblings as kids running and playing in the massive yard. Or riding the ranch's prized Andalusian horses in the pastures. Instead, he got a flash of his mom, of her dying when he was six years old.

She'd died in this home sweet home after losing her battle with cancer. Sometimes, Cal could still recall the sound of her voice. Her scent. Her smile. But not today. Apparently, his mind couldn't head in the direction of those good things. It was lingering on the last glimpse of her too pale, too thin face. A face that, he realized now, was etched with worry not for herself but for what would become of her four young children and her husband.

Cal liked to believe his mom would be damn proud of her kids. They'd all had decorated military careers. Had all excelled. Had lived up to the sky-high standards of the Donnelly name.

He was about to give those standards a proverbial black eye, though.

"Shit," he muttered when he saw what was on the front porch.

Or rather *who* was on it. Pretty much everybody in his gene pool, which meant they either knew he was coming or else this was some kind of impromptu family gathering.

Egan and his megapregnant wife, Alana. Blue and Marin were back from their jaunt into town, too, and they had their adopted seven-year-old son, Leo, with them, who must have been off from school because of some holiday. His Grammy Effie was staying in the shade of the porch with Maybell right next to her.

Front and center was his dad, and Audrey had clearly made it back as well, as she was by his side. Cal knew their marriage was going through a serious rocky patch because of some personal issues they were dealing with. Thirty years ago, shortly after Cal's mother had died, Audrey had had a one-off with Cal's dad, Derek, and had gotten pregnant. Audrey had not only kept the pregnancy from Derek, but she'd also given up the child for adoption.

Cal wondered if his own news would only add to that rockiness.

Most were all smiles when Cal parked and stepped from the truck. Leo even bolted off the porch to run and give him the first hug.

"Uncle Cal," he gushed with all the enthusiasm of a kid on a sugar high. "We get to eat cookies now that you're here."

"Sounds good to me," Cal assured him, and wondered how many of those cookies Leo had already sampled.

With Leo right by his side and chattering about lemonade and maybe nachos, too, Cal made his way to the porch and was engulfed in more hugs. This time from Effie and Maybell, followed by his brothers and their significant others. The smiles stayed in place, but Cal couldn't help but notice that they were tentative.

Audrey wasn't even attempting one.

She had on her general's face, which told Cal loads. She knew why he'd come home. Then again, maybe the slight edge of gloom and doom and cautious looks were because they were waiting to see how he was handling what had happened to Harper. He wasn't handling it well, and they would all soon know that.

"Something you want to tell us?" Blue came out and asked.

Cal glanced at Audrey to try to figure out if she'd already spilled his news, but in addition to a general's face, she also had a poker one.

"Yeah," Cal verified, and since that heat couldn't be good for his dad, Grammy or Maybell, he motioned for them to go inside. Nachos, cookies and lemonade weren't going to soften this particular blow, but those kind of treats wouldn't hurt, either.

Cal opened the front door, but no one else moved. Well, no one but Leo. The boy bolted inside, no doubt heading for the kitchen.

"So it's true?" his dad asked. "You're engaged to Charlotte Wilson?"

Cal nearly tripped on the single step he had taken inside. "What?" he managed to say.

Apparently, there was enough surprise in his voice and expression for the gathering to take some breaths of relief and to stop looking at him as if he'd grown a second nose.

"I knew it couldn't be true," his grandmother said. "Charlotte is Noah's girl, and I knew you wouldn't poach on a friend like that."

Cal mentally stumbled this time, and he decided to do some backtracking. "Who told you I was engaged to Charlotte?"

Effie whipped out her phone. "Six people texted me."

"I got a couple of texts, too," Maybell piped up.

"So did I," Alana contributed. "I was pretty sure it wasn't true, but I figured I'd hold off texting Charlotte and just ask you when you got home. Audrey had let us all know you'd be coming for a surprise visit."

Well, it clearly wasn't much of a surprise, but that explained how they'd known he was on the way. Soon, very soon, he'd have to address that part with them about the real reason he was home, but for now, he had another question.

"Who said I was engaged to Charlotte?" he asked, directing that at Alana.

"Apparently, Mr. Becker was in the feed store, and he mentioned it. I figured he just had it all wrong…"

Her words trailed off when Cal groaned, and he hoped like hell that someone hadn't filled Becker in on Charlotte not being his fiancée because it could cause the old coot to back out of the deal. It was obvious to Cal that Port in a Storm was important to Charlotte. Heck, it'd be important to Noah and his dad as well since it would give Alden a place to heal.

Ditto for Harper.

But that wasn't something he could think about right now. Best to clear this up. Well, clear it up as much as he could.

"Noah had to leave earlier than expected for a deployment, and he knew I was heading home, so he asked me to tell Charlotte that he was breaking up with her," Cal spelled out.

The news surprised exactly no one. Which in itself was a surprise. There were some shrugs and sounds of acknowledgment. From everyone but Effie and Maybell, anyway.

"But Izzie and Taggert are dating," his grandmother said, "and everyone who's got eyes and ears knows plain well that Izzie wants Taggert to ask her to marry him, and then she can make it a double wedding with Noah and Charlotte."

Alana rolled her eyes. "Charlotte hasn't even seen Noah in a year, and it's obvious from some of the pictures he posts on social media that he doesn't consider their relationship to be exclusive."

Cal hadn't seen such pictures, but he knew for certain that Noah hadn't lived the monk's life over the years. There'd been other women. Lots of them, actually. Cal had thought, though, that those were just flings and that Charlotte was the love of Noah's life.

Apparently not.

"Ah," Alana said as if she'd just had a light-bulb moment. "You went in to give Charlotte Noah's message, and Mr. Becker was with her. Becker's being a turd and won't sell to a single woman, so Charlotte pretended you two were engaged."

"Got it in one," Cal confirmed. "Charlotte asked me to keep the pretense a secret until the sale is a done deal." He frowned. "It will be a done deal, right?"

Alana lifted her shoulder, nibbled on her bottom lip for a moment. "Maybe. Egan and I would have bought the place and in turn sold it to Charlotte, but Becker won't do business with us. He doesn't seem to hold the same grudge against you as he does Egan and your dad."

"Becker won't sell it to me, either," Blue added. "I guess because he figures it'll end up in Charlotte's hands, too, and he doesn't want her to have the place as long as she's single." He stared at Cal. "Apparently, in

Becker's warped mind, Charlotte being single is worse than being wed to you."

"Apparently," Cal agreed. "Because he didn't nix the sale when he realized who her fiancé was." At least the man hadn't done that when they'd been face-to-face.

Egan huffed. "According to a couple of the texts I got, Becker was asking around to find out if you were an asshole." He whispered that last word, probably in case Leo was still in earshot. "You got resounding good-guy endorsements from everyone."

Cal lifted an eyebrow. "Endorsements even though an engagement to Charlotte would mean poaching on a friend?"

That brought on more shrugs and another eye roll from Alana, who continued. "Most people understand if Noah and Charlotte were ever going to marry, they would have done it by now. They're thirty-six, for heaven's sake, and have been in a holding pattern for more than two decades. I think people might be re-lieved that Charlotte has finally moved on. Or rather believe that she's finally moved on," Alana amended. "How'd she handle the breakup with Noah?"

"Better than I expected," Cal admitted. He'd thought there'd be tears. Then again, if Alana had seen those social-media pictures, then Charlotte probably had as well, so maybe she'd understood a breakup was inevi-table.

"Good," Alana muttered. "I'll give her a call and see how she's doing."

"I think Cal has something to tell us first," Audrey said when Alana took out her phone.

That sent all eyes back to Cal, and even though Audrey was giving him an admonishing look, Cal didn't do the same to her. No need. The decision he'd made had nothing to do with Audrey.

Again, Cal motioned for them to all go inside, and this time, they listened. They all filed in, not heading to the kitchen, where Leo likely was, but instead Cal led them into the family room. There were rooms closer, but those were more formal, better suited for parties and guests. He preferred the more casual space, surrounded by photos of the family. And surrounded he was. They lined the mantel of the large fireplace, were positioned on end tables and hanging on the walls.

You could never forget you were a Donnelly in this room.

Cal purposely didn't go to the center of the room or in front of the fireplace. He just stopped by the long leather sofas that faced each other, turned to look at his family and got started.

"I'm on thirty days' leave," he stated, after he took a long, deep breath. "But I also plan on putting in my separation papers." That got a blank look from all but Egan, Blue and Audrey. "I'm getting out of the Air Force," he spelled out.

That got the expected responses. Blank looks, followed by wide eyes and mutters of *what the hell?* sentiments. His dad was the first to voice that sentiment aloud.

"Jesus, Cal. You can't do that. You're a decorated fighter pilot. A hero. You'll be a damn general before you've got your twenty years in."

That all sounded similar to what Charlotte had said to convince Becker that he was a good guy. But Cal wasn't feeling it, and he tried to put this in a way that his family would understand.

"I'm tired," he admitted, "and I never wanted to be one of those ROAD guys. Retired on Active Duty," he spelled out for the nonmilitary folks. "I need a change. I need to be home," he added.

Hell. Effie had tears in her eyes, and Maybell's mouth was still open. The others were just giving him does-not-compute stares to go along with their blank expressions.

"Cal has a flawless record and will definitely be a general in a few years," Audrey finally said, and each word was dripping with disappointment for him. "You're throwing away chances that people would..." She stopped, thankfully not finishing that with the cliché of *die for*. "You have people who'll support you. People who'll help you get through this, and one day you'll be a fine general. You've got it all, Cal. Don't waste the gifts you've been given."

He'd figured that would be Audrey's opinion. Especially since she considered herself his guardian angel, a military way of saying *sponsor*. Audrey was behind him one hundred percent in his climb up the ranks.

"Audrey, I'll always be thankful for your support," he said, "but I need to be home."

The facial expressions in the room changed some. The looks softened, and there were some sighs. Sighs that alerted Cal of what was to come.

"This is about Harper," Egan was the first to say. But they were probably all thinking it.

And, hell, they were right.

It was about Harper, but not solely. It was about the

kind of man he'd become. The kind who had climbed, climbed and climbed and not given a thought as to the consequences. That didn't make him a good man, and it sure as hell didn't make him a hero.

"You can't blame yourself for what happened to Harper," Audrey insisted.

"I can blame myself for not seeing there was a problem, that she needed help," Cal was quick to answer. "If I hadn't been so focused on besting her, she might not have ended up like this."

And the grief came. Battering him in hard waves that made him feel sick. But Audrey either wasn't picking up on that or she was too focused on getting him to change his mind.

"Harper didn't let anyone know there was a problem," Audrey argued. "If she had, lots of people would have helped her. You can't help fix a problem if you don't know it exists."

"I should have known it existed," Cal argued right back. "Thirty-eight texts," he threw out there. "That's how many messages I got from Harper just in the month prior…" He stopped. Had to. "Prior to Harper attempting to end her life. I should have seen something was off. I should have realized she was too driven and that all those messages were a cry for help."

Audrey huffed. "You're a damn fine officer, Cal, but you don't have ESP. I read those texts," she added.

Cal was certain the surprise flashed in his eyes, but it shouldn't have. There had been an investigation after Harper's suicide attempt a month ago, and Cal had turned over all those messages to the investigation board along with giving a statement.

"There was nothing in the texts that would have clued you in that Harper had spiraled down," Audrey continued. "You couldn't have stopped her."

Cal didn't voice what he knew in his heart. Yeah, he could have stopped her if he hadn't been doing all that damn climbing.

"Uh, who's Harper?" Marin asked. "Sorry," she muttered. "But remember, I'm not from Emerald Creek."

Cal waited for someone to fill her in, and when no one did, he went for it. "Lieutenant Colonel Harper Johansen. I went to school with her, and we joined the Air Force at the same time."

He and Harper had done plenty at the same time. Not together, though, but as competitors. They'd gone to pilot school together with Cal earning the top graduate place and Harper just a breath behind him at number two. They'd both gotten fighter jets, and when they'd met in various air shows and competitions over the years, Cal had always managed to best her, barely. They had both made rank early, and Harper had been on that fast track right along with him.

Until a month ago.

"Harper left a suicide note and drove her car off a bridge and into a lake," Audrey explained to Marin. "Someone rescued her, but she sustained a lot of injuries. Head trauma, multiple broken bones and a damaged larynx. She's still in the hospital and not expected to make a full recovery. From what I understand, she'll be medically discharged from the military."

There it was. All spelled out. Mostly, anyway.

"Did you read the note?" Cal asked Audrey.

The slight tightening of Audrey's mouth confirmed that she had. "What happened wasn't your fault."

"Harper thought it was," Cal pointed out.

He glanced at his family. No way was he going to spell out the exact words in that note, but Harper had made sure that he knew she blamed him for her mental breakdown.

"Mercy," Marin muttered. "I'm so sorry."

Cal nodded to let her know he appreciated that. It didn't really help, but since nothing would, Cal preferred Marin's sentiment to Audrey's. She was clearly still seething that he was about to chuck in a fourteen-year career.

The silence came while everyone was trying to process this and maybe also trying to figure out what to say. Thankfully, no one had to come up with anything because Cal's phone rang. He'd never been so happy about an interruption in his life. His relief faded a bit when he saw Charlotte's name on the display, but even she was a welcome distraction.

"I need to take this," Cal insisted, hurrying out of the family room. He didn't answer until he'd gone a few rooms over. One of those fancy rooms for guests where he might have a moment to compose himself.

"Cal, I'm so sorry," Charlotte said the moment he accepted the call. "Have you heard about Becker's conversation at the feed store?"

"I have. A few people texted my family."

Charlotte groaned. "I'm so sorry," she repeated.

"Don't worry about it. I explained things to them." Though his other news had way overshadowed rumors of an engagement to *Noah's girl.* "What about Becker? Any idea if he knows the fiancé thing is a lie?"

"I don't know." There was a thick, frantic edge to her voice. "I tried to call him, but he doesn't have a cell phone, and I guess he's not back home yet. He doesn't have an answering machine on his landline so I can't even let him know I need to talk to him." She groaned again. "Becker will nix the sale if he even suspects I lied to him."

By the time Charlotte made it to that last sentence, he could hear the worry growing by leaps and bounds. This wasn't just the sale of a ranch. It was about a future she wanted to create to help people. Not compete with them. Not ignore their problems.

But help.

And at that moment, Cal knew what he had to do. He'd screwed up plenty of things, but he wouldn't allow a screwup on this.

"No, Becker won't nix the sale," Cal heard himself say. "Because we'll convince him and everybody else in Emerald Creek that we're engaged."

CHAPTER FOUR

"THE DENTIST CHAIR at Doc Wight's office gave me hemorrhoids and cellulite," the woman said. "I deserve legal compensation for that, right?"

Charlotte sighed, and she wanted to curse. She checked the time again. But she suspected Velma Sue Parsons wouldn't pick up on the subtle hints of time-checking and sighing. After all, Velma Sue hadn't paid a fleck of attention to the fact that when she'd waltzed into the law office Charlotte had been on the verge of waltzing out of it.

Or rather hurrying out of it.

Charlotte had had her purse hooked over her shoulder, her car keys in hand, and she'd had one thing in mind. Going to Saddlebrook Ranch to talk to Cal face-to-face about this notion of them convincing everyone they were engaged. There were oh-so-many pitfalls with that plan—hence the face-to-face deal—but Velma Sue had temporarily thwarted Charlotte's exit. Now the woman was blocking said exit by standing directly in front of the door.

Today, Velma Sue was wearing her usual pink yoga pants and top. Pink sneakers, too. And her hair had a pinkish tinge to it as well. Probably not by design, though. Charlotte knew from gossip that Velma Sue preferred to dye her own gray hair, and the results varied from month to month.

"It would be very hard to prove a dental chair gave you those things," Charlotte said, hoping beyond hope that would be enough to appease Velma Sue.

It wasn't.

"What's hard is that blasted chair. You can bet your sweet patootie on that," the woman countered. "Certainly you've had other clients who've complained about it and asked about legal compensation?"

Nary a one, Charlotte wanted to mutter. Then again, Velma Sue made a habit of encountering things that had offended her in some way. Last month, it'd been the toothache she'd gotten from the double scoop of Rocky Road she'd purchased at the town's candy and ice cream shop, the Jolly Lolly. The month before that, it'd been the water-weight gain from Sconehenge, the bakery that specialized in goodies guaranteed to sock on the pounds.

"No complaints about the dental chair," Charlotte said. "But if it's that uncomfortable, you should let Dr. Wight know. He might be able to add a pad or something for your next checkup."

Velma Sue made a hmm-ing sound. "I won't be getting back in that chair," she declared. "Not without legal compensation. Those ads on TV always make it sound easy to get money for wrongs, and hemorrhoids and cellulite are wrongs."

Again, Charlotte managed to hold back checking the time. Not the sigh, though. It came despite her efforts to squash it. "You should maybe try calling the number in the ads. I'm a small-town lawyer, but those city attorneys might take your case. Or you could try Carson, Elder and Carson just up the street."

Velma Sue's mouth tightened. "Already been there. They sent me here 'cause you work cheap and all."

That was true, and Charlotte could thank inheritance number two for that. She'd been left enough from one grandparent to pay for Port in a Storm, but she had inheritance number two from another grandparent that basically gave her enough of a modest monthly income to live on, which meant she didn't have to charge an arm and a leg for those needing legal services.

Velma Sue Parsons didn't need legal services.

Instead, the woman should opt for doing pretty much nothing that might cause her any distress, weight gain or other issues.

"I guess I could call the number in the ads," Velma Sue muttered.

And Charlotte decided to latch on to that as an exit line. She did check the time, gave her purse an adjustment and opened the door. "I hate to rush you out, but I have somewhere I need to be," she told Velma Sue.

Velma Sue got moving, at a snail's pace. "Guess you're busy because of your engagement to Cal Donnelly."

Good grief. If Velma Sue knew, then so did everyone in town. Yes, she had to speak to Cal ASAP, and when her phone dinged with a text from her mother, Charlotte realized she'd need to speak to her as well. Especially since the text didn't have any words but rather a string of question marks. If it hadn't been business hours, her mom would have almost certainly called to voice that particular punctuation.

"How'd Noah take you dumping him for his best friend?" Velma Sue asked.

"Noah dumped me first," Charlotte muttered without thinking. She wished she'd thought because that lit the gossip light in Velma Sue's eyes.

Since Charlotte couldn't think of any damage control or go back in time to change what she'd said, she just continued out the door. Velma Sue thankfully did as well, and Charlotte locked up. She got in her car to drive to the ranch, figuring that soon, very soon, it'd be all over town about Noah dumping her. That would lead to gossip about a rebound engagement and such, and maybe Cal would be able to help her figure out how to deal with it.

Of course, she'd need to do some dealing, too.

Since Cal had shown up at her office, she hadn't exactly had a moment to herself to process Noah breaking up with her, Becker's mule-headedness and the engagement ruse. But the ten-minute drive to Saddlebrook got her started on all of that.

She wasn't ready to start looking at alternative sites for Port in a Storm, but Charlotte had to concede that she might have to do just that. Especially if Becker heard this was all a ruse. Becker needed the money, or so the gossips had said, so if he sold the place, she could try to buy it from the new owner. Not ideal, but it was a backup, and no engagement ruse would be needed. That would get both Cal and her off the hook, especially since it was obvious Cal had his own worries.

With that checked off her list of things to process, Charlotte moved on to the whopper news of the day.

Noah sending Cal to break up with her. She had to put
that on pause for a moment when her phone dinged with
a text from Taggert.

What's going on?

Charlotte would need to respond but not until she'd
settled things with Cal. Ditto for the next text she got
from her good friend and work assistant, Mandy Men-
doza, who repeated Taggert's question. Charlotte put
those replies on the back burner and returned to her
musings about Noah breaking up with her.

She scowled, not because she was upset but because
she wondered why Noah hadn't just waited until he
could end things in person. Maybe there was an urgency
because he'd met someone? Charlotte had always considered the possibility of that.

Not just for Noah but for her.

But then the years had sort of just melted away, leading them to keep the same relationship status as they'd
had in high school, complete with on and off periods
where they'd both seen and dated other people. Even
when she'd dated others, though, most people just assumed she'd get back with Noah. And she had.

Overall, it had sucked but had been a comfortable
status that had probably stopped either of them from
having a deeper relationship. It certainly had done that
for her, even though she knew one thing for certain. She
wasn't in love with Noah, and she wasn't heartbroken
now that it was over. She was…

Relieved.

That was the first thing that popped into her head.

The next word popped, too, but she instantly tried to nip it in the bud. Because that word was *Cal*.

Yes, Cal.

Charlotte could blame the kiss on that particular thought. A kiss that was simply meant to fool Becker into believing that Cal was her fiancé. But it had backfired. Because the kiss had sent a trickle of heat and interest from her hair roots to her tippy toes. And neither the heat nor the interest should be there.

Nope.

Cal wouldn't want it. She shouldn't, either. But her body seemed to have a different notion about that. That meant she'd have to tell her body to take a chill pill. Not now, though. It'd have to wait because she pulled into the driveway of the sprawling Donnelly ranch and saw the reason for the heat and interest. Cal was walking toward one of the ranch's many barns.

He had his hands crammed in the pockets of his jeans, and his shoulders were slumped. Definitely not the straight posture he'd sported since he went into the military. When he turned toward the sound of her approaching vehicle, Charlotte got a good-enough look at his face to see that he wasn't his usual cheery, easygoing self.

Though he was still drop-dead hot.

Sighing, she had to shove that aside. Hard. And she thought she might have to keep shoving. What the heck was up with her? She'd been around Cal too many times to count and had never had this reaction. Then again, she'd never been around him as an adult who hadn't been in a semirelationship with his best friend.

She parked, and he stopped walking, clearly waiting

for her, and she watched to see if this visit was making his mood worse. It didn't appear to be. In fact, Cal seemed pretty rock-bottom right now, and she hoped his notion to make everyone believe they were engaged wasn't playing into his mood. If so, she could at least give him an out on that and maybe ease his mind.

"Three texts," he said when she started toward him. He didn't clarify what those texts were about, but Charlotte figured he was getting the same questions as she was.

"Ditto. There'll be more," she warned him.

He nodded in a not-a-news-flash sort of way and tipped his head toward the pasture. "I was going to take a look at some new horses."

She spotted the trio of magnificent Andalusians with their glossy pearl-white coats and manes, and while they certainly deserved some looking at, Charlotte figured this trek had more to do with Cal needing a moment to think things over as she'd done on the drive.

Or getting away from someone.

She glanced over her shoulder and spotted a whole bunch of people looking out the various windows on that particular side of the house. Cal's brothers and their partners. His grandmother and Maybell. And from the second floor, his father peered down at him. The one person who was missing was Audrey.

"I can come back at a better time," Charlotte offered. "I just wanted to talk to you about the engagement thing."

She patted his arm and turned to leave, but he took hold of her hand. Briefly took hold. Their gazes collided, and he let go of her darn fast.

"Walk with me to see the horses," he said, "and we'll talk."

Charlotte stayed put. "Honestly, the talk can wait. You obviously have other things on your mind."

"Walk with me," Cal repeated, his tone a smidge more insistent this time. "I have a plan for making this fake engagement work."

She did walk, and as she'd done, Cal glanced over his shoulder, no doubt spotting the family spectators. He muttered some profanity under his breath and then scrubbed his hand over his face.

"I'm guessing things are a little intense with your family right now?" she risked asking.

He made a sound of agreement but didn't add anything. Cal just kept them moving until they reached the pasture. "My family knows why we're pretending to be engaged," he said. He rested his arms on top of the white wooden fence, tucking one boot on the lower rung. "You should do the same for your mom. And for Taggert. No need to make them worry."

Charlotte made her own sound of agreement. But there'd be a different kind of worry for her mom and Taggert when they learned of the breakup with Noah.

"Everyone else in town should believe we're engaged," he went on. "At least until Becker caves and sells you the place. I'll go see him to move that along, since he doesn't seem to despise me as much as he does the rest of my family."

That was certainly true. However, there was a mountain-sized *but* in this. "Even a short engagement will disrupt your life, and I don't want you to have to deal with that right now."

"I want to deal with it," he insisted. "I want Port in a Storm to happen. Alden and Harper can benefit from it. Plenty of others, too, I'm sure."

She certainly hoped that would be the case, but Charlotte still wasn't sure about putting Cal through this. "I can try to find someone else to buy Becker's place."

Though she had already tried to do that and had come up with a goose egg. There were only a handful of people in Emerald Creek who weren't on Becker's shit list, but so far none of them had been willing to do something sneaky like this. Added to that, it would create a lot more paperwork and cost for her to rebuy the ranch. Still, she would do it if it spared Cal any additional pressure.

"It'll be faster to go the fake-engagement route," Cal assured her. "We'll just make it clear to our families what's going on, and I'll have that chat with Becker. I'm guessing we won't have to keep up the pretense for more than a couple of days. A week at the most."

Mercy, a week. And Charlotte got a flash of that kiss again. It probably wasn't a good idea for her to play lovey-dovey with Cal even for a minute, much less a week. Still, the prize for that particular torture was a whopper. She could actually get Becker's ranch.

"All right," she finally said. "The pretense is on." She paused a moment. "I'll also tell my mom and Taggert that Noah broke up with me."

Cal immediately shifted his attention from the horses to her, and she figured he was examining her expression to see how she was dealing with the breakup. Charlotte knew for a fact he wouldn't see any distress. Because she wasn't feeling any. Not for herself, anyway. But she was starting to get plenty for Cal. She'd never seen him down like this.

"I hope this doesn't add to your troubles, but I'm worried about you," Charlotte admitted. "Just how much should I be concerned? In other words, how okay aren't you?"

When he didn't answer right away, she was ready to tell him to forget she'd brought it up and then add an apology for poking her nose in his business, but Cal spoke before she could launch into the regrets and the *I'm sorry.*

"I'm getting out of the Air Force," he said. "Audrey's pissed off about that. Rightfully so, since she's opened some doors for me to make rank early. She's always seen me as her protégé." He paused a moment. "The rest of my family is just confused and, yeah, maybe pissed off because they probably think I'm making a hasty decision that's clouded with emotion."

Since Charlotte had already gone for a no-holds-barred approach to this conversation, she continued it. "Is your family right?"

He looked at her now, and the corner of his mouth lifted in a very dry smile. "Yeah," he repeated. "But it's the right decision. I can't give the military my all anymore. I can't be at the top of my game."

She could feel the pain of that admission. It was coming off him in hot waves. "I'm sorry."

When she didn't add more, he continued to stare at her. "What? You're not going to tell me to give it some time, that I might change my mind? That I shouldn't throw away this dream career?" The last two words went in air quotes.

Charlotte shook her head. "No attempts at mind-changing. I had too many battles with my mom over my life choices. Remember, she always wanted me to be a doctor like her dad and grandfather. She's mellowed some about that." She repeated *some* and put it in air quotes as well. "And she gives me at least weekly reminders that I should press Noah for marriage. Maybe those will finally stop when I tell her about the breakup," Charlotte added in a mutter.

"Why didn't you press for marriage?" he asked.

"Because I didn't want it." In hindsight, she probably should have mulled her reply over rather than be so blunt. But this didn't seem the day for pretenses. Well, except for their fake engagement.

"Noah always seemed to need that adventurous life away from here," she went on, making a sweeping motion with her hand to indicate places far and away. "I always needed Emerald Creek. He never planned for kids. I did. He never wanted what I did and vice versa. I just figured eventually we'd find someone who'd be more right for each other than we were." And that caused her to pause again. "Has Noah found someone else?"

Cal shrugged but dodged her gaze again. "Can't say. You should ask him about that."

She wouldn't be doing that. In fact, from here on out everything would be just plain awkward between her and Noah. That was a shame because, along with losing her relationship status with him, she'd also lost his friendship.

Again, the hindsight kicked in, and she realized the friendship was what she would miss most. But she wouldn't miss having to stake her future hopes on her feelings for Noah deepening again. On her falling in love with him again. Or wondering if that deepening and falling happened, whether it would ever lead to marriage and kids.

Now she knew it wouldn't, period.

She didn't want marriage without that mindless, overwhelming experience of head over heels in lust and love. For some unknown reason, her mindless brain flashed her an image of Cal. Nope, she assured her brain. Even if Cal was in a mental position to jump into heat, love and such, he wouldn't be the right man. In his mind, she'd always be Noah's, and in her mind, he'd always be...

Charlotte couldn't think of a word to finish that.

It didn't help her concentration that her phone dinged in rapid succession with more What the heck? texts from her mother, Mandy and some of her other friends. Cal's phone was dinging, too, but some of those messages might not have to do with the fake engagement. It was possible that members of his family were checking on him.

Cal turned his attention back to the horses. "Have you seen Harper?" he asked.

Charlotte wasn't surprised by the change of subject, since she figured Cal was doing plenty of thinking about Harper. But she was a little puzzled, and pleased, that he trusted her enough to broach these painful, muddy waters.

"Briefly," Charlotte answered. "When she was transferred to the rehab facility in San Antonio last week, I went to see her." A gut-wrenching visit. But she wouldn't be admitting that to Cal. In fact, she took a cue from him and dodged his gaze. "I told her about Port in a Storm and said that once it was up and running, she should consider finishing out her recovery there. She agreed."

Not with words. Harper wasn't capable of speaking yet. But she'd nodded. Of course, that nod had been in a vacant "leave me the heck alone" kind of gesture, but Charlotte intended to take it at face value.

"Have you seen her?" Charlotte countered.

"Briefly," he parroted, but he didn't elaborate. However, he did squeeze his eyes shut a moment as if to clamp off some horrible memory. Maybe lots of horrible memories.

Cal took out his phone, and for a moment, she thought he was going to check some of those texts he'd been getting, but instead he pulled up a photo and held it out for her to see. Except it wasn't a photo of a person but rather a letter. And Charlotte instantly knew what it was.

The note Harper had left before she'd driven off that bridge.

Cal, the playing field is all yours now. I'm bowing out of this shit show. No more looking over my shoulder and worrying about you besting me. No more losing to you. You win.

Oh, wow. Charlotte had figured Harper had to have been in a very dark place, but she hadn't expected the woman to put her final, sole focus on Cal.

"What would you do if you got a note like that?" he asked.

Charlotte swallowed hard. "Probably what you're

doing now. I'd know it wasn't my fault, but I'd blame myself anyway."

"It was my fault," he argued. Then he cursed, sighed and groaned, all in quick succession. "I knew the competition between us was intense. It fueled me. Pushed me. Made me do more than my best. I assumed it was doing the same to her. *Assumed*," he repeated like more profanity. "I didn't know I was shredding her to pieces."

"You didn't know because I'm guessing Harper didn't want you to know," Charlotte pointed out. "It's like that time she peed her pants in kindergarten."

Cal looked at her again, but his expression changed. "What?"

Going with the hindsight again, Charlotte wished she'd been able to come up with a different life lesson, but since she'd started it, she continued to launch right into this one.

"Her mom had put two apple juices in her lunch box, and Harper drank both right before recess. She was on the playground and didn't make it to the bathroom in time. So she wet her pants, but instead of telling the teacher what happened, she wore the wet panties all day. She ended up getting a rash and needed butt cream to stop the itching."

Charlotte paused, frowned. Okay, definitely not the best thing she could have recalled, but the story did support her assessment of Harper not asking for help with her problems.

"I think Harper's relationship with her father was a big factor in the way she handled challenges," Charlotte added. Maybe in the way she'd handled the wet-pants debacle, too. "You know how her father is."

Cal made a sound of agreement. Of course he knew. Everyone in town did. Paul Johansen wasn't a recluse like Becker, but he definitely fell into the SOB territory. A retired, decorated Green Beret, he'd had incredibly high expectations for Harper, and the talk was he ran his household with an iron fist. According to the gossips, that approach was the reason Harper's mother had walked out when Harper was sixteen.

"I drove out to see Paul," Cal volunteered.

Charlotte found herself holding her breath. "How did that go?" Because with Paul, you never knew. He'd always been civil to her, but then she'd always seen the man when they'd been in public. That civility might have taken a huge dive for a meeting in private.

"He wasn't home," Cal explained. "I don't have his phone number, so I left a message on his door for him to call me. So far, he hasn't."

Charlotte had no idea if that was for the best. Eventually, their paths would cross, and it might or might not turn out to be a confrontation that Cal was clearly dreading. Dreading, yet he'd gone to see the man. That was Cal, through and through. He'd never dodge anything ugly even when it was tearing him apart inside.

"Maybe this thing with Harper has softened Paul," Charlotte suggested. That wasn't a high-probability outcome, but, hey, this sort of thing could spur change. Possibly the right change.

Cal stayed quiet a long time. "I wish Harper had turned to someone. Anyone. Maybe Port in a Storm can give her the help she needs."

"That's the plan," Charlotte muttered. "Say, if you do get out of the military, maybe you can help me run it. I mean, the pay will be seriously lousy, the hours, too, but there'll be other perks. Like unclogging toilets, changing light bulbs, that sort of thing."

He turned to her again. "Are you saying this because you think I could use the services of Port in a Storm?"

"Maybe. Yes," she amended. "Do you need help?" she came out and asked.

"Probably," he said with a sigh. "I'm hoping I'll find it here at home."

Charlotte thought about that. "It might work, but if it doesn't, ask for help, okay?"

This time when he looked at her, the corner of his mouth lifted again. Not so much dryness this time. "I'm not going to do what Harper did."

"Good," she couldn't say fast enough, and she hugged him. It was a gesture of comfort. A good friends kind of thing.

Or at least that's what it should have been.

But the moment his body landed against hers, the annoying trickle of heat came again, and it caused her to tense. To pull back, too. Cal fully cooperated with the pulling back, but when he did, their gazes collided again. And held. Locked and loaded.

Moments passed. Slowly. The locked-and-loaded didn't. It stayed put, and the eye contact suddenly seemed intimate or something. As if the heat was zinging back and forth between them.

Cal frowned and muttered some more profanity. "Has this always been here?" he asked.

Charlotte couldn't pretend not to know what he was talking about. She matched his frown and nodded. "A latent thing," she admitted. "It's rearing its head now because I kissed you."

He certainly didn't dispute that, which, of course, only caused the latency to take a nosedive. The heat was coming out of hibernation and announcing itself big-time.

"It'd be a really bad idea," he muttered, but his voice came out as a drawl. All hot and cowboy-like.

"Oh, yes," she insisted. "Worst idea ever."

So why did that make her want to kiss him again? A forbidden fruit kind of thing? Maybe. But whatever it was, it definitely had a hard pull to it.

Charlotte was thankful for the ding of another text on Cal's phone, because the sound caused them to do some actual backing away from each other. Temporarily, anyway. When Cal looked at his phone screen and cursed, Charlotte moved back toward him to see what had caused that reaction.

The first thing she saw was that it was indeed a text. From Noah. And while Cal tried to pull his phone away, Charlotte caught a couple of words. *Dick*, *TLC*, *Elise*.

"Elise?" Charlotte had to ask.

Cal cursed some more, but this time the profanity was definitely aimed at Noah. He passed her his phone and let her read the entire text.

Feeling like a dick for asking you to do the breakup with Charlotte, but like I said, it needed to be done. Hope it went well. If she's taking it hard, do me another solid and give her a little TLC. Just whatever you do, don't tell her about Elise. That's news best left for later rather than sooner.

"Elise?" she repeated.

Cal looked as if he wanted to be anywhere but there and have to say anything but what he was about to say. "A woman Noah met a couple of months ago." He paused, did more cursing. "Noah plans to marry her, Charlotte, and Elise is pregnant."

CHAPTER FIVE

CAL FROWNED WHEN he checked his phone and saw that he didn't have any new messages from Charlotte.

Frowned and silently cursed.

Silently because he was at the kitchen table at his family's ranch, and with his Grammy Effie and Maybell at the stove, he didn't want to get any scoldings about having a potty mouth. However, he clearly didn't mute all of his reaction because Maybell looked over at him and grunted.

"You got a lot of reasons to be sighing, Cal," she said. "Want me to guess which one caused you to make that sound?"

He settled for shaking his head. No guessing desired, though Maybell and his family had no doubt observed his conversation the day before with Charlotte when they'd been by the corral fence and his family had been peeking out the windows at them. If those family members had been looking closely enough, they might have seen some of the color drain from her face. Might have noticed she'd abruptly ended their conversation and had headed back to her car.

Cal had gone after her, of course. Maybell and his family would have seen that as well and wondered what the heck was going on. If any of them had lip-reading skills he didn't know about, they would have noticed that he'd been cursing Noah, not only for making him the messenger but also for making him tell Charlotte the reason for the breakup.

Of course, Charlotte had brushed it off, saying it was a shock but that she was okay. She wasn't. No way. Here, all these years she'd wanted marriage and kids, and Noah—the supposed love of her life—had insisted he didn't want those things, only to then turn around and get them with another woman.

In the past eighteen hours or so since that bombshell, Cal had texted Charlotte to check on her. Six times and counting. She'd responded to the first five, assuring him she was fine. Short, clipped responses that were friendly enough if not soul-baring, but she'd yet to respond to his sixth. Maybe because she was tired of finding ways to repeat herself. Maybe because she was at this very moment sobbing her heart out and unable to see her phone screen. That made Cal want to throttle his old pal Noah.

"Another sigh," his grandmother remarked. "Is the fake engagement not going the way you planned?"

Actually, that was going just fine, as far as he knew. People who didn't know the truth were shocked and had been texting him. People who *did* know were texting and assuring him they'd keep his secret for this good cause. So far, Becker hadn't learned that it was a pretense, because Cal was certain that if he had, some of those texters and assurers would have let him know.

"Oh," Maybell muttered. "It's the one-month anniversary of what happened to Harper."

Cal certainly hadn't forgotten about that. Couldn't.

And, yeah, that was definitely hammering down his mood. It'd hammer even more once he had some time to himself to let the pain and memories wash over him. But time to himself wasn't possible this morning.

"I'm going out to see Becker today," Cal explained, finishing up the breakfast that Effie and Maybell had insisted he eat.

Pancakes and homemade maple sausage. It was delicious, of course. Everything they cooked was. But he'd hoped to get out of the house before anyone else in his family came down—

Too late.

Egan came in through the back door just as Blue made his entrance from the back stairs that led up to some of the bedroom suites. Since Egan was wearing his flight suit, that meant he was likely headed to the base where he was a squadron commander. Blue was in ranch clothes, which meant he would probably be going to the barns or pastures since he was working with the horses these days.

Both of his brothers instantly speared him with their gaze, and he could see the questions in their eyes. Cal decided to provide the answers to those questions. Some of them anyway.

"Yes, I'm still getting out of the military," Cal verified. "Becker hasn't yet agreed to sell his place to Charlotte. And Charlotte claims she's okay about Noah breaking up with her." He withheld the part about Elise, figuring that was Charlotte's bombshell to drop.

Or Noah's.

Considering that Elise was pregnant, Noah would

need to drop that one soon, if for no other reason than to let his dad know he was about to become a grandfather.

"I've texted Remi," Cal went on, "so she also knows about the fake engagement in case someone messages her."

Though, his sister's reaction had been a little odd. Remi had simply responded with a winky face. Cal wasn't sure if that meant Remi doubted the fake part or if she was amused by it all. Or if the quick response was all she'd had time to manage.

Egan and Blue continued to stare at him. Clearly, they planned on spending some time trying to figure out what was going on in his head.

"You're sure about the decision to get out of the Air Force?" Egan asked while he poured himself a cup of coffee. He did that while still managing to maintain the eye contact.

Cal would have assured him that the answer was still *yes*, but another family member walked in: Audrey. She, too, was in uniform, and those silver stars were awfully shiny on the epaulets that sported her rank. No way to miss those.

Like Egan and Blue, she zoomed in on Cal with her steely gaze. "I have to leave in a couple of minutes," Audrey said, "but I want you to do me a favor." She aimed that comment at Cal, and he figured he already knew what the favor was. "I want you to wait until the end of your thirty days of leave to put in your separation papers."

Bingo. Cal had known this was coming, but before he could tell Audrey that thirty days weren't going to make a difference, she rolled right over him in true general fashion. "Yes, I know you said you're certain, and if that's true, then waiting thirty days won't matter."

"I'm getting out," Cal stated.

Audrey shrugged. "Then waiting thirty days won't matter," she repeated right back. She added a huff to that, but then her expression softened. "Please," she added. "Do it as a favor to me. At the end of the thirty days, if you still want to get out, then I'll expedite the paperwork for you."

Until she added that last part, Cal had been about to do more affirming, but separation paperwork could take time. That time would no doubt be lessened considerably with a general's backing. Even if, in this case, the general wasn't in favor of it. Still, he didn't think Audrey would renege on something like that.

"All right," Cal finally said. "Thirty days. Twenty-nine," he amended when he remembered he'd already burned a day of that leave.

One huge eventful day where he'd become fake engaged, delivered news to crush Charlotte and sunk even deeper into a depression about Harper. Yeah, he didn't want to repeat the past twenty-four hours.

Audrey nodded, not expressing a whole lot of relief at his concession. She also didn't move. She volleyed glances at every person in the room.

"Since you're no doubt wondering, Derek and I haven't reconciled," Audrey said.

Cal had figured that was the case. If there had been a mending of the fences, then his dad would likely be back on his way to DC with Audrey.

"I'm not giving up on my marriage," Audrey went

on, "but I have to get back to work. I'm going to try to make it back here in six weeks or so."

No one in the room seemed surprised by that. Despite Audrey's previously infrequent visits to the ranch, the woman did seem to be trying hard to stay married to a man who was clearly still pissed off, and hurt, by what she'd done. Cal loved his father, but Derek could be a total hard-ass in certain situations. This was one of them. In his mind, Audrey had cost him his son by not telling him she'd had his child.

Audrey dragged in a long breath, glanced out the window. "I'm sure if any of you had heard from Rowan Cullen, you would have told me."

Maybell, Effie, Blue, Egan and Cal all made sounds of agreement. None of them had to question who Rowan was, either. He was the son that Audrey had given up for adoption.

"Other than the one phone call to me seven months ago, there's been no contact," Blue assured her.

It was old news. Because there were so many questions about this mystery half brother, Blue had been questioned and requestioned about that call. Apparently, it'd been a short conversation, and Rowan had indicated he was heading out on some kind of deployment and might get back in touch.

Might.

Judging from how little they knew about Rowan, he had been as shocked as the rest of them—minus Audrey, of course—about the circumstances of his conception. Cal figured his father knew a whole lot more about Rowan. No way would Derek have not put a PI on this to do at least a background check on his son, but Derek wasn't sharing anything, and no one was pressing.

"I did add my phone number to the genealogy site that Rowan used to get his DNA results," Cal volunteered. "Blue's is already there, but I thought it wouldn't hurt to have two numbers posted. Maybe it'd convince Rowan we're interested in talking to him."

Though Cal wasn't sure that *talking* was the right thing. It could open up a big-assed can of worms for all of them. Especially Rowan, since he apparently hadn't known he was adopted until he'd seen the DNA results. But Cal hadn't left his number for Rowan but in fact for their father. It was gnawing away at Derek that he had a son out there he'd never met.

"Rowan's military, right?" Maybell asked, not directing the question at anyone in particular.

It was Audrey who finally broke the silence and made a sound of agreement. Of course, she would have checked that once she had Rowan's adopted surname. No way would she have been able to resist.

"Rowan's an STO, an Air Force Special Tactics Officer," Audrey provided a heartbeat later.

Egan, Blue and Cal all made sounds, too, to indicate they were impressed. It was an elite special ops field similar to Remi's, but the STOs had a more direct combat role.

A dangerous one.

"I don't know where he is right now," Audrey went on. "It's classified. I could find out, but I don't want to dig too deep into him. It'd send up red flags, and while he's obviously aware that Derek is his bio-father because of his DNA match to Blue, he probably doesn't know I'm his...that I gave birth to him."

Her voice didn't exactly crack on that last part, but it was close. She had avoided saying *mother*. Even biomother. Maybe she was doing that to try to maintain some emotional distance. If so, it wasn't working, because Audrey's face was wracked with everything she had to be feeling.

"I have to go," Audrey abruptly added, and she headed out the door, moving fast. But not fast enough. Cal still spotted her eyes watering.

He considered going after her, to try to offer her whatever comfort he could give, but Cal also knew that would be a mistake. Audrey almost certainly wouldn't want to cry on his shoulder. In fact, she wouldn't want him or anyone else to see her cry, period. Egan, Blue, Maybell and Effie must have felt the same way because they stayed put as well, though Effie did shake her head and sigh.

Cal stood, went to his grandmother and gave her a hug. With the firestorm of emotions going on between Audrey and his father, it was sometimes easy to forget that Effie was no doubt also hurting, since Rowan was her grandson, too.

"I'll be fine," Effie assured him, patting his arm when she eased back from the hug. She met his gaze. "Will you be?"

"Yes," Cal said, though he had no idea if that was true.

Still, he didn't want his grandmother or anyone else worrying about him. Not when they already had so much on their plates.

"I need to go into town and see Charlotte," Cal told them. "Then I'll drive out to Becker's. Wish me luck. If I can convince him to sell the place to Charlotte, then we can drop the pretense of the engagement."

He frowned at the mention of that and thought of the comment Becker had made after Charlotte had made her announcement to him. "Anyone got a ring I can use for the fake engagement?" he asked. "You know, just to make it look more real to Becker."

"I've got that one I won at the county fair when I was twelve," Blue offered. "I'm sure it's in my room somewhere."

Cal rolled his eyes. He recalled the ring. Gaudy brass with a nickel-sized red stone that was probably plastic.

"You could just buy her one and then return it," Egan suggested.

"I've got some pretty charms that fit on the stems of wineglasses," Maybell contributed. "That might work."

"This will work better," Effie said, tugging out the gold necklace from beneath her shirt. A necklace that held her engagement and wedding rings.

"No," Cal was quick to say. "Those are the real deal."

"Yes, they are," Effie confirmed, unclasping the necklace. "Your grandfather gave them to me sixty-four years ago when I was just eighteen." She took out the engagement ring and held it out for Cal. "This belonged to his mother, so I'm guessing it's at least a hundred years old."

It wasn't a flashy piece. A simple round diamond set in etched gold. Cal supposed the style was art deco.

"I can't use that," he insisted.

Effie took his hand and pressed it into his palm.

"Yes, you can," she insisted right back. "If Becker's not a total idiot, he'll see it's a family ring, and that will help convince him that the engagement is the real deal. Once Charlotte buys the ranch, you can give it back to me."

Until she'd added that last part, Cal was about to refuse again. But he and Charlotte just might need some more fodder, and the ring did indeed scream *family heirloom*.

Sighing, Cal took the ring and brushed a kiss on his grandmother's cheek. "I'll keep it safe," he assured her, "and will return it as soon as it's done the job."

He squeezed the ring onto his pinkie finger, kissed his grandmother again and started out, only to have Maybell thrust a plastic container into his hands.

"A dozen lemon shortbread cookies," Maybell explained. "Guaranteed to soften up the worst of grouches."

Since Cal had eaten plenty of Maybell's cookies over the years, he knew that was usually true. The lemon shortbreads were especially tasty. But Becker was a couple of rungs above being a plain old grouch, so even these might not perform any mood miracles.

"Thanks," he told Maybell, figuring if Becker didn't want them, then he and Charlotte could have them.

He kissed Maybell's cheek as well, repeated his thanks and headed out to his rental truck, where he tucked the cookies beneath his seat. Audrey's own rental was nowhere in sight so she obviously hadn't lingered once she'd made her exit. Cal made a mental note to email her later in the week to check on her. He made another mental note to check on his father, even though Blue was already doing that.

Of course, his family was no doubt making some

mental notes to check on him, too. They were all clearly worried, and Cal would have liked to assure them that the worry wasn't warranted, but other than lip service, he couldn't do that. Because he definitely didn't feel as if he was operating on solid ground right now. He definitely wasn't in any mental shape to climb back into the cockpit and at the moment didn't even have the desire to.

Would that change in twenty-nine days and a handful of hours?

Cal knew it wouldn't. That love of flying was gone. Just gone. The problem was the love of everything else but his family was, too. He was sliding deeper and deeper into that dark hole and didn't know how to come out of it.

With that dismal thought, he drove away from the ranch and into town to Charlotte's law office. This time, he parked out front, but he still moved with some evasion since Cal didn't especially want to talk to anyone about his homecoming, Harper or his engagement. He hurried into the office, the bell announcing his entrance the moment he opened it.

And he immediately saw that Charlotte wasn't alone.

Her mother, Izzie, was there and so was Noah's father, Taggert. They turned toward him, and it seemed to Cal that they were all holding their breath, waiting for him to do exactly what he didn't know. In fact, not knowing what to do applied to Cal, too, since he wasn't sure how much Taggert and Izzie knew.

About Noah's breakup with Charlotte.

About the reason for the breakup.

About the fake engagement.

So it seemed like a good time for Cal just to stand

there and wait out the silence rather than blab something he'd regret. He didn't have to wait long. Taggert stepped toward him, extending his hand for Cal to shake.

"Welcome home," Taggert said in the deep baritone voice that had always reminded Cal of Darth Vader.

Taggert, however, was nothing like the often-intimidating, iconic character. He was more a silver-haired John Wayne in his well-worn brown leather vest, cowboy boots, Stetson and good ol' boy demeanor. Even though Taggert and his family came from money—and plenty of it—the man didn't wear or drive his wealth.

"Thanks," Cal said, but didn't add anything. He was still waiting to see what had already been said.

"Yes, welcome home," Izzie echoed, coming closer and hugging Cal.

As usual, she smelled of Chanel No. 5 perfume, a scent he would always associate with Charlotte's mom. Unlike Taggert, there was plenty of flash. Izzie was the current mayor of Emerald Creek and was wearing a powerhouse red sleeveless dress that showed off her toned arms and body. She looked as if she'd stepped off the pages of an AARP ad.

"They know the engagement is fake," Charlotte spoke up. She stepped closer, too, moving ahead of Taggert and Izzie, and Cal saw the nerves in every bit of her expression. "They understand why we're doing it," she added in a mutter.

"Though we don't approve," Izzie was quick to say. "Taggert and I want her to have a heart-to-heart with Noah as soon as possible so they can work out their differences."

Charlotte rolled her eyes, but Izzie and Taggert didn't

see it since her back was to them. "I was just explaining that there aren't any differences to work out. Noah took the chicken-poop path of sending you to do his dirty work of breaking up with me."

So, Charlotte had clearly moved on from the shock of Noah's news to the anger stage. Good. Cal was on the same page as her. He was plenty pissed at his old friend for this whole mess.

Izzie rolled her eyes, too. "Noah probably just wants Charlotte to have the opportunity to move on and have children. Her biological clock is certainly ticking away for that."

More eye rolling from Charlotte. A huff, too, that let Cal know this particular discussion with her mom hadn't been going especially well. Taggert wasn't huffing or making faces, but it was obvious that he, too, was displeased with what his son had done and was uncomfortable with this discussion.

"Noah still loves you," Izzie insisted, moving so that she could see Charlotte's face. "Tell her, Cal. Noah loves her."

Cal was certain he was showing plenty of nerves, too. He certainly couldn't make that assertion, not without going into other details that Charlotte had clearly withheld from them.

"If Noah loved me, he wouldn't have sent Cal to break up with me," Charlotte grumbled.

Izzie was quick to shake her head, and she took hold of Charlotte's shoulders. "On the contrary. This proves how much he loves you. Noah wants to give you the freedom to get married and have children." She added an annoying ticktock sound for her biological clock.

"I'm sure he's crushed, and I'm equally sure that if you tell him you want to reconcile he'll jump at the chance. Because I know you, Charlotte, and I know you love him, too."

Charlotte didn't respond, not with words anyway, but Cal could practically see cartoon steam coming out of her ears. "I haven't had sex with Noah in over two years," she finally snarled. "Does that sound like I'm in love with him? Does it?" She'd gotten louder with each word.

Then the silence came. The blush fired across her cheeks. And Charlotte grimaced, probably because she hadn't wanted to share that TMI detail with any of them. But it gave Cal a WTF moment. Noah had certainly been home during the past couple of years, probably two or three times, and he hadn't had sex with the woman he considered his girlfriend? It was a sort of sexual ghosting, and Cal had to wonder whose idea that'd been— Charlotte's or Noah's?

"Sex isn't the most important thing in a relationship," Izzie went on, and while Cal wasn't sure who was the most uncomfortable with this discussion, he thought it might be a three-way tie with Charlotte, Taggert and him. "Love is. And Noah loves you. Doesn't he, Taggert? Noah loves—"

"Noah knocked up another woman, and he's planning on marrying her," Charlotte blurted.

That stopped all other conversation, and Izzie's mouth froze just before the word *you*. Izzie stared at her daughter and then looked at Cal, clearly asking for some kind of clarification.

Cal settled for a nod.

"What?" Taggert demanded.

Cal gave him a nod, too. Charlotte went with actual words.

"Noah's girlfriend is pregnant," Charlotte repeated. She ended that with a heavy sigh. Obviously, the fit of temper had come and gone, and now she just looked spent.

Cal knew how she felt.

"That can't be true," Izzie muttered. She repeated a couple of variations of that, adding some headshakes to it. "Who is she?" she demanded, shifting her attention to Cal.

"I've never met her," Cal said. "But it's true about her being pregnant." He didn't add that Noah had been happy about that, because that would be like adding salt to Charlotte's wound.

Well, maybe.

Two years since she'd had sex with Noah? Cal had to go with another *WTF* on that. How the hell had Noah managed to keep his hands off her that long?

And that mentally stopped him in his tracks.

No way should he be thinking that. Heck, no way should he be linking Charlotte and sex, even when it was in a WTF context.

"You're still planning on driving out to see Becker?" Charlotte asked, obviously giving the conversation a big shift in topic. Well, not that there was actually anyone talking at the moment.

The news had stunned Izzie and Taggert to silence, and Cal wasn't volunteering anything more on the walking-on-eggshells revelation. Taggert would no doubt need time to come to terms with his impending grandfatherhood. Izzie would need equal time to wrap her mind around the big-assed life bubble that'd just been burst. No double wedding for Noah, Charlotte, Taggert and her.

"Yeah," Cal verified. "I'm going to see Becker. I just stopped by here first…" He wasn't sure how to finish that, but he'd come to check on her.

Charlotte took his unfinished sentence and ran with it. "To see if I wanted to go with you. Well, I do. Mercy, do I," she muttered in an "I've got to get the hell out of here now" tone.

"I'll call you later," Charlotte said, dropping a quick kiss on her mother's cheek. As she grabbed her purse from her desk, she looked at Taggert. "I'm sorry for dumping the news on you like that."

Charlotte added, "Please lock up when you leave," and headed out with Cal. Fast. She hooked her arm through his to get him moving and then practically jumped into his truck. She immediately let out a long breath that she'd clearly been holding.

"Drive, please," she said.

Cal complied, in part because he wanted to get away from Izzie and Taggert, too, to give them time to process what they'd just learned. But he also wanted to do whatever he could to try to soothe Charlotte. Driving away might help. Then again, maybe helping wasn't possible at the moment. She no doubt still had plenty of processing to do, too.

It was about a fifteen-minute drive to Becker's place, and Charlotte didn't say anything for the first eight minutes. "I'm sorry you ended up being part of that conversation."

Since her focus was straight out the windshield, Cal voiced a shrug instead of doing an actual one. "It's okay."

"No, it's not," she grumbled. "And trust me, I hadn't planned on telling my mom and Taggert this way about Noah's pregnant girlfriend. I shouldn't have snarled that out in anger."

"The anger's plenty justified," Cal assured her.

She glanced at him, maybe to see if he meant it. He did. Man, did he. "You deserve to rage on, to be so thoroughly pissed off that you yell at the top of your lungs. Or do voodoo curses for Noah's dick to fall off."

Her glance turned to a full stare, and then she laughed. "Mind reader. Because I did think of voodoo curses and dicks falling off." She stopped, and the smile faded. "Probably not something you want to hear about your best friend."

Actually, he agreed with her sentiment about the voodoo stuff, though he truly didn't want to discuss Noah's dick. And for reasons he didn't want to explore, he didn't want to think about Noah having once been Charlotte's lover.

But not for two years.

Yeah, that reminder wasn't going away anytime soon.

"I don't approve of what Noah did," Cal stated. "Especially the part about him not telling you in person about Elise and the baby. For the record, I tried to talk him into doing that, but he said the baby would be born by the time he got back from the deployment, and he wanted to be able to focus on that."

Which made Noah seem like an asshole and a happy

prospective father. Both of which had to eat away at Charlotte.

"Even if you're not in love with Noah, this all stinks," Cal added.

"It doesn't stink for Elise," she countered. "Or for Noah. He'll have a baby that he apparently wants." Charlotte stopped, swallowed hard. "He just didn't want the baby with me."

Cal silently cursed. Verbally did, too, and he would have launched into an attempt at some of the TLC that Noah himself had suggested. But Charlotte waved him off.

"I'm not in love with Noah," she spelled out. "And I'm sure once I get over the shock of what's happened, I can even be happy for him, his wife and baby. Eventually," she tacked on. "Okay, maybe not actually happy for him, but after a year or two, I might not want to call Noah every curse word in a sailor's vocabulary."

Yeah, that urge might fade. Might. But this had all been a hard blow to Charlotte, and she wasn't getting over it anytime soon.

"For now, Port in a Storm is my baby," she added a moment later, "and I want to put my mental energy there, not with Noah."

That didn't sound like lip service, which pleased Cal. He didn't expect Charlotte to just jump right into moving on, not when she'd spent most of her adult life and teenage years as Noah's girl. But this seemed like a positive step.

Just as Charlotte was taking that positive step, Becker's ranch came into view. Of course, *ranch* was a relative term, kind of like calling a potholed footpath a *highway*. Still, there was a house, a barn and even some fences. And weeds. Lots of them in the pastures, around the house, and some even sprouting on the roof of the barn. Mother Nature was trying to claim the place for herself.

He spotted Becker's rusty truck, a good sign that the man was home. Then again, the man usually was. Now he only hoped that Becker didn't order them off his land and slam the door in their faces.

Cal parked and was about to get out when the sunlight caught the diamond in the ring on his pinkie and flashed a rainbow prism around the cab of his truck.

"I nearly forgot," Cal said, tugging off the ring. "It's Grammy Effie's. It's a prop for the pretense." He held it out for Charlotte.

But she shook her head. "I can't wear that. It's real. It's an important piece of family jewelry."

"That's what I said, too, but my grandmother insisted. She said that Becker would be more likely to believe the engagement if he noticed the ring." Cal figured the noticing would be a long shot, but still it wouldn't hurt.

Charlotte finally sighed, then nodded and took the ring. Apparently, his grandmother had larger hands than Charlotte because it was too big for her ring finger. She slipped it on her middle finger instead, and when she looked at it, there was a whole lot of worry and caution on her face. Cal wondered what that caution was about, but before he could ask, his phone rang, and he saw San Antonio Rehabilitation Center pop up on the screen on his dash.

And his stomach instantly tightened.

He took the call on Speaker and waited. He didn't have to wait long before he heard a woman's voice.

"Lieutenant Colonel Donnelly?" she asked.

"Yes," Cal verified once he cleared his throat.

"I'm Dr. Meredith Kentrell," the woman explained. "I'm Harper's therapist."

"Yes," he repeated, though he had already guessed the caller had some kind of connection with Harper since that's where she was receiving treatment. "How can I help you?"

"I think it's more of a matter of how you can help Harper," the doctor quickly countered.

"How?" he managed, fully aware that Charlotte was studying him, and that this round of worry and concern was for him.

"Well, I was hoping you'd come to my office so we can discuss that," Dr. Kentrell answered. "Or I could come out to Emerald Creek to see you. Either way, if you're willing, I think it will speed up Harper's recovery if you'd consider visiting her."

"Visiting her?" Cal repeated. "Did Harper say that's what she wants?"

"No. I'm still working on that, but I believe it would be extremely beneficial for her to see you. After you and I have talked, that is. You'd need to understand what you might be walking into if you did agree."

Cal didn't answer. Couldn't. And the doctor must have taken his silence as a cue to continue.

"I was hoping you and I could talk tomorrow, around three or so. Do you think you could do that?" Dr. Kentrell asked.

Everything inside him was shouting a very loud *no*.

But that wasn't what came out of his mouth. "Yes," he told the doctor. "I'll see you. And Harper," he added, praying it wasn't yet another mistake.

CHAPTER SIX

CHARLOTTE DIDN'T SAY anything when Cal ended the call with Harper's therapist. Neither did Cal. They both sat there, the silence thick and heavy.

As if to try to cheer them up, the sunlight continued to bounce off the diamond in Effie's ring, and it sent beautiful rainbows fluttering around them. But Charlotte knew the ring wasn't going to cheer her up. Just the opposite. It was a reminder that her knee-jerk reaction of claiming Cal as her fiancé had turned into a huge emotional punch.

The phone call, however, was an even bigger emotional slam. No doubt about that. The visit to see Harper would carry with it a mountain of pain and grief for Cal. For Harper, too. But Charlotte was guessing that Harper might need a jolt like that to jump-start her recovery. The problem was the jolt might do the reverse for Cal. It could send him nose-diving deeper into guilt.

"I could go with you to the visit," she offered. "Not just with the doctor but with Harper, too."

Cal immediately shook his head. "No. Harper's likely to be angry. No telling what she might do or say if she's capable of speaking."

That wouldn't bother Charlotte. Well, it would, but it wouldn't cut her the way it would Cal. Her heart was incredibly heavy for what Harper was going through, but she suspected Cal didn't want her to witness whatever Harper might sling at him. He probably thought it was best not to have witnesses for that.

"Okay, but if you change your mind, the offer stands," Charlotte said.

He made a sound of agreement. What he didn't do was look at her. Or make her believe he'd take her up on that offer. No. Cal would go it alone. And it would rip him to pieces.

Charlotte reached over and put her hand on his. Of course, that sent the engagement ring into a color-burst dance again, and some of the sparkles were glittering around his face when he finally turned to her.

"Don't mention anything to my family about me going to see Harper," he said. "That would only make them worry more."

She wanted to ask if they should worry more, but she already knew that Cal wouldn't want that. Even if it was warranted.

"I won't tell anyone about the visit," Charlotte assured him. "Maybe when you see Harper, though, you could talk about us being kids. Nothing recent. I think she was happy when she was a kid, or at least *happier*, and it might help for her to tap into those memories."

Cal made another of those agreement noises, but then he stopped and shook his head. "Even when we were kids, Harper wasn't happy. Not like she should have been." He cursed and tugged his hand from hers so he could then use it to scrub it over his face. "We heard the way her dad talked to her, the way he berated her, the way he'd yell at her for anything and everything, and nobody, including me, did a damn thing about it."

"We were kids," Charlotte was quick to point out. Cal was already beating himself up enough without adding this. "And when someone would ask her about the verbal abuse, Harper would always insist he was a great dad, who loved her so much that he wanted the best for her."

Classic battering syndrome. Harper was covering for her abuser. Covering for her father, Paul. And what Paul wanted wasn't what was best for Harper but what would make her, and therefore him, *look* best. When she didn't live up to expectations, he struck out. Charlotte had no trouble recalling a recent incident of that.

"A couple of months ago, Desi at the diner wanted to name a burger after Harper, and her dad nixed the idea," Charlotte relayed. "Paul said she should come in first for that to happen, that the burger should be named after you."

Judging from the sound he made, Cal hadn't heard about that incident, but she hoped it made him see that Paul was also a driving force in this competition between Cal and her.

Charlotte wondered if Paul was still trying to supposedly motivate his daughter with the negative stuff. Or maybe he'd washed his hands of his daughter when Harper had driven off that bridge. For Harper's own well-being, that last scenario would probably be the best, especially if her father tried to continue his strong-arm approach when she was in therapy.

"Her dad drove her to be perfect," Cal muttered. "But

I took it up a lot of notches. I drove her to push herself too hard. I didn't want to see what it was doing to her."

Charlotte would have definitely tried to nip that guilt in the bud by reminding him that Harper had likely done her own driving toward perfection, but the front door of the house opened, and Becker stepped out onto the porch. He was clutching onto the collar of a barking, growling dog that was a German shepherd mix.

Both Becker and the dog were sporting scowls so she couldn't tell if their arrival was the cause or whether their faces were just naturally settled into that particular expression.

"What the hell are y'all doing just sitting there in my driveway?" Becker called out over the nonstop barking.

Sighing, Charlotte knew she'd have to push the pause button on any attempt to comfort Cal, and she stepped from the truck. "Cal and I came to pay you a visit." She tried to keep her voice oh-so-cheery while Becker clearly stayed in the oh-so-sourpuss zone.

"You're wasting your time and mine," Becker snapped. He had a tight grip on the dog's collar, but thankfully, the canine didn't seem to be trying to break free to charge at them. "I haven't made up my mind about selling to you."

"Good morning, Mr. Becker," Cal said, getting out as well and obviously ignoring the man's unfriendly welcome. "Maybell asked me to bring over some cookies." He took the container from beneath his seat and held it up.

"Maybell," Becker muttered, and while that was still a snarl, Charlotte detected just a smidge of softening.

She had no idea, though, if that was for Maybell herself or the cookies.

Becker no doubt knew who Maybell was, what with
this being Emerald Creek and all. That meant he also
knew the woman's baking skills were legendary.

Cal threaded his way around the weed-filled yard
and to the porch, and while still keeping his distance
from the dog, he extended his arm out as far as it would
go to offer the cookies to Becker. Again, she thought
she saw a bit of softening when Becker took them. He
muttered something that could have been thanks. Or a
belch. The dog quit barking, too, maybe in anticipation
of getting a treat.

"It's a pretty day," Cal went on, obviously pretending this was a friendly conversation, "and I hadn't seen
your ranch in years. I hope you don't mind that we just
dropped by without calling first."

"I wouldn't have answered my phone," Becker was
quick to let him know.

Cal nodded as if that was not only understood but
also perfectly acceptable, and he put his hands on his
hips and glanced around. Charlotte had to hand it to
him: Cal didn't scowl at the run-down state of the place.
He just added a few more nods, a smile and made it
seem as if this were indeed a paradise.

"And who is this guy?" Cal asked, tipping his head
to the dog.

"Jack the Ripper. Yeah, I know that's not a name
for a girl, but it fit her personality. Don't try to pet her.
She bites."

Cal didn't attempt any petting, but he stooped down,

smiling at the dog. "Hey, Jack. I'm Cal. You're doing a good job protecting this place."

The dog cocked her head to the side and began to wag her tail. All ferocity was gone, and Jack was apparently soothed by Cal's charm.

Becker, however, clearly wasn't soothed or charmed. His scowl returned in spades. "No more bullshit," the man grumbled, looking straight at Charlotte. "Why do you want my ranch? If you're marrying Donnelly here, you could be living on Saddlebrook." There was plenty of mocking tone at the mention of the name of the Donnelly ranch.

"Saddlebrook is beautiful," Charlotte answered, "but I don't want to live there. I love this place."

"Bullshit," Becker repeated, and that set off huge amounts of alarm bells for Charlotte.

Had Becker heard about her plans for the ranch? Had he learned the truth about her and Cal's engagement? Maybe. It was possible the BS was for her *love* remark. Anything she said to Becker could be a risk, but she went with something she thought might sway him into selling.

"Emerald Creek has a couple of wounded warriors who are looking for a place to recover and regain some peace in their lives," she admitted. Of course, her hope was that it would be more than just Alden and Harper. "Your ranch is big enough to offer them a place to stay while they're recovering."

And she waited. Holding her breath.

"This place is for livestock," Becker grumbled.

Charlotte gave an enthusiastic nod. "Oh, there'll be livestock." That was pretty much the extent of how she could answer that since she knew very little about running an actual ranch.

"My brother Blue recently purchased some rescue horses," Cal quickly chimed in, "and your land would give them plenty of room to roam. They could do some healing here, like the wounded warriors."

Charlotte didn't know if that was a real-deal offer or not, but she definitely liked the sound of it. It could end up being a mutually satisfying arrangement for the residents and the horses.

Becker's eyes narrowed some when he stared at Cal, and then he seemed to relent again. "Yeah, I heard about those horses. You got some fancy-schmancy horse whisperer working with them."

"Marin," Cal provided. "She's made a lot of progress, but my brother found another group of neglected horses. Not Andalusian like we usually raise at Saddlebrook but a mixed-breed lot that was pretty much left to pasture when their owner had to be put in assisted living. Blue's bought them, and they'll be transported to Emerald Creek once we have a place for them."

"The Donnellys have got plenty of land." That came out as yet another snarl from Becker.

"We do," Cal readily admitted, "but at the moment we also have a lot of livestock that we won't be selling off for at least another four months."

Becker still didn't look convinced. "I figured you Donnellys would be cutting back, considering what happened to your daddy." He tapped his chest. "I heard about his bad ticker."

Cal nodded. "Yes, he's had two heart attacks and is taking a break from ranching. My brother Egan took over running the cattle side of the business. Blue's managing the Andalusian horses. We'd need a place for these new rescues and any others we might end up buying."

Becker kept his steely gaze on Cal, but the man also opened the plastic container and plucked out a cookie. The air was suddenly filled not with pollen from the weeds but with the scent of lemons.

"So, the Donnellys are looking to expand onto my land," Becker threw out there like a challenge.

"We are, but the biggest reason we want your place is that Charlotte is looking for a new home. A home that will keep what you've built here and add to it," Cal said, slipping his arm around her waist and inching her closer.

Charlotte took the closing-in cue and lifted her hand to take hold of Cal's arm. In doing so, she made sure the engagement ring was in Becker's line of sight. Thankfully, the sun cooperated again and caused the diamond to flash.

"I see you finally got around to getting her a ring," Becker told Cal.

Cal nodded and snuggled even closer to Charlotte. So close that the side of her left breast brushed against his chest. It wasn't a whole lot of contact, but it still packed a wallop. Mercy, did it. She felt that blasted tickle of heat again. That tug below her belly.

The lust.

For the past two years it was as if her body had gone dormant when it'd come to men and sex, but it sure as heck wasn't dormant now. At least she didn't have to kiss Cal. That would make things so much worse—

Cal leaned in and kissed her.

Holy moly. Even though it was barely a touch of his lips to hers, the heat zinged its way from her mouth to all parts of her. Especially the wrong parts, and Charlotte had to remind herself and her body that this was all for show. Well, the kiss was anyway. The lust was the real deal. And completely one-sided on her part.

Wasn't it?

Charlotte would have sworn that it was, but when Cal pulled back from the kiss, their gazes met. She saw some heat. Maybe. But, no. She had to be wrong about that. Had to be.

Unless this was pity lust.

It was possible. Cal might believe she was crushed about what Noah had done. And Noah had put in that text for Cal to offer up some TLC. So she wasn't seeing actual heat but rather a snowball of emotions.

"I'd rather you do your smooching somewhere other than my porch," Becker grumbled. The grumble was toned down, though, because he was chowing down on the cookie. "And it ain't necessary to show me you're in love and all. I got eyes, don't I? I can see it for myself."

A laugh nearly burst out of Charlotte's mouth. *In love and all?* Really? That's what Becker was seeing? If so, either the man had seriously bad eyesight or else she and Cal were very convincing.

She waited, hoping this would be the moment when Becker would finally say he was selling her the place. He didn't. "It's time for one of the TV shows I watch," Becker muttered, tipping his head to the container of cookies he'd tucked under his arm. "Tell Maybell I said thanks for these."

He turned to go back inside just as Jack started barking again. Charlotte automatically moved back from the dog, who began straining to get out of the grip Becker still had on her collar.

"Dang squirrel," Becker grumbled. "Settle down, Jack."

But the dog didn't settle. Just the opposite. Jack bolted, causing Becker to tumble forward. Cal and Charlotte both reached for him but weren't in time. Becker landed with a hard thud on the porch. Charlotte heard the sickening sound of what she was certain was a bone snapping.

Becker howled out in pain, and that thankfully caused Jack to stop. The dog ditched all efforts to get at the squirrel and turned back to her owner. No more barking; Jack started to whimper.

Cal stooped down, examining Becker but not touching him. Probably because he didn't want to risk making the man's injuries any worse. There was a gash on his head, and his face was now twisted in pain. He'd dropped the cookies and was trying to clutch his leg.

"It's broken," Becker gutted out.

Yes, it almost certainly was, and there was blood on the knee of the man's jeans. Blood, too, from the head gash.

"I'm calling an ambulance," Charlotte insisted, figuring that Becker would balk about that.

He didn't.

Becker just continued to lie there on the porch and moan in pain while she tapped 9-1-1. The emergency dispatcher answered on the first ring, and within just a couple of seconds Charlotte had the reassurance that an ambulance was on the way and would be there in about fifteen minutes. She relayed that to Cal and Becker and went back closer to Becker to keep an eye on him.

"It's okay, Jack," Becker muttered to the dog, who was also keeping careful watch of her master.

The man's gentle tone was certainly a surprise, and while still whimpering, Jack lay down next to Becker and rested her big head on his shoulder.

"Do you think anything else is broken other than your leg?" Cal asked.

Becker shook his head, squeezed his eyes shut and groaned. He started to shiver, probably from shock. The color had drained from his face as well. "I don't think so, but it's bad. I can feel it. It's bad," he repeated.

Charlotte couldn't argue with that. It was possible the man had a compound fracture, and if so, he might end up needing surgery. She felt totally selfish when she thought of how this might affect the sale of the ranch. She shoved that notion aside and stepped around them to go to the front door.

"I'll get a blanket," she offered.

She stepped inside, and as she'd already learned from the one showing Becker had approved for her and the Realtor, the interior was not a companion piece to the weed-filled yard. It was surprisingly clean and uncluttered, though the furniture was well past merely being outdated. In fact, some of the pieces had come and gone back into style several times.

There weren't any throws or such on the sofa, and since she didn't want to go poking around in any of the bedrooms, she grabbed a jacket from a peg near the door and came back out. Becker was shivering even more now, and she draped the jacket over him, hoping the slight pressure of the fabric didn't do more harm than good.

"If y'all hadn't been here," Becker said, gulping in a series of quick short breaths, "I would have had to crawl my way back into the house to the phone." He shook his head. "I'm not sure I could've done that. I could have ended up dying out here."

Charlotte braced herself, figuring that Becker was about to say that it was all their fault for paying him this impromptu visit. But he didn't.

"This is a life-pact," Becker added a moment later. "Neither of you might even know what that is."

"We know," Cal and Charlotte said in unison.

Mercy, did they. Cal's life-pact to Noah had been a biggie in Cal's life, and without it, she and Cal might not have even ended up here, since he likely wouldn't have played messenger for Noah.

Becker managed a weak nod. "Good. Then, you know I owe you," he said. He looked at Charlotte, and even though his eyes had watered from the pain, he lifted his hand toward her. It took her a moment to realize he wanted her to shake it.

She did.

"That's a done deal, then," Becker muttered. "I'm selling you the ranch."

CHAPTER SEVEN

CAL TUCKED THE container of cookies under his arm, plastered on the best "I'm okay. Really" expression and stepped into the hospital. He'd figured he would see people he knew, and he was right. The seeing started almost immediately.

Jenny Bell, a longtime nurse at the hospital and his late mom's best friend, was crossing the lobby. She spotted Cal and made a beeline toward him. With each step she took, her arms opened wider, her smile broadened, and once she reached him, she gave Cal a bear hug.

"There you are," Jenny gushed. "I heard you were back in town and hoped I'd see you." She let the hug linger a few moments before she pulled back and met his eyes. Cal hoped he'd succeeded in his attempt at looking calm.

"It's good to see you, Mrs. Bell," he said.

She kept staring, kept smiling, though she did take it down a notch. "I heard about your engagement. Figured it was malarkey," Jenny added in a whisper. "But my lips are sealed. You and Charlotte did a fake-a-roo to convince old man Becker to sell his place, right?"

"My lips are sealed," Cal repeated, adding a grin that he figured would cause Jenny to giggle. It did.

"Well, it worked," Jenny went on as if he'd confirmed

the fake-a-roo. "Word's all over town that Becker caved after his come-to-Jesus meeting with that bad fall he took yesterday when you and Charlotte were at his place. Is that why you're here, to see the old geezer?"

Cal nodded. "Is he allowed visitors?"

"Sure is." Jenny hooked her arm around him and got him moving toward the hall with the patients' rooms. "Not that he's had many. Only Charlotte and Sally Daughtry, who's the real estate agent."

Good. Well, not good about the few visitors, but good that things seemed to be moving along with the sale. Cal had worried that Becker might renege on his life-pact once he'd had some time to think. Twenty-four hours in a hospital bed would give him plenty of thinking time.

Of course, if Becker had waffled, Charlotte would have almost certainly let Cal know. Since the accident, Cal and she had stayed at the hospital until Becker had come out of surgery. After they'd parted ways, there'd been lots of text exchanges with Charlotte keeping him updated about the sale and Becker's condition.

There'd also been some restless hours.

On Cal's part, anyway.

He blamed those blasted fake kisses—which hadn't felt the least bit fake to him. He'd gotten lost in the last one on Becker's porch. Lost and hot. Not a good combo when it came to Charlotte.

"I was so sorry to hear about Harper," Jenny went on as they walked. "You doing okay with that?"

Figuring he couldn't pull off a convincing lie, Cal went with a sound that could have meant anything. Thankfully, Jenny didn't push him. But that didn't stop Cal from thinking about Harper. That included being reminded of the visit he had with her therapist. He checked the time: it was scheduled to be in less than a half hour. A half hour, and he'd no doubt have to hash and rehash things he wished hadn't happened. Hard to unwish through a lifetime of junk when that junk was wrapped up with all his other memories.

At least the visit wouldn't be taking place at the San Antonio facility where Harper was a patient. Cal had instead arranged to have Dr. Kentrell come to Emerald Creek. Not to the ranch. He hadn't wanted his family in on that. Instead, he was meeting Harper's therapist at Charlotte's law office. It wasn't exactly neutral ground, but since her office was closed today, it would at least give him some privacy.

"Well, if you want to talk about any of it, I'm here for you," Jenny said, stopping outside a door. Becker's name had been written on a little dry-erase board attached to the wall. "If you want to talk about Noah, too. I'm hoping he's okay with the fake-a-roo engagement?"

No need for a sound this time. Cal nodded. "He is."

Or rather he would be okay with it if he knew about it. Noah was all wrapped up in his new life but would probably applaud the pretense since it'd been put into place to allow Charlotte to start something new as well, with Port in a Storm.

"It was good to see you," Cal said, giving Jenny a hug before he knocked on Becker's door.

"If you gotta come in, do it," Becker grumbled. "But if it's not important, leave me the hell alone." Obviously, Becker was back to his usual self.

After Jenny wished Cal luck, he stepped in and immediately spotted Becker in the bed. Not a pretty sight.

The man's head was bruised and bandaged, and his leg was in some kind of elevated sling. Cal could see the bandage there, too, that covered his surgical incision.

Becker had already opened his mouth, maybe to continue being ornery, but his expression changed, and he seemed to throttle back. Maybe because he remembered that life-pact deal.

"Donnelly," he said with a lot less venom than usual. "Charlotte told me you had Jack. How's she doing?"

"Good." And that wasn't a lie. "I took her to Saddlebrook, and she's been getting a lot of attention." Mainly from Leo, who was thrilled at having a dog to play with, but some of the ranch hands were also enjoying it.

Becker's forehead bunched up. "Well, don't give her too many treats and spoil her rotten."

"I won't." Cal set the cookie stash on the bed next to Becker. "From Maybell. Snickerdoodles. Unless maybe you think you shouldn't have too many treats, either." He reached as if to take back the cookies.

"No," Becker was quick to say, and he slid his hand over the container. "Tell Maybell I said thanks."

"I will," Cal assured him, and he tipped his head to the sling. "So what's the verdict? How long will you be in here?" Cal already knew the gist of it from Charlotte, but he wanted Becker's account of it.

Becker's forehead did more of that bunching up. "At least a week, and then they're clamoring on about moving me to a rehab center. A stupid name," he grumbled. "Makes me sound like I use drugs, and I don't. I'll be there to get physical therapy."

That meshed with what Charlotte had said. Apparently, the therapy would be needed to help him walk again, and because of Becker's age, it wouldn't necessarily be a speedy recovery. Or perhaps even a complete one.

"Well, don't worry about Jack," Cal said. "I'll take care of her as long as needed."

Becker eyed him with skepticism. "What about when your leave is up? I figured that wouldn't be more than a week or so. What happens to Jack then?"

No way did Cal want to get into the whole deal of leave and his separating from the Air Force. "My brother Blue will watch her. And Maybell." Cal tacked on that last bit not only because Maybell would indeed volunteer to help but also because he thought it would please Becker.

It did.

The man smiled a little. It was sort of creepy and looked unnatural on his craggy face, but it confirmed something Cal had suspected: Becker had a crush on Maybell. Or maybe the crush was for the woman's superior cookies.

"Closing on my place is in two weeks, maybe less. I'm not sure how I'll get my house cleared out by then," Becker went on a moment later. "Charlotte said she'd help with that, that maybe I could supervise the move by looking at her computer while everything's packed up. I don't like the sound of that, but I also don't want to delay the sale, and Lord knows when I'd be able to get back to do it myself."

"I'll help, too," Cal assured him, and then frowned. Help would likely mean more close contact with Charlotte, and his gut instinct told him he should be distancing himself from her. And he would. As soon as the sale was final.

So why did that only deepen his frown?

Because he was stupid, that's why.

"I'll use the money from the sale to pay off some stuff," Becker continued. "And I want to buy a camper trailer. I've got a cousin outside of Austin who said I can park it on his land."

Becker didn't exactly seem thrilled about that, but Cal didn't hear or see any hint of the man backing out. Good. Because the sooner the sale went through… He stopped, frowned again and didn't bother to swear to himself that he would start distancing himself from Charlotte.

And speaking of Charlotte, Cal's phone dinged, and he saw her name pop up on the screen. But this wasn't an update about the sale or Becker.

Dr. Kentrell just arrived early. No need for you to hurry. I can show her the plans for Port in a Storm to make sure it'll have what Harper needs.

Yeah, the therapist would no doubt be interested in that, but Cal didn't want Charlotte to have to entertain the doctor. It was best to get this appointment over, and then he could deal with the aftermath.

There would be an aftermath. No doubt about it.

"I have to go," Cal said after he replied to Charlotte that he was on his way. "But if you need anything, just have one of the nurses call Saddlebrook." That was a better option than leaving his number, since Becker didn't own a cell phone. "Oh, and I'll thank Maybell for the cookies."

Becker opened his mouth again, but then he waved off whatever he'd been about to say.

"I'll also tell Jack you said hello," Cal said on a guess, and judging from the man's nod, he'd hit the nail on the head.

Cal smiled at Becker's obvious devotion to his dog, muttered a goodbye and headed out. Charlotte's law office wasn't far, only about six blocks away, but Cal didn't want to risk being stopped for chats along the way, so he intended to drive straight there. His plan went south, however, when he went into the parking lot and saw a man waiting by his truck.

Harper's dad, Paul.

Hell, Cal had figured this meeting would happen sooner or later, but it wasn't the best time. Then again, maybe no time was best, and it was long overdue.

"Mr. Johansen," Cal greeted him.

The man didn't respond, not verbally anyway, but he kept his hard stare on Cal. "Got your note you left on my door," he finally said. "I'd been meaning to call you or something, but I just didn't get around to it. I got an appointment for a checkup in a few minutes, but when I saw you coming out of the hospital, I decided now was as good a time as any for us to talk."

Cal didn't pick up on any immediate bitterness, but it had to be there. Paul had essentially lost the version of his daughter that he'd tried to shape and mold. Of course, the shaping and molding had never been a high enough standard for the man, but that wouldn't matter. He had lost his daughter, and he probably wanted someone to blame.

Cal was more than willing to take that blame.

"I wanted to tell you how sorry I am for what happened to Harper," Cal stated, and despite Paul's indecipherable body language, Cal went closer. If Paul punched him, then he'd take that, too. In fact, it might feel damn good if Paul took out his anger on him.

"Yeah," Paul said, his tone still not conveying a whole lot. But then, he glanced away, fixing his gaze on the roof of the hospital. "Have you seen her since she made this mess of herself?"

"Briefly," he muttered, repeating the response he'd given Charlotte.

He considered telling Paul that he was on his way to see Harper's therapist and that might end up with an arrangement for Cal to see her, but he didn't want Paul horning in on that meeting. Especially since Cal wasn't sure what the therapist wanted to say to him.

"You've seen her?" Cal asked.

Paul grunted in a way that confirmed it. "She can't talk. Can't walk. Hell, she can hardly move, and she just stares off into space when I tell her she shouldn't…"

He stopped, waved that off, and it seemed to take him a couple of seconds to regroup. "Nothing I say gets through to her, but that's my problem, not yours. I just wanted to let you know that I got your note. And thanks for saying you're sorry for my daughter's screwup," he muttered. With that, he turned and walked away.

Cal didn't even consider going after him since he was reasonably sure there was nothing he could say to the man that would help. Nothing he could do. And with that dismal thought racing through his head, he got in his truck and made the drive to the law office.

Since the drive was indeed a short one, he didn't have much time for his body to settle from the impromptu meeting, but he figured that wasn't the last he'd see of Paul. After all, they lived in the same small town. During those future meetings, Cal was certain he'd be doling out more apologies, and while they'd be heartfelt and would slice him to the core, his words wouldn't help.

A mountain of apologies wouldn't get Paul back his daughter and wouldn't fix Harper the way Paul wanted. But maybe Harper could be fixed in other ways, and that's why this meeting with the therapist was so important.

He parked behind a sleek silver Audi that was in turn behind Charlotte's Fusion. The moment he stepped out, he spotted the Sorry, We're Closed sign on the door, and through the window, he saw Charlotte and a tall brunette woman peering at the plans that Charlotte had on her desk.

He stepped in, the jangling bell alerting the women, who both turned in his direction. The mood for the day was apparently uneasiness since both had that in their expressions. Cal figured there was plenty of it in his, too.

"Dr. Kentrell," Cal greeted, and he shook her hand when she extended it to him.

"Lieutenant Colonel Donnelly," she greeted right back.

"Cal," he offered, though part of him wanted to keep this strictly professional. She must have as well, because she didn't offer her given name. "Thanks for agreeing to this meeting in Emerald Creek."

"No problem," she said. "Thanks for seeing me."

The politeness didn't settle Cal's nerves one bit. The same for Charlotte, who fluttered her fingers toward an office. "You two can talk in private in there if you like."

The doctor glanced at both of them. "It might be beneficial for you to hear what I have to say. I mean, since I know Harper and you are friends."

Charlotte shrugged. "We were when we were kids, but we grew apart after high school. Actually before that," she admitted. "My dad ran off with Harper's mom when we were sixteen. We didn't exactly avoid each other after that, but we quit connecting."

"I think that's possibly true for all of Harper's friends," Dr. Kentrell admitted. "And that's part of the problem. Normally, I like to involve a client's family and friends in the therapy, but so far, the only person who's come to see her has been her father." Her mouth tightened a little. "I'd like for her to have visits that are of a more positive nature."

Cal groaned. Apparently, Paul was at it again, and those bullying tactics wouldn't help. In fact, they could hurt.

"I'm not sure a visit from me would be a positive-nature thing," Cal pointed out to the doctor.

"On the surface, it wouldn't be," she agreed. "I can't get into the specifics of Harper's diagnosis, but I'll give you the broad strokes. I believe her anger is imped-ing her recovery of her mental state and of her speech and mobility, and that she needs to start facing some of that anger." She looked directly at Cal. "Just seeing you could be the jump start she needs."

"Or it could set her back," he quickly countered.

The doctor sighed. "Possibly. But I don't think so. Her recovery has stalled. In fact, there's regression in some areas."

That gave him another gut punch. From everything he'd heard, Harper had a long, hard road ahead of her, and even with stellar care, she might not ever have a normal life. Then again, she hadn't had much normalcy before driving off that bridge.

"Uh, can Harper even communicate?" Charlotte asked. "I understand her vocal cords were damaged."

Dr. Kentrell nodded. "She doesn't speak, but she has use of several fingers on her right hand and can type out vocal responses either on the computer or as a text. She's also been able to draw some things with a stylus in an art app we use for some clients." She paused and took out her phone. "I took photos of some of what she's drawn, but I'm not sure what they mean, and she won't explain. I was hoping you'd be able to help."

The doctor held up the photo for Cal to see, and he instantly recognized it even though it was a crude drawing. "It's the cockpit of an F-22."

But he also saw something else. Harper had drawn it at an angle so it looked as if the fighter jet was in a nosedive. The pilot's helmet had the call sign on the back instead of the front.

"*Lone Wolf*," he muttered. "That's Harper's call sign." Not exactly a flattering one since the perception was that she wasn't a team player. Then again, plenty of call signs weren't flattering. Cal's included.

"Am I mistaken, or did she draw the jet about to crash?" the doctor asked.

"You're not mistaken," Cal verified.

She nodded and pulled up the next photo. Another F-22 cockpit, this one on a steady course, though, and Cal groaned when he saw the call sign on this particular helmet. "*Halo*," he said. "That's mine."

Both Charlotte and the doctor lifted eyebrows, clearly questioning it.

"Can't do any wrong," he provided. "Trust me, in that context, it's not a compliment."

Cal figured his early promotions had caused some resentment. That, and he'd had sort of a golden career. Well, he had before Harper had tried to end her life. And then there was Audrey. No one in his current squadron was going to forget that his stepmother was a two-star general with her own golden career that came with lots of pull.

"So in your picture, all is well, and in hers, she's crashing," the doctor summarized. She met his gaze. "I see that as positive. Harper's not aiming any ill will at you."

Cal wished he could agree with that. Or that the insight made him feel better. It didn't. Then again, there wasn't a lot that was going to make him feel good at the moment.

"There's a third picture," the doctor continued, pulling it up, and she showed it to both Charlotte and him.

Again, the drawing was crude, but Cal picked out four sticklike figures, trees and some water. Since one of the stick figures was sprawled in the water and had tears or some kind of drops spewing out of his eyes, this was probably a depiction of the incident at the creek when they were kids.

"That one must be me," Charlotte offered, tapping the stick figure with the long hair. "That's Noah." He was reaching out to Cal.

The fourth figure with short hair was likely Harper, and she was standing back as if observing. Cal couldn't recall if that's what she'd done that day, but he doubted it. It seemed to him that all three of his friends had come rushing to save him.

"When we were eight, I nearly drowned at the creek," Cal explained, tapping each stick figure and identifying them.

"Interesting," the doctor murmured. "Was this an incident Harper talked about a lot?"

Cal had to shake his head. Charlotte did the same. "I don't remember Harper ever mentioning it," Charlotte provided. "So why would she draw it?"

"That's what I need to find out," Dr. Kentrell concluded. "If you two agree to visit Harper, I'd like for you to bring up that incident. It's possible she drew this because she wants to reconnect with you or because she saw this as some kind of important moment in her life."

Cal still wasn't convinced. "Has Harper actually agreed to us visiting?" he came out and asked.

"No." She tapped the photos. "But you're clearly on her mind. It takes a lot of effort for her to draw or do anything with her fingers. It would have been painful for her to do these, and yet here they are."

The doctor put her phone away. "I told Harper I was coming here to talk to you today and that I was going to encourage you and Charlotte to go see her. She didn't respond to that, but now that I know what the photos mean, I'll talk to her about them and then try to arrange a visit. If you're both willing to do it, that is?"

"Of course," Charlotte murmured.

Cal made a barely audible sound of agreement, but he followed it up with a firm nod. If his seeing Harper might possibly help her, then he'd do it. No matter how hard it would be. He sure as hell hadn't helped her before, but he would now.

"Good," Dr. Kentrell concluded. She shifted her attention to Charlotte. "And thank you for showing me the plans for Port in a Storm. When it's up and running, I think it'll be the right place for Harper."

"Good," Charlotte said. "If you think her room needs any modifications I haven't added, just let me know."

"I will," the doctor assured her. "Harper can physically take care of a lot of her personal needs. Showering and such. But will there be someone around if she needs help?"

"Yes," Charlotte verified. "I'll have some LVNs and nursing assistants. There'll also be a therapist on call and a personal trainer who has experience working with traumatic injuries. Do you think Harper will need more than that?"

"Maybe. But if anything comes up that you or your staff can't handle, then let me know, and I'll try to arrange for it."

The doctor seemed to want to say more. Maybe more about exactly what kind of long-term care would be needed, but that would probably get into too much of Harper's condition.

"I think we all just want the best for Harper, and that's a good start," Dr. Kentrell added.

With that, the doctor said her goodbyes and walked out. Cal and Charlotte stood there, watching as Dr. Kentrell got into her car, and Cal figured Charlotte was doing exactly what he was: trying to process what they'd just learned. Trying to figure out what Harper had meant when she'd drawn that picture of the creek.

Harper had certainly known about the life-pact between him and Noah. Was the drawing about the pact itself, or was she secretly wishing that Cal had died that day? If it was the latter, Harper hadn't voiced that over the years. Well, not until the suicide note, anyway.

"You okay?" Charlotte asked after some long moments of silence.

Cal didn't bother with a lie. "Not really." His mind was whirling, the thoughts crashing into each other. Thoughts of how Harper had been when they were kids. Thoughts of the person she'd become.

"Yeah," Charlotte muttered, and at that moment the sunlight caused the ring she was wearing to flash. "Oh, before I forget, you should get this back to your grandmother since we don't need it anymore. Please thank her for me again."

Cal looked at the ring, and sighing, he tucked it into the front pocket of his jeans.

She slipped her arm around his waist, drawing him closer until they were side to side while they continued to stare out the window. "You've got a lot to deal with right now."

"Not nearly as much as Harper," he whispered.

She made a sound to indicate she didn't quite agree

with that. "If the doctor drove all the way out here, she must be devoted to helping Harper. It's only been a month, so maybe she'll end up recovering more than her initial prognosis."

"Maybe," he echoed, also echoing Charlotte's previous skeptical sound. Harper would have to want recovery, and Cal wasn't sure she did. After all, she'd drawn herself in the nose-diving F-22.

Charlotte kept her arm around him but turned to face him. No more side to side. This was body to body, and it didn't seem to matter that their centers weren't actually touching. Didn't seem to matter, either, that they were dealing with an emotionally heavy moment. Nope. Parts of him reacted. Parts of him felt the heat.

Parts of him—well, his mouth, anyway—wanted to kiss her.

"You know, this has all the makings of a rebound disaster," he spelled out.

She gave a quick nod. "It could ruin our friendship and complicate things that are already too complicated. Added to that, neither of us has time for sex and stuff."

Again, parts of him reacted. Specifically, one part that wanted to seriously disagree about them not having time for sex. His dick seemed to think it was an amazing idea.

It wasn't.

Still, Cal didn't move away from her. He just stood there like the idiot he was and continued to stare at her mouth. Obviously, over the years he hadn't felt this heat bath of lust when he'd looked at her. There'd been an attraction. No way could he deny that. Charlotte was a stunner with a good heart. A bad combo for him. In fact, it was his exact type, he had to admit.

"When you were with Noah, I didn't have these thoughts about you," Cal admitted.

"Ditto," she confessed right back, and Charlotte continued to stare at his mouth, too.

The tapping sound had them flying apart, and they both whirled toward the window to see a familiar face pressed against the glass.

Remi.

Cal groaned. Not his usual reaction when he saw his sister. Normally, seeing her would give him a jolt of joy that she was safe and home. He got a jolt of a different kind this time because Remi was giving him a *What the hell are you doing?* look. Unfortunately, Cal didn't have an acceptable answer.

"Remi," Charlotte called out, and she hurried to the door to open it. The moment his sister stepped in, the women gave each other hugs. All the while Remi kept her gaze on Cal.

"I didn't know you were coming home," Charlotte said.

"My deployment was delayed, so I decided to come and check on my brother." She volleyed glances at Charlotte and him. "Should I ask why you two were within a breath of kissing each other's lights out?"

"No," Cal was quick to say. He pulled Remi into a hug as well and held on for a couple of moments.

Remi chuckled when she eased back. "I heard about the pretend engagement, so I'll just assume the two of you were practicing so you'd be a convincing couple."

Neither Charlotte nor he jumped to agree. Or deny it.

That brought on a shrug from Remi, and her attention settled on Charlotte. "I was on my way to the ranch but decided to drop by here first to check on you." She paused. "Noah asked me to check on you," Remi amended.

"You've seen him?" Charlotte asked.

"For a couple of minutes." And Remi left it at that. Since both she and Noah were Combat Rescue Officers, it was possible they'd been heading on the same now delayed deployment. Remi had chosen to spend the delay at home, but Cal suspected Noah was with Elise.

"Are you handling the breakup okay?" Remi wanted to know.

"It was a long time coming," Charlotte was quick to say, and Cal hoped that she truly did feel that way. It was possible, however, that she was shoving down her true feelings because she didn't want to deal with the pain. "Uh, how's Noah?"

"I'm not sure," Remi answered. "I only saw him for those couple of minutes after the debriefing."

Cal studied his sister's expression to determine if she knew about Elise. She did. But he didn't press her for any further info.

"So, care to guess why I decided to come home?" Remi added, looking at Cal now.

No guess required. "You heard I'm getting out of the military."

Apparently, that was enough for Charlotte to decide this was a private conversation. "I've got some calls to make about the renovations at the ranch." She didn't give them a chance to object to that. Charlotte hurried into her office, the one that Cal knew she didn't use, and she shut the door.

"Why?" Remi immediately pressed.

He figured a picture was worth a thousand words, and he took out his phone to show her the note that Harper had left. He watched as Remi read it.

Cal, the playing field is all yours now. I'm bowing out of this shitshow. No more looking over my shoulder and worrying about you besting me. No more losing to you. You win.

"Well, I can see how that would be a kick to the balls," Remi muttered.

"It was," he assured her.

She handed him back his phone but continued to study him. "And you don't think you can get past this?"

"No. This isn't something you get past."

Remi nodded. Shrugged. "You believe getting out of the Air Force will help you better deal with it?"

There was no snark or admonishment in her tone or expression, but like everyone else in their family, she was probably trying to work out how giving up his career would fix this.

It wouldn't.

"I just can't face going back to the cockpit," he spelled out. "I'm spent, Remi."

She nodded. Hugged him again. "Then, maybe you just need some time off. Or are you one hundred percent sure you want to throw it all in?"

Yesterday, he'd been positive. But today, there was doubt. And Dr. Kentrell's visit was the reason for it. She'd given Cal a sliver of hope that Harper might recover. Of course, her recovery shouldn't be the catalyst for what he did or didn't do with his career, but Cal thought he might be able to climb out of this dark hole if Harper started showing signs of getting better.

"All right, change of subject," Remi said when he didn't respond. "Want to tell me what's going on between you and Charlotte?" Now there was a smidge of snark.

Cal's initial reaction was to return the snark, but Remi would just keep digging until she got to the truth. "We've been doing the lovey-dovey act. Spending time together, touching, a chaste kiss," he spelled out.

She raised an eyebrow. "Judging from your expression, I'm guessing it wasn't chaste enough?"

Nail, hit right on the head. "Anything that could happen now would just be a rebound, and I don't want to put Charlotte through that." Didn't want to put himself through it, either.

"You're sure about that?" his sister pressed. "When I saw you two through the window, that didn't look very reboundy to me."

Cal looked her straight in the eyes and tried to make sure there were no visible doubts. "Think it through. In the town's eyes, Charlotte will always be Noah's. She'd have to live with daily gossip if she stepped out with me."

"And yet she's dealing with daily gossip now because of the fake engagement," Remi was quick to point out. "Is Charlotte getting a lot of objections about that? Are there people clamoring for her to get back with the scum-butt cheating Noah, who was too chickenshit to do his own breakup with her?"

Cal's stare turned to a flat look. "I suspect most

people know the engagement is a sham. And as for clamoring, well, Izzie certainly voiced her objection to the breakup."

Remi groaned. "Izzie wants the fairy-tale image of her and Charlotte's wedding to Taggert and Noah. *Image*," she emphasized. "Izzie's up for reelection, and there are some who are not so happy about her snooty ways."

Izzie could indeed have some snootiness, but Cal hadn't heard anything about her waning in the polls. Especially since the woman had run unopposed for the past two elections.

"The pitiful mayor whose husband deserted her, marrying the long-suffering widower rancher," Remi went on, "while her daughter is marrying the special forces military hero." She put the last word in air quotes. "The fairy tale loses some punch when said daughter instead has a fling with the hero's crestfallen best friend. By the way, do Izzie and Taggert know the truth about Noah?"

Cal had been about to address the *crestfallen* remark, but he nodded in response to the question she'd tacked onto that. "They know, but I don't think Izzie fully believes that it's over between Noah and Charlotte."

And that led Cal to another thought. He wasn't sure *he* believed it was over. That's why he was disgusted with these urges to kiss Charlotte. It was possible, if Noah came waltzing back into her life and asked her to forgive him and reconcile, that Charlotte would do just that. Yes, she was hurt and angry over what Noah had done, but she and Noah had been a couple for a very long time, and even the hurt and anger might not be enough for her to throw that away.

All right, now he was indeed crestfallen. And what a stupid word that was. He would have cursed that word and his rock-bottom mood, but his phone dinged with a text. It wasn't a saved-by-the-bell moment, however. Cal realized that when he saw *San Antonio Rehabilitation Center* on the screen.

And when he saw the message.

Harper here. The shrink said you might visit. Well, don't waste your time. I'm not worth saving, Cal, so just give the hell up.

CHAPTER EIGHT

IT WAS CHAOS. But Charlotte smiled anyway. A wide, genuine smile since this particular chaos was the start of having her dream come true.

Only eight days ago today, Mr. Becker had taken that nasty fall and had agreed to sell her the place. That had created a flurry of medical attention for him and a flurry of paperwork for her. Even though the expedited closing was still another five days away, Becker had given her the written okay to start renovations along with agreeing to sell her any and all furniture in the house that she wanted to keep.

Now there was a full work crew in the barn and more workers on the second and third floors to update the three bathrooms that were already there. Painters were in the rooms where the personal items had already been packed up.

Vehicles for the various workers were parked willy-nilly, crushing the weeds and making the surrounding areas of the house and barn look like a parking lot. The electricians, plumbers and carpenters were all going full speed ahead with lots of sawing, drilling and buzzing. The spring air was filled with sawdust, latex paint, sweat and chewing tobacco.

But not text dings.

She knew that for certain because Charlotte had been checking her phone. Nothing from Cal, which was far more disappointing than it should have been. After all, she and Cal had sort of unfinished business. Becker had agreed to sell her the place, so there was no need for a fake engagement. Added to that, Cal was probably busy with his family and the ranch. She'd caught whiffs of gossip about him working on a deal that would bring in yet more rescue horses to the ranch. So a good cause.

Still, she kept checking her phone—like now, for instance—to see if she'd missed a message from him. Nope. Nor was there one from her mother. That wouldn't last. Izzie had been either texting daily reminders or calling to press Charlotte to contact Noah and try to get back together with him, and she was certain Izzie wouldn't go a full twenty-four hours without another round of pressure.

She glanced back through the texts and smiled when she reread the latest one from Alden. Charlotte had not only sent him the plans for the place but photos of the bedroom that would be his. Unlike her mother, Alden gave his approval with some thumbs-up emojis and "Can't wait" comments.

Charlotte looked up from the box of Becker's things she'd just packed and was hauling out onto the porch, and she spotted Mandy making her way from the barn toward the house. She no longer had the huge bags of sandwiches that Charlotte had had delivered so hopefully the workers approved of getting a free lunch and would work even faster.

Because they'd closed the law office for the day, Mandy was wearing ratty jeans and an equally ratty shirt, just as Charlotte was doing. Fitting, since they'd taken on the chore of packing item after item into boxes so they could then be put in storage. For now, though, they were moving them onto the porch where the plan was for them to be picked up by a moving company later that day.

Becker had declined Charlotte's offer to let him watch the packing process on a computer—or rather a "gall-danged boob tube"—which Charlotte had been relieved to learn wasn't a reference to breasts but rather what some people had once called the TV. She considered it a blessing for both of them that Becker had opted out of the boob-tube viewing. He probably wouldn't have liked watching her paw through his things, and she certainly wouldn't have liked him watching her do the sorting. That'd been especially true since she'd been the one who'd packed his underwear.

Both pairs of it.

Apparently, the man didn't see the sense in owning a lot of duplications, which considerably lightened the packing load. One pot, one frying pan, one plate, a single set of silverware. She'd found boxes of other similar items already packed away in one of the bedrooms, and she could only guess that Becker had done that sometime in the past thirty years since he'd been the sole occupant of the place.

"How are things going in the barn?" Charlotte asked Mandy.

Mandy shook her head, causing her long ponytail to swish. Like Charlotte, her face was past the glistening stage, and they had moved on to full-fledged perspiring. The house had AC, thank goodness, but with all the box hauling, it was still sweaty work.

"There's a whole lot of cursing going on in there," Mandy said. That put some alarm on Charlotte's face, but her friend instantly waved it off. "The gist is they're not used to working together like this, and while the sandwiches were a hit, the cursing and grumbling are still the main form of communication."

No, working together like that wasn't the norm, and the contractor had emphasized that to Charlotte. But Charlotte had stressed that she wanted the place up and running as soon as possible. The barn was a key part of the facility since it would house the exercise, training, therapy and rec areas, complete with an indoor hot tub to help those who were going through physical therapy.

"How's it going in there?" Mandy asked, tipping her head to the house. "Find any porn, illegal weapons or anything interesting?"

"Depends on your definition of *interesting*. I found two sets of dentures in one of the bedrooms. Mr. Becker appears to have his own teeth so I'm not sure who they belong to."

Apparently, that didn't qualify as interesting for Mandy, and she came up the porch steps, no doubt to get started on yet more packing. However, she stopped right in front of Charlotte and looked at her.

"Why don't you just call or text him?" Mandy asked. "I saw you checking your phone again," she tacked on.

Charlotte didn't bother pretending that she didn't know who Mandy was talking about. Cal, of course. "Because he's busy."

Mandy muttered an exaggerated *uh-huh*. "Word is he's checking his phone a lot, too."

Charlotte frowned. "Who would notice something like that?"

"Hello? In Emerald Creek, who wouldn't notice?" Mandy insisted. "Cal is under a gossip microscope, what with the fake engagement and buzz about Harper."

Of course, Charlotte had heard some of that. No way for her to avoid it. But to notice that Cal was checking his phone? He could have been doing that because of something work-related. It might not have anything to do with her.

But Charlotte wanted it to be because of her.

She wanted Cal to be thinking of her as much as she was thinking of him. And that was a lot. Heck, she was even dreaming about it, and she had this giddy buzz that she hadn't gotten since way back in high school. It was because of that buzz and the talk about Cal that she at first thought she might be hallucinating when she saw an approaching truck with Cal behind the wheel. But it was the real deal. Cal himself. And he wasn't alone.

Becker was in the passenger seat.

"What the heck is Becker doing here?" she muttered.

Last she'd heard the man was still recovering in the hospital after having yet a second round of surgery. Charlotte felt fear shiver through her, and her first thought was a horrible one. That Becker had insisted Cal bring him here so he could call off the sale.

"Everything's okay," Cal said as he stepped from the truck. "He hasn't changed his mind."

The relief caused her legs to turn to jelly for a moment, and maybe because she looked ready to drop into a puddle, Cal hurried to her. "Everything's okay," he repeated in a murmur. Well, actually it was a sexy drawl where his mouth seemed to kiss each word.

Mercy, it was good to see him. Especially good when he wasn't in the bad-messenger mode. Well, hopefully he wasn't.

She welcomed the hug Cal gave her. Except it wasn't actually a hug. More of a bracing because she probably still looked ready to topple over.

"Becker just wanted to see the place one last time," Cal explained. "He has strict instructions from his doctor not to walk yet so I put his wheelchair in the back of the truck."

"They let him out of the hospital?" she asked.

"He more or less insisted on it. *More* than less," Cal muttered.

He looked at her. Full eye contact, and the corner of his mouth lifted into a smile. Then he cursed himself and moved back away from her.

Since that had basically been her reaction to thinking about Cal over the past week, she totally understood. He was glad to see her. Wasn't so glad that the seeing qualified as the ultimate *It's complicated*.

"How's it going, Mandy?" Cal called out while he went back to the truck to hoist out the wheelchair.

"Lots of cursing in the barn, but other than that, it's okay," Mandy said, using her forearm to swipe the sweat off her face.

As Charlotte had done, Cal frowned at the cursing remark. "Want me to go check on things?"

"Yes," Mandy said with conviction, just as Charlotte said, "Thanks, but don't trouble yourself."

Apparently, she was less convincing than Mandy, because Cal muttered something about doing that check in the barn as he lifted Becker off the truck seat. Becker wasn't a heavyweight by any stretch of the imagination, but he was a grown man. Still, Cal obviously had some upper body strength because he maneuvered Becker into the waiting wheelchair.

Jack, the dog, barreled out right behind his owner, and apparently she was glad to be home because she yapped, danced around and then took off running to check out the other vehicles.

"Stay close, Jack," Becker warned her. "And don't get in anybody's way. This isn't our place anymore."

There was more of a tinge of sadness in his comment, and again, Charlotte hoped he wasn't regretting the decision to sell the ranch to her.

Becker must have already had some training on how to use the automatic function on the chair because he immediately started toward her. The chair bobbled a bit on the uneven ground. Uneven because the clumps of weeds were now basically stomped down.

"If you find any dolls, they're not mine," Becker insisted.

Charlotte glanced at Mandy, who shook her head. "We haven't found any dolls."

"Well, if you do, they aren't mine," he repeated. "My cousin Gertie lived here when my folks were still alive, and she was always making these creepy dolls and hiding them in places where they'd end up scaring people."

That would have certainly added some excitement to the packing. "No dolls, creepy or otherwise," Charlotte assured him. "But I did find two sets of dentures."

"Gertie's," Becker promptly provided. "She used to work in an old folks' home over in Bulverde, and she'd take discarded teeth, eyeglasses, wigs and such and use them on the dolls." He shook his head in disgust. "Damn weird, if you ask me."

Charlotte had to agree, and part of her wished she'd find one of the dolls just to see if they lived up to Becker's description.

Becker eyed the boxes stacked up on the porch. Eyed the steps, too, that were in no way user-friendly to someone in a wheelchair.

"I'm having a ramp built," Charlotte explained, pointing to the right end of the porch. "It's on the schedule for the end of the week. Well, it is if the carpenters finish in the barn," she added in a mutter.

Cal immediately glanced in that direction. "I'll check and see how things are going. If they're falling behind, we have a couple of hands with carpentry experience, and I'll have them come over."

Charlotte smiled, thanked him and felt the warmth wash over her. It was temporary, though, since Cal got that "It's complicated" look in his eyes again, and he headed for the barn.

"I'll do some more packing," Mandy announced, and she went inside the house, leaving Charlotte alone with Becker.

"Thank you again for making all of this possible," Charlotte started, intending to follow it up with the offer to drag some of the boxes down the steps so he could examine the contents. "And thanks for allowing me to buy some of the furniture. I'm keeping most of the beds."

She would replace the mattresses and bedding. But

the bed frames themselves were sturdy antiques that she hoped would give the rooms a homey feel, especially once all the walls had fresh coats of paint and the rooms had thorough cleanings.

"If you're still on board, I'll donate the furniture in the living areas," she went on. She'd already ordered sofas, chairs and such that were scheduled to be delivered as soon as the painting was finished.

"Your engagement's a big-assed fake, isn't it?" Becker said, mentally stopping her in her tracks.

She automatically glanced down at the bare spot on her ring finger. "Yes," she admitted, hoping that wasn't the wrong response. "And I'm sorry about the lie. How did you find out?"

"People yapping outside my door. Hard not to hear some of what they're saying." He shook his head in disgust. "Depending on who's doing the yapping, you're going after Donnelly for real because of your former beau crushing your heart or something. Other yappers claim that every bit of your lovey-dovey stuff is bullshit."

Charlotte refrained from saying *Not every bit.* Yes, the engagement itself hadn't been real, but the heat between Cal and her certainly was. Whether or not that would lead to anything lovey-dovey, she still didn't know. Cal was being awfully sensible in keeping his distance, and in her case, his absence certainly wasn't creating an out of sight, out of mind scenario.

"What about your real fella?" Becker went on. "Taggert's boy Noah," he spelled out. "I'm guessing you didn't tell me you were engaged to him since he's got a smart mouth on him, and you knew I wouldn't approve."

Charlotte wasn't aware of any specific incident between Becker and Noah, but then again, almost everyone in town had had some kind of run-in with Becker. Everyone except her and Cal. However, she quickly added one more name to the list when she saw Maybell drive up. Becker clearly saw her as well, and the man sat up straighter in his wheelchair. He even ran his hand through his hair as if to make sure it wasn't standing on end.

So that's the way it was. Becker had a thing for Maybell. Charlotte didn't point out that over the years, plenty of other men had as well, and that one by one, Maybell had shut down all of those men. She apparently enjoyed her single status and had no plans to change it.

"Charlotte," Maybell greeted as she stepped out of the truck. "Mr. Becker," she added, and he muttered a greeting back to her. One that was missing his usual crotchetiness.

Just as Cal had done earlier with the wheelchair, Maybell hauled something out of the back of her truck. A wooden sign, Charlotte realized, and when she also realized it was heavy, she hurried to the woman to help. Maybell, however, waved her off, probably because she was more than capable of carrying pretty much anything. Her sturdy Viking build was a serious contrast to Becker's bony one.

"Effie and I had this made for you," Maybell said, holding up the sign. *Port in a Storm* had been painted in matte gold on the pale ash wood.

"It's perfect," Charlotte assured her. "Thank you."

"You're a whole lot of welcome. We figured you'd want something more personalized for later, but we thought this would do for now." Putting her hands on her hips, she glanced around. "You got plenty going on. I'm guessing Cal's helping?" she asked as Cal came out of the barn.

Maybell glanced at the now bare spot on her finger where there should have been an engagement ring, and even though she didn't come out and ask, Charlotte knew what she wanted to know.

"Mr. Becker knows the engagement is fake," Charlotte spelled out.

"Fake sometimes doesn't feel so fake, I'll bet," Maybell muttered, causing Charlotte to look at the woman. And what she saw was Maybell volleying glances at Cal and her.

Crud.

The heat was there again. A smoldering look from Cal. Then again, maybe he wasn't capable of being anything but smoldering. Charlotte was certain her own expression was filled with lots of lust and longing.

And Maybell clearly saw all of it.

Since Charlotte was positive neither Cal nor she wanted any matchmaking nudges, she tried to readjust her expression and redirected the moment by asking a nonheated question.

"Is everything okay enough in the barn?" she wanted to know.

Cal made a so-so motion with his hand. "There *is* a lot of swearing going on."

"Like we said," Charlotte remarked. "Anything I can do to help with that?"

"Not you specifically," he said as he continued walking toward Charlotte. He nodded a greeting to Maybell.

"But I'm supposed to go up to the third floor where Darrin McKenzie is working on a toilet and have him go to the barn and help his dad with something. His dad's tried to text him, but Darrin's phone might be dead or something."

Darrin was indeed on the third floor. Or rather that's where Charlotte had last seen him. "I'll be right back," she said to Maybell and Becker, and she wasn't sure if she should be surprised or not when Cal followed her in. However, she was glad he did.

"The place is a mess right now," she muttered, stepping around some boxes. She heard Mandy in one of the downstairs bedrooms where she was no doubt doing more packing. "But soon, it'll come together."

Cal nodded. "It's a big place."

"It is, and it's one of the main reasons I wanted it." She took him through the living room and kitchen, giving him an unofficial tour. "There are two living areas, a library and two bedrooms on this level. Four bedrooms on the second and four more on the third. I'll save these two lower ones for Alden and Harper, but the plan is to put in an elevator so that all three floors will be accessible to anyone."

Cal continued to glance around as they made their way up the first flight of stairs. He tested the newel posts, which stayed firmly in place, and ran his hand over the whitewashed shiplap walls.

"Becker's kept it in surprisingly good shape," she remarked, and paused again on the second-floor landing. She could hear work going on here as well as in the bathrooms. "All four bedrooms here have nice views of the ranch, and I'll use one of them as a combination sitting-and-rec room."

They moved on and stopped again on the third-floor landing. "Darrin?" she called out.

A moment later, the young man with curly red hair stuck his head out from one of the bathroom doors. "Yeah?"

"Your dad needs your help in the barn," Cal relayed.

Darrin crammed what appeared to be a handful of gummy worms into his mouth so Charlotte wasn't sure what he said when he walked past them and barreled down the stairs with all the energy of an oversugared preschooler.

With the message delivered and Darrin gone, Charlotte should have probably considered ending the impromptu tour of the place, but she wanted to show Cal one more thing, so she motioned for him to follow her to the third floor hall.

"The bedrooms here are much like the ones on the lower levels, but there's an addition up here." She glanced back over her shoulder at Cal. "Any idea why the Beckers would build such a big place?"

"Probably for the same reason my ancestors built Saddlebrook. That whole notion that bigger is better." He stopped in the hall, his attention shifting to yet another staircase. A spiral one that coiled straight up into the attic.

"I'm not sure whose room this was," she explained. "But the moment I saw it, I knew I wanted it to be mine."

"You're going to live here?" he asked.

"That wasn't the plan until I saw the room, and it

changed my mind. I'll sell my house in town and move here." Which wouldn't please her mother, but that was a battle for a different day.

"Wow," Cal muttered when he reached the top of the stairs and stepped out into the huge open room that had once been the attic.

Emphasis on *huge*.

It covered a good portion of the entire width and length of the house. But that wasn't why Charlotte wanted it. She twirled around, pointing at the windows that were seemingly everywhere. Added to that, there were skylights.

"I came up here last night," she said, "and the view was amazing. Stars galore. And I think the lights I saw in the distance over there were Saddlebrook."

She took hold of his hand and led him to the window that looked out over a vast stretch of pasture. It didn't look so weedy and unkept from up here.

"Yeah, that's the direction of Saddlebrook," he confirmed. "You can't actually see the house, but you'd be able to see the lights. Same for me. My bedroom faces this place."

Charlotte had no idea why that felt romantic, she and Cal looking at each other's lights, but it seemed like something people in an old-fashioned courtship would do. Ironic since there was nothing old-fashioned going on with Cal and her. There was no courtship, either. But there was something that she figured neither one of them wanted to voice.

She did anyway.

"I've been trying not to call or text you," she said.

"To give you time to deal with, well, everything. How are you dealing, by the way?"

"Minute by minute," he admitted. "Which is really sort of a weird expression, since it's how everyone has to live their lives." He paused, stared at the window. "Things are so unsettled now, and all that unsettling hasn't stopped me from wanting to call and text you as well."

She smiled. Not the brightest reaction she should have had, but she was quickly losing the battle in this "resist Cal" campaign. Added to that, she was having a hard time recalling exactly why resisting was necessary. That fuzzy recollection had her moving closer to him. She wasn't the only one doing it, either. Cal was leaning in as well, and while she could tell he was still fighting it, he apparently lost that battle.

He brushed his mouth over hers.

And there it was. That slam of heat. That jolt of pure pleasure. All that from something that barely qualified as a kiss.

It occurred to her, though, that it was their first real kiss. The others had been for show, an embellishment for the fake engagement. But there was nothing fake about this. Ditto for the real-deal stuff when Cal slipped his arm around her waist and eased her to him. No hurrying. He was clearly giving her, and maybe himself, the chance to rethink this.

Rethinking failed, however.

A big-time failure.

Because any and all resistance dissolved. So did the slow rethinking of this pace. It was as if something snapped, and they launched themselves at each other.

This time, it was a whole lot more than a touching of lips. It was a full-on, mouth-to-mouth kiss that caused the heat to skyrocket.

He tasted amazing, like something she'd always longed for but never knew she wanted. Like a thousand desserts all rolled into one. And he was good at this kissing, too. Just the right amount of hunger. Just the right amount of pressure from his body as he pulled her even closer to him. Until they were right against each other. Until the need was firing on all cylinders, causing an urgency to make the kiss hotter. Deeper. Longer.

So that's what they did.

They were kissing each other's lights out when Charlotte heard a slight gasping sound. She was surprised she could hear anything what with her pulse thrumming in her ears, but the gasp had managed to cut through that thrumming.

Cal must have heard it, too, because both of them whirled toward the doorway where Mandy was standing. The open doorway. And she wasn't alone. Nor was she the one who'd made the gasp. Nope, Charlotte was pretty sure the sound had come from the man next to Mandy.

Noah.

CHAPTER NINE

CAL'S BRAIN FROZE for a moment. Just plain froze. His eyes were seeing the two people in the doorway, but it took a while for the rest of his body to catch up.

Catch up and realize that Noah was there.

Right there. Staring with his mouth open at him and Charlotte. Apparently, Noah was having an issue with being frozen, too, because other than that soft gasp, he didn't make a sound.

Charlotte managed to make a sound. One word, actually. "Shit." That was it for several more seconds.

"Uh," Mandy piped in, "Noah made a surprise visit, and I brought him up to see you. I'm so sorry, Charlotte," she muttered.

That apology jump-started more talk. Unfortunately, it was the four of them talking at once.

"I should have called out to you," came from Mandy.

"Noah, clearly I wasn't expecting you," from Cal.

"What the hell is going on here?" Noah's contribution.

"Shit," Charlotte repeated.

For some reason, Charlotte's reaction stung, even though it was a perfectly normal response. Still, it seemed to be some sort of apology and *What have I done?* rolled into one. Had she forgotten that she had a right to the kiss that had caused the *What have I done?* response? Had she also forgotten that Noah had dumped her for another woman and had sent Cal to do his dirty work?

Possibly.

Her mind had to be whirling right now, so it was possible none of those thoughts were getting through the muck.

"What the hell is going on?" Noah repeated, and this time there wasn't so much shock, just more of a pleading tone that he aimed at both Cal and Charlotte since he was volleying gazes at both of them.

"I kissed Charlotte," Cal fessed up, though that was a big-assed duh since Noah had seen the kiss.

Noah's frozen expression completely thawed, and he started cursing. Cursing and pressing his hands to the sides of his head as if trying to stop it from exploding.

Cal automatically moved in front of Charlotte. As far as he knew, Noah had never been aggressive toward her, but then, he'd probably never walked in on her kissing another man. Except it wasn't just another man. It was his best friend. But Cal was certain that his best-friend status would soon carry the label *former*.

Charlotte didn't stay put behind him. She moved to Cal's side and faced Noah. "Obviously, we weren't expecting you," she said.

"Obviously," Noah snapped, and oh, the anger was rolling in fast. "My deployment was delayed so I decided to come home and see you." He stopped, and it seemed to take a couple of moments to get his mouth working again. "What the hell, Charlotte?"

Cal was about to intercede and defend Charlotte, but

she managed it herself. "Noah, you and I are no longer together," she spelled out.

So she did recall the breakup after all. Good. Because Cal didn't want her to feel any guilt over what had just happened. Even if he was feeling plenty of it himself. And he was. He was drowning in guilt here.

No way should he have kissed Charlotte when it'd been only a little over a week since the end of her really long relationship with Noah. Cal wouldn't even mentally add that he sure as hell wasn't in any position to dive into a romance. Especially a romance with the one woman in Emerald Creek who wasn't in any position, either.

Noah started pacing, and occasionally he would stop and fire looks at them. His mouth would open and shut just as quickly. Apparently, like Cal, he was having a hard time figuring out what to say. He finally settled on a question.

"Was that kiss part of the fake engagement my dad told me about?" Noah demanded.

"No," Charlotte answered before Cal could speak.

Mandy must have decided that this conversation was too private for her, and she muttered something about having packing to do, and she hurried out of there darn fast.

Noah huffed and shifted his attention to Cal. "What the hell? I asked you to break up with Charlotte, not seduce her."

Again, Charlotte jumped in. "Cal didn't seduce me. I kissed him because I'm attracted to him." Noah howled out some profanity, but she rolled right over him. "And remember, you broke up with me. How's Elise, by the way?"

Noah stopped howling and looked at Cal as if this was yet another betrayal.

"No, Cal didn't tell me about her," Charlotte was quick to point out. "I saw her name in a text you sent and filled in the blanks."

That wasn't entirely true. Cal had done some blank-filling, but no way would he have brought up Elise if Charlotte hadn't seen the text.

"So this is payback," Noah snarled, jabbing his index finger at them. The jabbing settled on Cal. "You were pissed at me asking you to break up with Charlotte, and you thought this would be the way to repay me."

This time, Cal was the first to answer. "I wasn't thinking of you or repayment when I was kissing Charlotte. I was only thinking about her and the kiss."

That brought on more howling and headshaking from Noah. "I can't believe this," he muttered, spicing that up with some raw profanity.

"That was sort of my reaction when I learned you'd gotten another woman pregnant and were marrying her." Charlotte folded her arms over her chest and glared at Noah. "When's the wedding, huh? And when will you hear the pitter-patter of little feet?"

Noah didn't answer. He just continued to glare at Cal, but that expression softened considerably when he looked at Charlotte. "There's no baby. Elise lied so she could manipulate me into marrying her, and when I found out the truth, I ended things."

That was a lot of information in just a pair of sentences, and if that kiss with Charlotte hadn't happened,

Cal might have gone to his old friend and doled out some sympathy.

But the kiss had occurred, and it'd changed everything.

Well, for him anyway. Cal wasn't so sure it had for Charlotte. She certainly wasn't muttering any condolences or reassurances that all would be well. But then, she wasn't telling Noah to get lost, either.

"I feel like an idiot," Noah said. He groaned and scrubbed his hand over his face. "I threw away what I had with you for a liar." His gaze locked on Charlotte. "Please tell me I haven't ruined everything."

When Charlotte opened her mouth, Cal was very interested in what she had to say. But she didn't get a chance to say anything because there was a blood-curdling shriek from somewhere else in the house.

"Mandy," Charlotte blurted, and she broke into a run.

Cal was on her heels, and Noah was right behind him. Whatever the heck had happened, it was no doubt bad because Mandy let out yet another shriek, and before they even reached the second floor, Cal heard the running footsteps. Mandy was going so fast that she nearly smacked right into them.

"In there," Mandy said. "It's alive. The creepy thing is alive."

That got Cal's attention, and he considered all sorts of possibilities from spiders to snakes to bats. Charlotte must have been considering that as well because she slowed a little, enough for Cal to overtake her.

Cal hurried into the room where Mandy was pointing, and once he looked in the open closet door, it didn't take him long to see, well, he wasn't sure what it was.

An acid-green thing with big teeth and curly red hair. It was bobbling up and down, its little feet making scraping noises on the top shelf of the closet.

"What is it?" Charlotte asked, moving next to Cal.

"I think it's some kind of animated…thing," he settled on.

Charlotte sighed. "This must be one of the dolls Becker mentioned."

They moved closer, studying it. Yep, in the strictest sense of the word, it was a doll, all right. The sort that could be used on the set of a horror movie.

The doll did a few more dancing jig steps, and the movement must have propelled it forward because it plunged off the closet shelf and smashed onto the floor. Its false teeth and wig went flying. So did the little mechanical device that it'd been attached to. Cal looked closer and saw that it'd been connected to some kind of trip wire that activated the device when the closet door was opened.

"Well, it's definitely creepy," Charlotte muttered just as Becker called out.

"Did y'all find one of Gertie's dolls?" he shouted.

"Yes," Charlotte confirmed. "A green, dancing one."

Cal thought he heard Becker groan, and the man said something else that Cal couldn't make out.

"He said Gertie sometimes used motion devices," Maybell relayed, her voice a lot louder than Becker's. "And that she used to put little sacks of corn and such in the dolls so the mice would crawl in there to eat it and cause the dolls to move around."

Cal couldn't remember crossing paths with Gertie, and he was glad of that.

"By the way, Izzie and Taggert are here," Maybell added a heartbeat later.

"Great," Charlotte muttered, and she turned away from the doll as if just remembering that Noah was there.

It didn't take long, just a couple of seconds, before there were yet more hurried footsteps. No shrieks, though, when Izzie and Taggert came rushing up the stairs.

"Good," Izzie declared when she saw Noah and her daughter. "You two are together. Noah told you that it's over between him and that other woman?"

"He mentioned it," Charlotte said with plenty of sarcasm. Not aimed at her mother, but rather at Noah.

"Good," Izzie repeated, clearly ignoring the sarcasm. "Then, that sets the stage for the two of you to get back together. Noah's very sorry for what happened," she tacked on as an afterthought.

"He mentioned that, too," Charlotte muttered, and Cal could practically see the mix of emotions coming from her. Anger, for sure, and annoyance, but he thought there was some hurt in the mix.

"Now that Becker's sold you the place, there's no need for the fake engagement," Izzie went on. "You can let everyone know you're with Noah again."

"Izzie," Taggert muttered like a warning. Not an especially stern one, but the man was definitely telling her to throttle back.

Izzie didn't. She shot Taggert a dismissive glance before she reeled back around. Not to face Charlotte this time, but Cal.

"Do the right thing, Cal," Izzie begged. "Tell Charlotte not to throw away all these years. Tell her not to throw away a man who loves her."

A week and a half ago, Cal might have agreed that Noah loved Charlotte. And maybe he actually did. But Noah hadn't just made a little mistake. Then again, his kissing Charlotte might fall into the same non-little category, too. Yes, Charlotte wasn't running into Noah's arms, but she sure as heck wasn't hurrying into his, either.

Izzie huffed when Cal didn't respond, then turned to Charlotte. "Do I need to remind you of your father?"

Of all the things that Cal had thought Izzie might say, that wasn't one of them. "Her father?" Mandy and Cal asked in unison.

Izzie's stare stayed on her daughter. "Charlotte knows what I'm talking about. Some things can't be undone, and the consequences can be devastating."

Clearly, Cal didn't have the big picture here. Yes, he knew that Charlotte's father had left her and Izzie when Charlotte was a teenager. That'd been over twenty years ago, and as far as Cal knew, Charlotte and Izzie hadn't heard a peep from the man since. But Cal couldn't figure out what that had to do with Noah dicking around with another woman and then slinking back to beg Charlotte's forgiveness.

"My father," Charlotte muttered, and this time there was a different emotion in her voice. Really pissed-off anger, and even though Cal didn't know the details, he was pissed for her. Izzie was clearly trying to manipulate her by dragging up something that'd happened in the past.

"My father," Charlotte repeated, and it seemed to Cal that she wasn't even trying to rein in her anger.

Charlotte whirled toward Cal, and in the same motion as the whirling, she hooked her hand around the back of his neck, dragged him to her.

And she kissed him.

Right there, right on the mouth. Right in front of her mother, Noah, Mandy and Taggert. From the corner of his eye, Cal saw that even Jack was watching.

Unlike the kiss upstairs, this one was all for show. And that told Cal loads. That Charlotte obviously had way too many unsettled feelings for Noah, and she might end up forgiving him and taking him back.

Hell.

Cal voiced the *Hell* aloud when Charlotte broke away from him and stormed out.

CHARLOTTE JUST KEPT WALKING. Down the stairs. Out of the house. Into the yard. Thankfully, neither Maybell nor Becker tried to engage her in conversation. Probably because she looked ready to rip off someone's head, and they didn't want to risk that. She wouldn't have lashed out at them, but mercy, she wanted to at someone.

Noah for starters. Then her mother. Then this crappy situation that was also known as her personal life. Great day in the morning. Things had certainly gone to hell in a handbasket very quickly.

Well, partly it had, anyway.

She hadn't wanted to deal with Noah or her mother. She'd only wanted to focus on the renovations and continue to lust after Cal. The latter was because her body hadn't given her much of a choice about it. But she'd been enjoying the tingle and sparkle of attraction. She'd been enjoying just being with him.

And now she'd ruined it.

That anger kiss had been all wrong. She'd used him, and not only did Cal not deserve that, he was likely now feeling plenty of anger of his own. Added to that, she'd left him to clean up the mess with Noah and her mother. Soon, very soon, she would have to go back in and deal with it, but for now, she just needed some space. And really loud music. She cranked up her go-to, My Chemical Romance's *Black Parade*, and she sped away from Port in a Storm.

At the moment, it didn't feel much like a port or a peaceful place to recover.

Then again, nothing did.

How dare Noah come back like this. How dare her mother take his side. And bring up the holy grail of guilt trips, her father. Izzie had no doubt thought that would whip Charlotte into submission. It had certainly worked at other times over the years. Izzie probably hadn't bargained on the father card prompting her to kiss Cal in what had to be the worst kiss ever.

Well, maybe not that bad. After all, it'd been Cal, and she wasn't sure he was capable of a bad kiss, even one that had been fueled with so much anger that it was possible it'd bruised their mouths.

Yes, she would owe him a huge apology.

First though, the drive. The music. And maybe trying to wrap her mind around everything that'd just happened. Charlotte started with a mental list.

Noah was back. He had broken up with Elise. He wanted to reconcile.

That was problem number one. Part of her—the really angry part—wanted to just tell Noah to go to hell, but that seemed a little extreme since he hadn't actually broken her heart. Hadn't come close to doing that. In fact, if she was being honest with herself, the breakup had been a relief. Now here he was, apparently wanting to undo the breakup and therefore the relief.

Mental list number two was all about Izzie. Izzie wanted her to get back with Noah. Maybe because of that whole double-wedding deal. But there seemed to be more to it than Izzie being her usual Izzie self.

Mental list number three. Cal. Before Noah's arrival, Cal and she had ditched any trace of caution and kissed. Had it meant anything other than lust? And would Cal back off now that Noah was back?

Charlotte might have started whittling her way down the lists to try to come up with some answers, but her phone dinged with a text. She was ready to curse, but then she saw it wasn't from Izzie or Noah. It was from the San Antonio Rehabilitation Center.

"Harper," she muttered, and Charlotte instructed her phone to read the text aloud.

It's me, Harper. Dr. Kentrell showed me pictures of the room where I'll be staying at the ranch.

Charlotte had indeed sent photos to the doctor so she was glad Kentrell had shared them with Harper. The room had an amazing antique bronze bed and was currently in the process of being painted a soothing sea-mist green.

Since she wanted to take time with her response to

Harper, Charlotte pulled off the road and onto one of the many ranch trails that threaded through the area.

"The room will have a seating area and some work-space for a computer," Charlotte dictated verbally through the Bluetooth. "And the door's wide enough to both the room and the en suite bath to accommo-date a wheelchair if needed." In fact all of the down-stairs rooms had had that modification, since Becker's mother had needed the use of a chair during the last few years of her life.

Charlotte sent the response and waited. And waited. Because Harper couldn't speak and had only limited use of her hands, Charlotte imagined that it was taking the woman a while to type out the response.

I'm supposed to say it's nice and thank you, Harper finally texted.

Charlotte frowned. "Supposed to?" she repeated. "What do you actually want to say about it?"

There was another long wait, and Charlotte wished she could see the woman's face so she'd have a clue what Harper was actually feeling. It was possible that Harper was just in a mad-at-the-world mood, but it felt like more than that. It seemed as if Harper was reach-ing out to her for more than just a remark on her soon-to-be living quarters.

It took several minutes for Harper's response. I don't want to be around people just yet.

"That's all right," Charlotte assured her. "The room is large, and your meals can be brought in to you. You can do your physical therapy in the room as well."

Though the hope was that eventually Harper would want to leave the main house and use the facilities in the barn. Or make use of the walking trails that would also be wheelchair-friendly.

Heard you were hooking up with Cal. Gossip or truth?

Charlotte froze for a moment, and her first reaction was to ask who'd told Harper that, but it was possible it'd come from Paul or from another family member who was keeping in touch with her.

"I'm not sure what's going on when it comes to Cal," Charlotte answered.

That caused Charlotte to groan, and again she wanted to kick herself for kissing him in anger. It was entirely possible that it'd riled Cal enough that he would want to wash his hands of her. Especially since he had his own problems to deal with. Especially, too, now that Noah had returned.

Cal has that effect on people, Harper responded.

She stared at the reply. And stared. Not sure how to answer it. However, it turned out that a comeback wasn't necessary because several seconds later, Harper ended the conversation with a simple Bye.

Charlotte continued to sit there, wondering if she should contact Dr. Kentrell to check on Harper. It was possible that checking on her wasn't even necessary, but the whole text conversation had Charlotte wondering and worrying. She was still doing that when she saw the car pull in behind hers.

Izzie.

"Great," Charlotte muttered.

She definitely hadn't wanted to see her mother, and now with Izzie parked behind her, she was trapped.

Well, unless she was ready to start a jogging trek down the rugged ranch trail. Which she just might do after she got a glimpse of her mother's expression. Izzie seemed to be spoiling for a fight.

Izzie didn't wait for an invitation. She waltzed right to Charlotte's car and tried to throw open the passenger's-side door. It had automatically locked, and Charlotte considered keeping it that way. A childish response for sure, but then, her mother probably wouldn't be on her best behavior, either. Still, after Izzie tapped on the window multiple times, Charlotte finally unlocked it.

Her mother slid onto the seat, and Charlotte geared up to defend herself. Izzie put a stop to that with two words. "I'm sorry," she said.

That threw Charlotte. She definitely hadn't been expecting that, and then it occurred to her that the apology wasn't for the things she'd said but rather for something that'd gone on at the house after Charlotte had left. It was possible Cal and Noah had gotten into some kind of altercation that'd turned physical.

"Is Cal all right?" Charlotte had to ask.

Izzie blinked, clearly surprised by the question. "As far as I know. He left right after you did. I assumed he'd come after you, but then I saw you parked here and realized he hadn't. That's good. He didn't need to be crowding you when you obviously need time to think."

Charlotte gave her mother a blank stare that should have conveyed that Izzie was crowding her, but she clearly didn't pick up on it.

"Noah left, too," her mother went on. "Oh, Charlotte. He's positively crushed to the bone over what he did to you. You got him back, though, by kissing Cal, so I hope you'll see that as a score settled."

So, Izzie's apology hadn't been real. She'd likely said it to throw Charlotte off balance so she could continue the browbeating.

"Mom, I don't want to talk about Noah or Cal," Charlotte spelled out. "You've made it crystal clear that you want me to get back with Noah, and I've made it equally clear that's not going to happen."

"But you haven't," Izzie insisted. "You were hurt and angry enough to kiss Cal in front of Noah, so you must still have feelings for Noah."

Charlotte was sure she blinked. "How do you figure that?"

Izzie blinked, too. "Well, because if you didn't still care for Noah, then you wouldn't have tried to lash out at him that way."

Charlotte huffed and wanted to say she'd done it purely out of anger. Something that'd just popped into her head. But she was certain that spelling it out to her mom wasn't going to help, so she went with a different approach.

"I haven't been in love with Noah for a long time now. Truth is, he did me a favor by breaking up with me."

Izzie stared at her a long time and then sighed. "Noah made a mistake with the breakup, period. A mistake he deeply regrets. And as for not loving him, well, that's because you haven't been around him much over the past couple of years. Once he's around again, I'm sure the love will return."

Charlotte did her own round of staring. "It won't."

She would have added more, but her mother talked right over her.

"I'm worried about Taggert," Izzie said out of the blue. "He loves his son, and all of this has put him between a rock and a hard place. I'm not sure how Taggert would feel about you breaking his son's heart."

It took Charlotte a moment to process that jumble. It didn't land well, and she felt the anger seep through her again. "And you and Taggert weren't worried when you believed Noah had broken my heart?"

Izzie rolled her eyes. "Of course we were concerned, but we knew Noah would come to his senses. And he did. He came back to make amends with you." She paused only a heartbeat. "This is nothing like what happened with your father."

And there it was. Her mother's secret weapon that she pulled out any time she needed an emotional hammer.

Sadly, Charlotte knew that it usually worked.

That's what happened when there was so much unresolved guilt, and her mind flashed back to the note Cal had shown her on his phone. A copy of the one Harper had written before she'd driven off that bridge.

The playing field is all yours now. I'm bowing out of this shitshow.

Charlotte had gotten a similar note when she was sixteen. Oh, the words weren't the same, but the gist was. And it'd come from her father, who hadn't driven off a bridge but had instead disappeared from her and Izzie's lives forever. He hadn't left the note for Izzie, either.

But for her.

Because her father had blamed her for the reason

he was leaving. So, yeah, lots of unresolved guilt, and she didn't need the note to recall each and every word of what he'd said.

I can't do this anymore. You've made it impossible for me to stay.

Hard not to give that the worst interpretation possible. That if she'd been a better daughter, then he wouldn't have left, and her mother wouldn't have lost her husband.

Charlotte waited for her mother to go into steamroller mode. It could take a couple of different directions. Izzie could drone on about how hard it'd been to be a single parent and that Charlotte hadn't made it easy. Which she hadn't. Nothing major, just normal teenage-angst stuff, but Izzie had a way of using that to make Charlotte believe she owed her. However, before Izzie could begin steamrollering, or anything else for that matter, her phone dinged with a text.

Huffing, Izzie yanked her phone from her purse. "Oh, God," she muttered a moment later.

Charlotte tried to see the message that'd caused her mother's reaction, but Izzie pressed her phone to her heart, hiding the screen.

Izzie's tear-filled gaze flew to Charlotte's. "Oh, God," she repeated on a hoarse sob. "You've ruined everything *again*."

CHAPTER TEN

CAL PUSHED THE STALLION, Ice Man, into a gallop, and the horse lived up to the hype he'd been hearing. Arrogant but top-notch. Ice Man was certainly in that mode now as he practically flew over the pasture.

It didn't give Cal quite the adrenaline hit as flying a fighter jet did, but it was darn close.

He'd always enjoyed riding, always enjoyed working with the horses, and as Ice Man continued to deliver the thrill of speed, it reminded Cal that this would be how he would get his adrenaline fixes in the future. No more fighter jets. No more competition and hungry rise to the top. He was okay with that because he had to be. He just didn't have that hunger, that need or drive, and he could trade it all in to make his place here at Saddlebrook.

Of course, some members of his family weren't going to understand that. They'd think his separation was still about Harper. And it was. For now. But Cal thought he could move past that and give himself a good life as a rancher.

At that thought, the image not of Harper but of Charlotte flashed into his head. Whether he wanted it or not, Charlotte was now playing into his mood. The real kiss they'd shared had opened up a small crack of possibilities. And given him a mother lode of lust for her. But he couldn't shake the notion that if he stayed in Emerald Creek, there might be more kisses. For that to happen, though, she'd have to get over Noah, and Cal wasn't sure she was anywhere close to being able to do that.

Since the angry fake-kiss the day before, Cal hadn't actually spoken with Charlotte to find out her state of mind. She'd sent him a text that simply said, I'm sorry. Will talk soon.

Maybe the apology was for the kiss. Maybe for everything else going on. But her *talk soon* was now going on twenty-four hours so she obviously hadn't worked things out yet.

He rode Ice Man toward the barn and spotted someone waiting for him by the pasture fence. Not Charlotte but rather Remi. Since she was in uniform, she was likely getting ready to leave and had come to say goodbye. A goodbye with conversation, no doubt, and since she had a serious expression, Cal figured she had some serious things to say. Considering what was going on, this could turn out to be a chat about multiple things— all serious.

Remi wasn't totally alone. Jack was with her, sitting right by her side while she rubbed the dog's head. Thankfully, Jack had fit right in at the ranch and hadn't taken to barking at or chasing livestock as some dogs did. In fact, she had settled in so well that she'd be missed whenever Becker had recovered enough to take her back.

Cal reined in, dismounted and gave Ice Man a few pats on his neck before he headed to his sister. "Magnificent," Remi muttered, her attention on the horse. "Truly one of a kind."

"Thanks, I try my best," Cal said, hoping to add some levity to the start of the conversation.

Remi sneered in only a way a kid sister could manage. "You smell. You're sweaty, and your desperado stubble looks weird on your usually baby-butt face."

"Baby-butt?" he said. He went to the corral fence, resting his arms on the top of it.

"Smooth. You usually look like a military recruitment poster. Clearly not now, though."

No. The stubble wasn't intentional. Cal had just decided he needed a long-ride thinking session so he could try to burn off some of this restless energy, and he'd left the house without shaving.

"FYI, Dad's watching from the window," Remi said several moments later. "So let's keep this all smiles and happy goodbyes before I have to leave for the airport."

He glanced up and did indeed spot his father, and Cal did smile and added a friendly wave. It might or might not have been convincing. Remi's attempted smile made her look a little deranged.

"Dad's worried about all of us," Remi went on, turning so that she no longer had to fake a smile. "Me for the job, Egan because he's burning the candle at both ends, and Blue because he's still in physical therapy from his injury..."

"But he's mainly worried about me," Cal finished for her.

"Yeah," Remi confirmed, still smiling. "You're his biggest concern right now. I'm guessing you're still hell-bent on getting out?"

"Still hell-bent," he muttered, though it was hard to say that with a smile.

"By my calculations, you've only gone through about a week and a half of your leave," Remi pointed out. "That means twenty-one more days for you to change your mind."

"Twenty," he corrected. And while three weeks was a long time to mull things over, Cal knew it wouldn't make a difference. "I'm getting daily texts from Audrey to say she's working to find me a dream job. She won't accept that there isn't one."

"Really?" Remi challenged. "I recall you had a few options for your dream jobs."

He had, but even those wouldn't tempt Cal now.

"Running the test-pilot program," Remi provided.

"That was mainly so I'd be Blue's boss," Cal joked.

It was more than that, though. Once, it would have indeed been a prime assignment. All that speed and adrenaline. Testing out the next-generation modifications that would not only break records but begin the path for new norms. It would have been the ultimate ride, which was probably why Harper had always said she wanted it as well. In fact, on the single occasion that he and Harper had ended up talking at a bar about their dream jobs, hers had been almost identical to his.

"And you've always wanted to be a Thunderbird," Remi continued.

Yep, another truth. The Thunderbirds was the Air Force's premiere demonstration team, and it'd been on his wish list for years before he'd realized it'd basically be showboating. Of course, it had diplomatic appeal in that the team were ambassadors for the Air Force, but a degree of *Hey, look at me, look at me* was needed to reach that purpose and appeal.

"Let's not forget you always wanted to be a time-traveling superhero, too, with a talking dragon side-kick," Remi went on.

His sister had reached way back in the past for that one, but Cal could recall that around age eight that had been his number-one dream. His mother had died when he was six, so for years after that, he'd latched on to plenty of fantasies to help him cope with the loss. Then he'd joined the military and had found his element.

Or rather he'd thought he had.

"You must have something more recent than that for your dream jobs," she went on.

"Helping people," he said before he even knew it was going to come out of his mouth. "It seems as if I've spent a lot of time reaching and taking but not much time giving back."

Remi stared at him. "There are jobs like that in the military, you know."

"I know," he confirmed, although one hadn't come up in his career options. "There might be something for me here at the ranch."

"There's always something here," his sister assured him. "Always something for all of us. The question is will it be enough when you could still be ready for a whole lot more?"

Cal wanted to insist the answer was *yes*, that it would be enough, but at the moment he could only hope it was true. The problem with running from something ugly and dark was that the ugly and dark followed right along with you.

Remi turned from him, glancing back up at their dad's window, and she sighed. "He's still watching, still worrying." She looked at Cal. "I know we all agreed not to push Rowan to make contact, but it would probably do Dad a lot of good if we heard from him."

"Maybe," Cal agreed. "But it's possible Rowan will make contact only to say he wants nothing to do with any of us."

"But then at least Dad would know. Right now, it must feel as if he's in…limbo."

When she trailed off for a moment, Cal followed his sister's gaze and saw that her attention had landed on Jesse Whitlock, the ranch foreman. Remi quickly looked away from Jesse. A reaction she hadn't always had, because Cal could recall a time when Remi and Jesse had been seeing each other in what had to be the worst-kept secret ever. Jesse probably hadn't wanted everyone to know he was sleeping with his boss's daughter, and Remi likely hadn't wanted her three brothers and dad in her private business.

Maybe it was the pressure of being involved with someone so close to home and in their dad's direct chain of command that had caused the breakup. Cal didn't know since both Remi and Jesse had kept that close to their vests. Still, he was pretty sure he saw heat still zinging between them.

"Don't ask," Remi warned Cal when she saw that he was darting glances between Jesse and her. She looked over her shoulder again. "Besides, you've got your own personal issues to deal with, and one of them is driving up right now."

Cal turned toward the driveway and spotted Charlotte's car coming to a stop in front of the house. He silently cursed the way his internal organs reacted. Racing pulse. Fluttering stomach. Heat galore.

He tried to tamp down, well, everything since it was entirely possible that Charlotte had come here to spell out that she was putting an end to whatever this was between them. She could be there to tell him she was getting back together with Noah. Or taking a long break from anything remotely involving romance. Any and all of those were possibilities.

"Gotta go," Remi said, giving him a hug and a not so gentle headbutt, her substitute for a goodbye kiss. She headed away from him just as Charlotte started his way. When the two women reached each other, they stopped, hugged.

No headbutt, though.

Cal couldn't hear what they said, but whatever it was caused Charlotte to laugh. Fluttering a wave, Remi went on to her rental car while Charlotte continued to him.

He was still on the other side of the corral fence, and he stayed put, bracing himself for anything and everything. Or so he thought. But Charlotte didn't launch into an apology or a speech about why she had to end things with him here and now. Instead, when she reached him, she surprised the heck out of him.

She leaned in and kissed him.

Not that anger stuff that'd gone on the day before. Not the fake stuff, either. This was more like the kiss in her room at Port in a Storm. Hot, long and, best of all, the real deal.

Cal forgot all about the complications anything real would cause. Hell, he forgot where he was. Who he was.

He just sank right into the kiss, both hating and loving that it made too many things inside him feel right. He shouldn't be relying on Charlotte and her kisses to make his life better.

But they did. Mercy, they did.

When she finally eased back from him, she wasn't exactly smiling, which told him she was probably having her own internal battle about whether or not they should be doing this. Again, though, he was wrong.

"I probably shouldn't have kissed you with your dad and Jesse watching," she muttered. "Neither are gossips, but you probably don't want something like that announced in such a hot, tasty way."

Now she did smile. So did Cal. "It was indeed hot and tasty." And he wanted to dive right back in. Not a good idea. For now, anyway.

She glanced down at the fence between them and then at Ice Man. "Wow, he's a beauty."

Cal didn't go for the joke as he had with Remi. "He is, and he knows it. You can probably tell from the smell that I just finished a ride and was about to brush him down."

"This is probably the kiss talking, but I like the smell," she insisted. "Saddle leather, a little sweat. You could probably market it as one of those designer manly scents called Leather Forever or Cowboy Dreams."

"Yeah, it's probably the kiss talking," he agreed, "since I'm pretty sure I stink."

She smiled again. He smiled again. And Cal figured he should just bash his head against a fence post to try to knock some sense into himself. His body was in the full-throttle mode when it should be reining in, taking things slow, because both he and Charlotte needed to get their respective footings.

He tipped his head for Charlotte to follow him into the barn. That would get them away from any spectators and give them some privacy for whatever it was she had come to say. Charlotte went through the front of the barn, and Cal led Ice Man in through the side.

"Obviously, I've come to apologize," she said while he began taking the tack off Ice Man. "Pissed-off kissing is rarely a good idea, and I used you to vent and stand my ground with Noah and my mother. I'm sorry."

Cal nearly said that venting had never tasted so good, but he decided that wasn't reining in stuff. "I might have done the same thing if I'd been in your shoes."

She shrugged. "Doubtful. You would have figured out something else that wouldn't have led to chapped lips, gasps and Izzie's ire."

Cal sighed. It would have been more than enough for Charlotte to have to deal with Noah's return, but Izzie would have added an extra layer of dealing.

"Maybe," Cal muttered, "but whatever happened would have probably led to Izzie's ire." Well, unless Charlotte had offered Noah blanket forgiveness and an immediate reconciliation. "How hard did your mom come down on you?"

"Hard," she replied, and Charlotte picked up a brush to help him with the grooming. "You heard the part about her bringing up my father."

"I did. And I'm sorry." Cal didn't push for any info about why her mother would have done that, he just provided Charlotte silence in case she chose to fill him in.

Charlotte wasn't quick with a reply, and when she

did finally speak, she didn't look directly at him. "My father left me a note when he walked out. Not a good note," she qualified. "I'll spare you the details, but the gist was I was the reason he was leaving."

"Shit," Cal blurted so loud and fast that it caused Ice Man to whicker and give Cal a dirty look. "Sorry," he added in a mutter. Then he lightened his tone with Charlotte. "What a crap thing to do. You were a kid."

There was no humor in the smile she attempted. "No, I was a moody, mouthy teenager who pushed him over the edge. And Izzie has never let me forget that," she was quick to add. "My dad apparently didn't leave her a note, so it's clear where Izzie has put the blame."

Yes, and it was also clear that Charlotte had accepted that blame. But Cal wasn't convinced it was hers and hers alone. "Your dad ended his marriage, not just his relationship with you, so he must not have been madly in love with your mom."

Charlotte made a sound that definitely wasn't of agreement. That was more proof of the blame.

"Have you ever talked to your dad about why he left?" Cal asked.

She shook her head. "I haven't talked to him at all since he walked out. And he certainly hasn't gotten in touch with me. Over the years, I've done internet searches for him, but there are a lot of Anthony Wilsons out there. Even more when I put in the usual nicknames of Tony or Andy."

Of course, her father didn't have that disadvantage of having to search for her whereabouts. Izzie and Charlotte had stayed put, so if he'd wanted to get in touch with them, he could have. In Cal's mind, that made the man a selfish bastard. Then again, he had left his wife and daughter for another woman, so the groundwork for selfish bastardhood was already there.

"Anyway, over the years Izzie has been quick to play the dad card," Charlotte went on a moment later, "and she's trying to use it with Noah."

Everything in Cal went still. "Is it going to work?"

Charlotte looked at him, and the sound she made now was more of a *duh*. "A thousand gallons of no. I wouldn't have kissed you if I'd been planning on giving in to the pressure about Noah." She paused, locked eyes with him. "And I wouldn't be thinking about kissing you again."

Oh, that brought on the heat. Man, did it. But Cal forced himself to stay put. If he got his mouth and hands on Charlotte now, there was no telling how many rules he'd break. And there were rules, he assured himself. Rebound boundaries. Windows of necessary time to think. If he pressed Charlotte with kisses and sex, she certainly wouldn't have much of a clear head to deal with what she was facing.

And neither would he.

"My mother came after me yesterday when I left Port," she continued a moment later. "She played the dad guilt card, and then she got a mystery text that she wouldn't show me or say who it was from." Charlotte paused, and he could tell whatever she was about to say was eating away at her. "After Izzie read the text, she looked at me and said, 'You've ruined everything again.'"

Cal growled out another "Shit" and tossed the brush aside so he could go to Charlotte. He would have pulled her into his arms for a comforting hug, but she waved him off.

"It's okay," she insisted. "Don't dole out too much TLC and pity right now because it might make me cry. I don't want to cry in front of you."

"Cry if it'll make you feel better," he offered.

"It won't. It'll only clog my nose and make my eyes red. Also, I'm wearing foundation and mascara so it'd be ugly crying with streaks involved."

It twisted away at him that she was trying to keep this light when it was obvious that it was anything but. He silently cursed Izzie for saying something like that.

"I think the text was from Taggert," Charlotte continued after she'd swallowed hard. "He might not be happy with me for not jumping to reunite with his son."

Cal shook his head. "More likely Taggert wasn't happy with the way Izzie tried to pressure you."

She stayed quiet, obviously considering that. "Either way, I'm at the center of it again, and now Izzie has another guilt card to play."

"Don't let her play it," Cal heard himself say. It was the truth. He didn't want Charlotte to give in to pressure from her mom, but he knew his motives were mostly selfish. He didn't want Charlotte reunited with Noah because he wanted her with himself.

And talk about a selfish attitude.

He was an emotional land mine right now, and she was in the middle of a breakup and a project that would have plenty of people pulling out their hair. Charlotte didn't need any other complications in her life. That didn't stop Cal from brushing a kiss over her mouth, however.

Thankfully, the kiss had her smiling. Then, not so thankfully, frowning. Cal was right there with her.

"I'm not sure what's going on between us," she admitted.

He had to nod. "Same. I just don't want any of this to be because of Noah. Or your mother."

"A tall order, but it's not. Trust me, it's not," she added in a mutter. "I have really hot fantasies about you that don't have a thing to do with either one of them. Only us."

Hell. Of course, that alerted his dick. Alerted other parts of him, too, and his brain piped up with a big caution flag. He didn't need to jump headfirst into this. It wouldn't be good for him, but it especially wouldn't be good for Charlotte. She could end up getting hurt if he wasn't able to sort out his life.

She brushed a kiss on his mouth, too, and ended the kiss with some muttered profanity when her phone dinged. She glanced at it. "The contractor. He needs me back at Port in a Storm. Want to give me a call later today to see if we can carve out some time to…? I'll just leave it at that," she added, flashing him a grin.

Cal kissed that grin, lingering a moment to savor her taste. Her phone dinged again. "Plumber," she muttered. "The electrician will probably be next." Charlotte waved and headed out, just as her phone dinged again. "Wrong. It's the carpenter."

He went to the barn door to watch her leave, and Cal saw her come to a stop when a truck pulled up in front of the house.

Noah.

Great. Just great.

Noah stepped out, his gaze immediately zooming in on them, and he froze for a moment, probably muttering his own gripe at seeing him and Charlotte together. Well, sort of together.

"No, I'm not getting back together with you, Noah," Charlotte announced right off, and Cal went toward her in case there was trouble.

Noah didn't shout or curse. He dipped his head down and shook it. "Charlotte, I'm so sorry," he said.

She didn't have any snarly comeback and didn't give in to what was one of the best puppy-dog expressions that Cal had ever seen on a human. Sad eyes, remorse, pleading. Nope, she didn't react to any of that.

"If you try to pick a fight with Cal over this," she stated, "I will start a permanent shit list and put you on it. I'll never, ever forgive you, understand?"

Charlotte waited for Noah to nod, probably the only response he figured he should give. She confirmed his nod with one of her own and then walked to her car. She drove away, leaving Noah and Cal facing each other down like Old West outlaws about to have a shoot-out. Despite Noah's nonverbal assurance that he wouldn't pick a fight, Cal could see that was exactly what Noah wanted to do. Pick a fight and work off some of his anger. Well, Cal had some anger, too, at the way Noah had treated Charlotte, and he wasn't convinced trying to play nice was possible here.

"Well?" Cal said after the stare-down had gone on long enough.

"Well," Noah repeated with a heavy sigh, "you heard what she said. She's not getting back together with me. Is that because of you?"

Cal gave him a flat look. "Just a guess, but I think it's because of you. You broke up with her because you were planning to marry another woman."

"And you took full advantage of that and moved in on her," he snapped.

Yeah, it would be impossible to keep the anger out of this, but Cal managed to keep his tone a lot more civil than he thought possible. Probably because he couldn't forget that Noah was his lifelong friend. Or rather he had been, before things had started to heat up between Charlotte and him.

"I didn't move in on Charlotte," Cal stated. "We were thrown together because of the fake engagement, and things just happened very fast after that."

He frowned at his own explanation because it made the real kissing sound as if they'd tripped and their mouths had accidentally landed against each other. The first two kisses had been calculated as part of the engagement ruse, but everything after that was the real deal.

The real, hot deal.

And that caused Cal to mentally pause again. What the hell was he doing by having real, hot stuff with Charlotte? He didn't have time to mull that over because Noah broke the silence with a string of profanity.

"I want to kick my own ass," Noah snarled. "So stand in line if you want to do the same. I screwed up bigtime, and I deserve multiple ass-kickings. From Charlotte, from you, from her mom and my dad."

That took some of the fire out of Cal's own anger, but he doubted he'd be taking Noah up on this particular offer. It would be too close to picking a fight, and he didn't want to end up on Charlotte's shit list.

Noah did more cursing. More groaning. And he pressed his hands against the sides of his head while he paced. "I don't know what the hell I'm going to do to fix this. I would ask you for your advice, but I think we can agree that you no longer have my best interests at heart."

"Yeah, we can agree on that," Cal assured him. But, of course, that wasn't totally true, and that's why Cal sighed and let go of even more of his anger. "I do want what's best for Charlotte, though."

Something flashed in Noah's eyes. Not all temper, either, but some snark that questioned Cal's motives for wanting that for Charlotte. Cal couldn't say his motives were selfless—the kisses precluded that—but he definitely wanted her to be happy.

"Trust me, I want what's best for Charlotte, too," Noah said, his tone and words a little tight. "She and I were together a long time, and we were happy. Happy until I screwed it up," he added harshly.

That brought on more groaning, more cursing, more pacing. After several moments of that, though, Noah seemed to compose himself, and he whirled back around to face Cal.

"I'm working on a plan to get Charlotte back," Noah said. "The deployment's been rescheduled, and I have two weeks of leave. I'll use that time to get her to forgive me and work on us being a couple again."

Cal got a nasty mix of feelings about that, including jealousy. Sadly, it was there. But he was also pissed because getting Charlotte back sounded as if Noah was going to try to pester her and goad his way back into her life.

Would it work?

Maybe. That was the reason for the jealousy. The reason for the guilt, too, because Cal didn't want it to work.

"How do you plan on getting her back?" Cal came out and asked.

"By reminding her of what we had together." Noah was quick enough with that answer to let Cal know he'd given it some thought. "She was in love with me... once. And I could maybe make her feel that way about me again."

"Are you in love with her?" Cal was quick enough with that, too, but he wished he'd kept the question to himself because it brought on another flash of anger in Noah's eyes. They were back to the Wild West showdown mode.

"I can fall in love with her again, too," Noah snapped.

Cal apparently hadn't learned from his previous question because he continued to blurt. "So you're not in love with her now at this moment."

"No, but then, neither are you." Noah's glare dared Cal to deny that.

He couldn't. He cared deeply for Charlotte, but he was sure Noah could say the same thing.

"Don't hurt her, Cal," Noah said. There was a different mix of emotion in his voice now. Worry and regret. "Don't mess up her life the way you did Harper's."

The arrow didn't miss. It smacked right into Cal's heart, rendering him speechless enough that he couldn't respond. Noah must have realized he wasn't going to get a better parting shot than that, because he went back to his truck and drove off, leaving Cal standing there and doing his own mental cursing, groaning and pacing.

Because Noah was right.

Cal could hurt Charlotte. He could mess up her life. Then again, Noah had been willing to do the same thing to her when he'd planned on marrying Elise. And that meant Charlotte wasn't going to end up being happy with either Noah or him. Noah because of what he'd done to her, and him because of what he couldn't give her.

Cal mentally repeated that. He couldn't give Charlotte much of anything. Kisses, yes. Maybe even sex. But he was nowhere in the realm of being able to offer her love. And that's what she deserved. The real-deal package with a man free to love her and give her that family she'd always wanted.

Now, that led to one big-assed question.

How the hell was he going to walk away from her?

CHAPTER ELEVEN

CHARLOTTE WALKED OUT on the porch of Port in a Storm and cursed the smell of the roses. Normally, that wasn't a curseworthy scent, but it was overpowering. That was just one of the reasons she hadn't allowed the bouquets into the house.

All fifteen of them.

Not little bunches, either, but the whopping big ones that people sent for weddings, funerals, major celebrations or groveling. The last category was the clear winner here as the arrangements were from Noah.

Thankfully, Noah hadn't done the delivering himself. He'd relied on the town's florist, Petal Pushers, for that. Good thing, too, since the fifteen deliveries would have meant three daily trips out to the ranch, and simply put, Charlotte just didn't have the time or inclination to see him. Noah, however, clearly had the time, because he'd spent the past five days not only buying flowers but also texting at an hourly frequency.

Or rather he had done that before she'd blocked him.

Before the blocking, though, Noah had thought it wise to text her old photos of them together. There was no shortage of those, since they'd been together for more than two decades. He'd probably hoped the memories would stir old feelings. It hadn't. Neither would the flowers, especially since she was cursing them.

"They're starting to attract bugs," Mandy remarked as she walked past the sea of yellow, pink, red and white roses.

Mandy was carrying yet two more gallons of paint that she'd just picked up from the hardware store, and like Charlotte, she was covered in splatters of A Hint of Sunshine washable latex, the color choice for several of the guest rooms. Charlotte had underestimated the amount of paint required when she'd done the initial order, which meant trips back to the store. More than once since she'd also underestimated Scottish Highlands Mist for the bathrooms and Barely There Bluebonnets for the kitchen and dining room.

Charlotte made a sound of agreement about the bugs, some of which were bees, which was the main reason she hadn't dumped the flowers in the trash. That, and the fact that she didn't want to take up coveted trash-bin space on flowers, not when there were so many other things that the work crews were having to haul away. Besides, the flowers would make good compost once they got the heap going in a spot she'd picked out behind the barn.

"All went well with the closing?" Mandy asked, making her way up the porch steps.

"It did," Charlotte confirmed, motioning to the pocket of her overalls where she'd stashed her phone. It held the huge volume of paperwork that her Realtor had emailed her.

Charlotte hadn't actually been at the closing because she'd presigned everything. Becker had done the same, and he hadn't gone to the closing, either, despite being discharged from the hospital. In fact, he was supposed to be at the rehab facility getting physical therapy but instead he was in the barn doing heaven knew what. Apparently, he was helping in some way or she was sure the contractor or some of the crew would have complained about him by now.

There were certainly no complaints about Cal, either, who'd been putting in a lot of hours with the renovations. She was thankful he was so eager to get the place finished, but Charlotte thought the work might also be a way of distancing himself from her. There'd been no kisses over the past five days since the scalding one at the corral fence. Just plenty of heated looks between them and some wincing, grunting and sighing at the body aches the work was giving them.

"We'll celebrate soon," Charlotte assured Mandy, who was wincing, grunting and sighing as well from the weight of the paint cans. "Maybe a girls' night out with champagne. Or some hot-stone massages," she added while rubbing her back.

"I vote for massages with champagne," Mandy said, but her words trailed off when something by the barn caught her attention.

Or rather someone. Speak of the devil. Or rather *think* of the devil and there he was.

Cal.

He came out of the barn, and as many of the workers had done throughout the morning, he headed to the hose. First to have a drink and then to pour some of the water over his head. Water that slid down his face and then his chest. Charlotte had no trouble watching the water's journey because Cal had unbuttoned his shirt, no doubt as a way of keeping himself cooler.

It had the opposite effect on Charlotte.

Mercy, the man was, well, hot.

As she always did when she looked at Cal these days, she got a mixed bag of emotions. All of the mess with Noah came tumbling back, but that was starting to be an annoying gnat of a thought compared to hot-cowboy-guy-with-unbuttoned-shirt who was working hard and unpaid to make her dream come true. That itself was a form of foreplay, but Cal could spur plenty of stimulation just by breathing.

Or apparently by moving.

He shifted a little, going for a second round with the hose, and Charlotte watched his chest and ab muscles respond. She responded, too, and she was certain she had a serious lustful expression when he glanced her way. He waved, the gesture freezing a little, no doubt when he realized he had an audience of both her and Mandy. They weren't exactly drooling. Well, not so that he could see, anyway.

Charlotte waved back and kept her attention on Cal when he turned to go back in the barn. While there were no exposed muscles with this view, it was interesting to see the way his jeans molded to his butt.

"Well, that might give me smutty thoughts for a while," Mandy remarked. "But don't worry, I'll keep my hands off since he's yours." She paused. "Uh, is he yours?"

"No," Charlotte said and sighed. "I'm not even sure where I stand with him. He's been avoiding me lately."

Just as she said that, she got another speak-of-the-devil moment when Cal opened the barn door, but instead of going right in, he turned to look at her again. Things passed between them. Steamy, unspoken things that whispered of forbidden lust and all that.

Mandy chuckled. "He's not doing a very good job of avoiding you," she muttered, heading inside with her paint stash.

Charlotte could have disagreed with that comment since there'd been no actual human-to-human contact between Cal and her in days, but the avoidance clearly hadn't done anything to douse the heat.

She smiled at that and muttered, "Good." Because she intended to do something about that heat very soon.

Charlotte hoisted up her own cans of paint, but she stopped when she saw the approaching truck. At first, she groaned because it belonged to Taggert, and she thought Noah might have used it to drive to the ranch. But, no, it was Taggert himself.

"Charlotte," he greeted her when he stepped from his truck.

"Taggert," she said back, but she kept her tone a little cool if he'd come here to plead Noah's case. So far, he hadn't done that. In fact, it seemed to Charlotte that he'd been avoiding her as well.

"I hope I'm not interrupting you too much." He slowly made his way to her while he glanced around. "A busy day for you."

"Yes," she quietly agreed, and did more waiting for the Noah shoe to drop. Thankfully, it didn't.

Taggert hitched his thumb to his truck. "I hope you don't mind, but I went ahead and brought over some things from Alden's old room. He's so excited about being able to come here. I can't thank you enough for making this happen."

She relaxed. A lot. "I just wish it'd happened sooner, but better late than, well, even later." Charlotte tipped her head to the front door. "Would you like to see Alden's room?" She'd sent Alden some pictures, but she wasn't sure if he had shared them with his dad.

Taggert didn't hesitate. "I'd love to see it."

He came up on the porch, glancing at the flowers and saying "Noah?" in a headshaking, exasperated tone.

"Noah," she confirmed with a scoff. "Too bad he didn't send paint instead." That wouldn't have turned the tides in his favor, but Charlotte would have been slightly less annoyed with him.

They stepped into the house, and Taggert followed Charlotte to one of the bedrooms on the main floor. It was one of only two fully finished suites in the house. Barely. She'd finished the painting in there a couple of hours earlier, and she'd had a work crew move the furniture back in.

"It's close to the kitchen and the main living area," she pointed out, hoping that Taggert didn't just see the mess of the place but also the potential.

Charlotte ushered him into the large suite that had gotten the Sea Spray walls to complement the white-washed bed and navy blue sofa and chair. The two windows had great views of what would be the garden, once that was up and going.

"Oh, he's going to love this," Taggert said, taking it all in.

Charlotte's breath of relief was a little louder than

she'd intended. "Good. Because I want him to be happy here."

"I think he will be." Taggert turned toward her. "He's anxious to move out of the rehab facility, but he didn't want to move home. Not yet, anyway. He says thirty is too old to be moving back home." He stopped, gathered his breath. "But I suspect it's because he doesn't want me to see how much pain he's in. How much he has to struggle just to get through the day."

Charlotte didn't say *Bingo*, but she thought Taggert was one hundred percent right. Here, he'd be with other wounded warriors. The therapy and services were geared specifically to people like him. Of course, there'd be some pity, sadness and empathy from the staff and fellow residents. From her, too. But she imagined those reactions would skyrocket if his dad were around to witness it.

"Alden might eventually want to return home," she settled for saying. "Or getting his own place nearby." Now she paused. "Though, if things go as well with him as I hope, I'm planning on offering him a job as an in-resident therapist of sorts."

It surprised her when she saw tears appear in Taggert's eyes, and he held up his hand in a "give me a second" gesture while he regained control of his emotions. "Thanks again. For that. For everything."

"You're very welcome. From the moment Alden was sent to a rehab facility, I've wanted to do something like this. For him, yes, but for so many others like him."

Harper, for instance, though Charlotte was reasonably sure Harper wouldn't be arriving with high hopes and a positive attitude like Alden.

"You're thinking about your uncle Rob," Taggert said when she stayed quiet. "You're doing this for him."

"I am," she admitted. "Of course, I wish this place had been here for him. If so, he might still be alive."

The regret resurfaced. And some guilt because she hadn't been able to save him. She'd been too young and hadn't had the resources. But that failure might end up saving others. Charlotte had to be satisfied with that.

"Rob would have loved this place, too," Taggert said, reminding her that he had known her uncle. Heck, he'd known her father, too, since Taggert had lived in Emerald Creek his whole life.

He looked at her again. "Anything you want to ask me about Noah?"

Charlotte didn't even have to think of her response. "No, thanks." But since she and Taggert seemed to be in heart-to-heart mode, she went with a question she did want answered. "What's going on with you and my mom?"

The breath he dragged in was long and then even longer when he repeated it. Clearly, he was going to need a lot of oxygen to spill about this. "I told Izzie that I thought it was a good idea if we stopped seeing each other."

There it was. Exactly what Charlotte had thought. "Stopped seeing each other for good or just a short break?" And she hoped for the break, the shorter the better. Her mom could be a pain in the butt, but Izzie had seemed happier with Taggert.

"Probably for good," Taggert said. "Yesterday, after the big blowup here with Noah, I texted your mom and told her we needed to talk."

Izzie must have known what was coming when she'd said, *You've ruined everything again.*

"I asked Izzie to meet me," Taggert went on, "and I told her things were over." He squeezed his eyes shut a moment. "She didn't say anything. She just walked away." He paused. "Is she all right?"

Charlotte wasn't sure as she hadn't talked to her mom since she'd blurted out the stinging remark. She'd thought it best to give them both some time and space. Lots of space because Charlotte was still reeling from her mother accusing her of ruining another of her relationships. Ruining the first one, with her father leaving, was indeed on her, but Charlotte didn't think she was responsible for this second one.

Or was she?

"Did you break up with Izzie because of me?" Charlotte came out and asked.

"No," Taggert was quick to say. "I just didn't like the way Izzie talked to you, how she was trying to browbeat you into getting back with my son."

Charlotte groaned. So this was partly on her after all. She should have just left when Noah showed up yesterday. Left and then confronted him later when they were alone. Then her mother wouldn't have tried to jump in and save things.

Well, crap.

She was quickly becoming the Typhoid Mary of her mother's relationships.

"I don't want you to blame yourself for any of this," Taggert continued. He was obviously correctly interpreting her expression. Her *crap* mutterings likely clued him in, too. "I know Izzie wanted me to ask her to marry me. And I nearly did. But after what happened with Noah and you, I figured if I took marriage off the table for Izzie and me, then she might back off trying to pressure you to reconcile with Noah."

Yet more confirmation that she was the reason for the breakup, and again Taggert was astute enough to pick up on what she was feeling.

"I'm making things worse," he said. "It's not your fault," he assured her. "If anyone's to blame, it's me. I knew Izzie was high-strung, but I thought I could get past that. In hindsight, I should have never started up things with her, since I'm pretty sure I ended up breaking her heart."

Charlotte had no idea if that last part was true, but it prompted her to take out her phone and fire off a quick text to her mother. Are you okay? she came out and asked.

No immediate answer came, but Izzie might be in a meeting or something. Hopefully, she would see the text soon and get in touch. Then again, it was possible Izzie was just as heartbroken by her as she was with the breakup with Taggert.

Charlotte turned at the sound in the doorway and not only saw who was there—Becker—but also got a strong whiff of the roses. She looked at his wheelchair and saw crushed petals on the wheels.

"I used the new ramp," Becker said, following her gaze. "But I ended up crushing some of the flowers. They were in the way," he added in his usual snarling tone.

"They were," she agreed. "Sorry about that. Did you need something?"

"Nope, but I found this in the barn, and I thought you might want it for some of the doors."

Becker handed her a rusted tin that had likely once held candy or cookies. The lid had already been pried open, and she saw the dozen or so old skeleton keys. She was in the process of having new locks put on the doors, but it could be fun to keep some of them as is.

"Those were the spares when they first got put in that box," Becker explained. "I used to play with them when I was a kid."

"Thanks," she muttered, and she didn't miss the wistful way he looked at both the keys and the room. It was obvious he was having a little trouble dealing with the big changes in his life. "And thanks for helping with the barn reno. I hope you're not overdoing it. I know you were supposed to be at the rehab facility starting today."

"A waste of time," he grumbled. "And it's all the way in San Antonio. I'd rather just see somebody here in Emerald Creek."

There was indeed a physical therapist, Renee Bilbo. Charlotte had gone to school with her and had contracted with Renee to provide services to the clients coming into Port in a Storm. Renee would also keep her practice in town and would likely be able to treat Becker, but that would be as an outpatient. Added to that, Becker couldn't even drive himself to appointments yet. Cal had driven him here today.

"Where will you stay when…" Her question tapered off when Becker dodged her gaze, and she mentally sighed. "Do you have a place to stay?" she amended.

"I'll figure something out," Becker insisted, and he started turning his wheelchair around.

Charlotte stepped in front of him, and she so hoped she didn't regret what she was about to say. "You could stay here."

The surprise flashed in his eyes, and she thought she saw a sliver of hope to go along with it. But then he shook his head. "I wouldn't feel right staying in the house now that it's not mine."

"Then how about one of the rooms in the barn until you're back on your feet?" she quickly countered. "Both of those rooms are finished enough that you could stay there. It'd mean putting up with work crews for a while, but you'd get your physical therapy without having to go to a rehab facility."

She could tell that her offer had touched him, but this was Becker, so he didn't have an overjoyed reaction. "I wouldn't feel right just staying here for free."

"Then help the work crews in any way you can." And then she thought of something that might seal the deal. "It'd be like you fulfilling that life-pact for me and Cal getting you to the hospital after you broke your leg."

Of course, she hadn't needed to spell all of that out. Nor did she want any deeds done in the name of the life-pact. But in this case, it was apparently the way to go, because Becker wasn't turning it down. Wasn't grabbing it with both hands, either, but there was a glimmer of gratitude in his eyes.

"I'll think about it," he finally grumbled. He got his wheelchair moving and added a barely audible *thank you* once his back was to her.

"That was good of you," Taggert said once Becker was out of earshot.

Charlotte shrugged and was ready to move back to

her conversation about Taggert and her mother, but he checked his watch. "I have to leave to go see Alden." He glanced around the room again. "Can't wait to get him here."

She made a sound of agreement and followed Taggert out. She still wasn't able to bring up her mother as she spotted Cal making his way toward them. He'd buttoned his shirt, which meant no peep show for her, but Cal could give her a punch of lust even fully dressed.

"Taggert," Cal greeted him, and he extended his hand for the man to shake but then pulled it back when he saw the paint smears. Apparently, Cal had been doing some painting as well.

"Cal," he greeted back. Taggert opened his mouth, closed it and seemed to rethink what he'd been about to say. He settled on, "It's good to see you." He repeated that he needed to leave to see Alden and headed out.

Charlotte had trouble finding her own words when she looked at Cal. Then again, that was starting to be a trend. Her mouth and the rest of her just seemed to get flustered and downright giddy whenever she was around him. The giddy sexual buzz was fun, but they clearly had some not-fun things they needed to discuss. Charlotte started with an item she'd just added to her list of topics.

"I told Becker he could stay in one of the rooms in the barn," she explained. "Please tell me that's not a massive mistake and that Becker's surliness won't cause the work crew to leave."

The corner of Cal's mouth lifted. "The crew will stay. And Becker's helping in his own way. Whenever anyone finds something light that needs to be moved to the junk pile, Becker moves it there." He paused. "I'm sure he appreciates your offer. In his own way," he repeated.

That caused Charlotte to smile, too, and the smiles added to the buzz. Unfortunately, that feeling couldn't take over because there were other points on her list.

"Tell me the truth," she said firmly. "Did Noah pick a fight with you after I left you two alone the other day?"

"No," Cal was quick to say. "So there's no need for you to start a permanent shit list and put his name on it."

At the time, she hadn't been sure if Cal had heard that, but obviously he had. Better yet, Noah had heard it and heeded her warning. Well, he had if Cal wasn't fudging, and she didn't think he was.

"Did Noah use the life-pact to try to get you to back off from seeing me?" she pressed.

Cal shook his head. "He might have realized he's sort of overplayed that card over the years." He paused again, and his expression turned more serious. It turned out, though, that serious Cal was just as hot as the smiling one.

Oh, mercy. She really did have it bad for him.

"But Noah said he was going to try to get you back," Cal added. He reached out and moved a strand of hair off her cheek. The touch zinged through her almost effectively as a kiss.

Almost.

"He's trying with flowers," she confirmed. "He was also trying with texts until I blocked him. There's more than one form of shit list," she added, causing Cal to give her another of those temporary smiles.

"Noah also warned me not to hurt you," Cal shared, and his expression turned serious again. Very serious.

Which told her that there might be more to Noah's warning than Cal was saying.

And then it hit her.

The zinger that Noah would have used.

"Noah said for you not to hurt me like Harper," she guessed. She got confirmation that she was dead-on when a muscle flickered in Cal's jaw. "Well, my permanent shit list is up and running, and Noah's the number-one shit on it. He shouldn't have said that to you. It was a chickenshit thing to do. And, yes, I'm aware I'm using the word *shit* a lot, but it applies."

Sighing, Cal slipped his arm around her and eased her to him. She was glad he did. Not because of the ever-stirring, ever-escalating heat but because he had turned to her for comfort. Anything she could do in that department was a bonus.

"Noah doesn't want to lose you," Cal muttered. "He's pissed off at himself. Pissed off at the world right now. He used Harper as sort of a Hail Mary pass."

She heard the pain in his voice. Felt it in the way he was holding her. So the Hail Mary had worked. It'd hurt Cal. It'd brought back his guilt and his pain. Oh, yes. Noah was totally on that shit list.

"What about you?" he asked, touching her face again. This time, there wasn't a strand of hair to remove so it was just direct-skin contact. "Did Taggert ask you anything about getting back with Noah?"

"No." She stopped, sighed. "Taggert broke up with Izzie because of me."

Cal stared at her as if she'd sprouted some extra facial parts. "You're not going to tell me that Taggert is secretly in love with you or something."

That had the intended effect. It got her to smile. For a second or two, anyway. "No. He broke up with my mother because of the way she pressured me to get back with Noah."

"And you blame yourself for that?" Cal asked.

"Rightfully so," she stated.

"Unrightfully so," he objected. "Taggert made that decision, and it was probably because he didn't think he could handle a future of dealing with your mom. Izzie can be a handful."

Charlotte couldn't argue with that last part, but still this breakup felt as if it was on her. Izzie would see it that way, too, which was probably why her mother hadn't texted her.

"Part of me wants to say to heck with it," she admitted, "to let my mother wallow in her sadness and strike out at me for contributing to it in any way. Another part of me wants to block her the way I did Noah."

"Which part is winning out?" he asked. This time he touched her cheek not with fingers but his mouth. It was a nice escalation.

"I'll let you know," she said, and did some escalation of her own.

Charlotte slid her hand around the back of his neck and pulled him down to her for a real kiss. Full-on contact. Lots of heat. Those were the markers for a kiss with Cal, and this one didn't disappoint. The taste of him slid right through her, all the way to every nerve in her body that could get excited by such things.

Apparently, there were lots of them.

She deepened the kiss, immediately feeling the deeper jolt of heat, too. Sweet. It was amazing that something so simple could ignite so much. Then again, no kiss stayed simple when it came to Cal.

The heat started to roar. Nothing gentle about that. Heat was a greedy sucker who wanted more, more, more. So did her body. Her pulse galloped. Her breath was heaven knew where. And a whole lot of tingling was going on.

The greedy sucker urged her to go even deeper with the kiss. She did. It urged her to add some body contact. Charlotte did that, too. Her breasts against Cal's toned and perfect chest. It was sweet pressure. And some torture because it made her realize she wanted more of that pressure. She wanted his naked body against hers.

She wanted sex.

Yep, heat was doing its thing and escalating this much too fast. After all, the door was open, and with all the work crews around the place, someone could come walking in at any second. If they did, though, Charlotte wasn't sure she'd be able to hear them. A galloping pulse meant her heartbeat thudding in her ears that could block out pretty much any sound.

It couldn't block out the pleasure, however.

And hallelujah for that. Because she was all into the pleasure right now, and Cal was the supreme pleasure-giver. That deep, hungry kiss. The chest thing, too. He didn't stop there. No. He pressed her against the wall, anchoring them so he could do all sorts of stuff to her without the risk of their legs giving way and them falling on their butts.

He slid his hand over hers, cupping it and easing that part of her forward so that it created a whole bunch of contact between her center and his. Delicious, incredible contact that was on the verge of making her drag him to the floor.

But then, Cal stopped it.

Just stopped.

With his breath gusting and while whispering some profanity directed at himself, he stepped back. "Sorry," he said through those breaths. "Sorry."

Charlotte blinked and looked surprised at him because she couldn't figure out why an apology was needed. "We seemed to be on a good track there." Mercy, her breath was gusty, too, and her words hadn't had a lot of volume.

He nodded, cursed some more and looked at her as if he might dive in for another round of all that kissing and touching. He didn't.

"You need time to think," he said.

Another surprise. This didn't appear to be a thinking situation. And the moment that thought came to mind, she realized that it should have been just that. A situation where some thinking had been involved.

Because this was big.

This was foreplay. This was one snap, one heartbeat, away from sex. Not scheduled sex-date stuff, either, but the wild, impulsive kind that might lead to some regrets. Not during or immediately afterward. Later, when they'd had time to process it.

"Any regrets I might have wouldn't be about Noah," she assured him, and she hoped that made sense.

Apparently she was clear, because he nodded. "But I don't want us to have regrets of any kind or for any reason. That's why you need time. We both do."

Until he'd added that last part, Charlotte had been about to suggest they go on a date or something to test the romantic waters. But his use of *both* stopped her. Yes, Cal needed that, and it wasn't as if she didn't have a whole bunch of stuff on her plate right now.

The universe seemed to confirm that, because her phone dinged with a text. Maybe from her mother to start the guilt-flinging. But it was just as possible it was from someone doing the reno.

It wasn't.

"It's from Dr. Kentrell," she relayed to Cal, and since he would likely want to know anything the therapist had to say, she went ahead and read it aloud.

"'Charlotte, I was hoping you'd be able to come up with a firm date to have Harper moved to Port in a Storm. Harper's having some adjustment problems with her physical therapist. She fired her. Actually, she fired me, too.'"

Charlotte paused, groaned and then kept reading.

"'The physical therapist and I are staff, so Harper can't actually fire us, but she's insisting that it's either her or us. She says she'll text her father to come and get her if something isn't done soon.'"

Now it was Cal who groaned. Adding Paul to that mix would be putting gasoline on an already-blazing fire.

"'Anyway,'" Charlotte continued to read, "'I think the sooner you can move Harper in with you, the better. Harper agrees. She says she wants to go back to Emerald Creek, and for better or worse, she says she's ready to face Cal down.'"

CHAPTER TWELVE

Nine days.

That wasn't written down anywhere, and Cal hadn't actually looked at a calendar, but he knew his leave was ticking away. Literally. The first three weeks of it had gone by in a blur. Well, except for the kissing he'd done with Charlotte.

Definitely no blurs there.

Those memories were right there in the front of his mind and were encouraging other parts of him to go back to her for more. *More* would no doubt be sex, and that was the reason Cal was trying his level best to throttle back. Three weeks wasn't nearly enough time for her to get past whatever she was feeling or had felt for Noah.

Was it?

Those memories and the mindless part of him behind the zipper of his jeans assured him that it was. That Charlotte hadn't loved Noah in a long, long time. That their relationship had technically been over long before Cal had shown up with the Dear John official breakup. Still, it'd been three weeks.

Three long weeks where Charlotte's life had changed. Where she'd started her dream of Port in a Storm. Where Izzie and Taggert were no longer getting married, which meant there was no dream double wedding on the horizon. When Cal laid it all out there like that, it seemed like these three weeks had been in doggy time and had stretched out into months.

Of course, that rationalization only gave his mouth and dick encouragement he didn't want them to have, so Cal tried to push it all away, dry off from his shower and get dressed. By now, he had enough splattered jeans and shirts, but he went with something paintfree, and he didn't even try to pretend it wasn't because he wanted to make a good impression.

Because he did.

And because Harper would be arriving at Port in a Storm today, and according to Dr. Kentrell, she was ready to face him down. Whatever that meant, Cal was more than ready for it. Or rather he was just anxious to get the meeting out of the way.

Harper likely wouldn't be impressed by clean clothes, but Cal thought they might at least make him feel less grubby. That might help with his overall mood. Might. It seemed a lot of pressure to put on fresh laundry.

Dr. Kentrell had been the one to suggest that Cal go ahead and visit Harper as soon as she arrived. The therapist had thought it would be good for Harper to have that initial contact so she could understand right from the start that this wouldn't be just a single meeting, that she might end up seeing Cal and other people she knew on a regular basis. If Harper couldn't cope with that, then it was best for them to know up front. And if she couldn't cope, then they would need to come up with strategies to temporarily minimize her contact with him and move her to yet another facility.

Charlotte had already offered Cal an out by letting him know that she didn't expect him to visit Harper. That she knew how hard such a visit would be on him. But Cal had no intention of taking Charlotte up on that out. He needed to at least try to see Harper, to let her know that he would help her in any way. If she wanted his help, that is.

And, yes, it would be hard.

Not just for him but for Harper and Charlotte, too. Cal suspected they were all in for a high-stress kind of day.

He finished dressing and walked out of his room, nearly smacking into Blue, who seemed to be pacing outside his door. "Were you waiting for me?" Cal asked at the same time Blue said, "I wasn't sure you were alone. Is Charlotte in there?"

Cal sighed. He wasn't a fool, not generally anyway, so he figured that gossip about him and Charlotte would get around. No way to stop that. But if Blue thought there was a possibility that Charlotte was in his bedroom, then his brother obviously thought the relationship had escalated.

Which it had.

It just hadn't gotten to the bedroom-overnight stage.

"Charlotte's not here," Cal assured him. "What's wrong?"

"Dad got a PI to do a full background check on Rowan," Blue provided.

Cal shook his head and swore under his breath. "Please don't tell me Dad's tried to contact him." Because Cal figured the contact should come from Rowan, not the other way around.

"Not that I know of, not yet anyway. But I don't know what's in the report, and Dad's not sharing. I just thought we should keep an eye on him in case something he learns about Rowan hits him hard."

Cal frowned. "Like what?"

"Like maybe Rowan never wants anything to do with any of us. Especially with Dad and Audrey. I'm not sure he could handle that right now."

Cal had to agree. Two serious heart attacks, a marriage on the rocks and learning he had a son he'd never met. News that the son never wanted to see him might trigger both medical and psychological problems, and his dad sure as hell didn't need any more trouble than he already had.

"I'll keep an eye on him," Cal promised. "And I'll try to talk to him about it. Maybe see if I can get him to stop digging into Rowan." Though the lack of digging likely wouldn't stop his dad's need to know anything and everything about his son.

"Good. Maybe talk to Audrey, too. I've already done both. So has Egan. But maybe if they hear it from all three of us, it'll sink in that they're not doing themselves any favors by pushing these particular buttons right now."

Of course Egan and Blue had already had those conversations with their dad and Audrey, and they would have probably asked Cal to intercede a whole lot sooner had he not been going through his own crap.

Cal gave his brother another assurance he'd help, said his goodbye and headed down the stairs and onto the side porch that was closest to where he'd parked his truck. Again he nearly smacked right into somebody. Or rather two somebodies.

His dad and Noah were on the porch, and judging from their expressions they'd been having a deep conversation. Cal didn't have to guess what they'd talked about. Nope. Charlotte and he were a solid bet.

"Everything okay?" Cal automatically asked, which was a dumb question since it was obvious that both men had more than their share of problems.

"Your dad was just telling me that you're planning on getting out of the Air Force," Noah threw out there. "Why the hell would you do something like that?"

Cal just gave him a flat stare and waited for Noah to recall what'd happened to Harper.

"That's why you're getting out?" Noah demanded, and it sounded like the tone of a current, worried friend rather than a former friend who might hope that Cal would dissolve into a puddle of goo. "How will you getting out fix Harper?" But he didn't wait for Cal to respond. "It won't, that's how."

"No, but it might fix me," Cal said.

That had Noah's shoulders snapping back, and Cal saw the surprise morph to something else: disgust. "You'll be around to pursue Charlotte after my leave is up, and I have to return to duty."

Cal was certain there was some disgust on his own face. "Pursue? No. Just no. If she wants to see me, however, I won't stop her."

Well, probably not. Cal doubted he could work up enough resolve if Charlotte did end up wanting to go through with a relationship. That said, she might be working up enough of her own resolve to stop it in its tracks.

Noah bit off a string of swear words, probably because of the dirty look he got from Cal's father. Everyone who knew Derek knew he wasn't a fan of cursing.

"Sorry," Noah grumbled. "I should be going, anyway."

"Don't you first want to tell me why you came?" Cal asked. "Because I figure you're here to see me and not my dad."

Noah locked eyes with him. "No, I came to see you. I wanted to ask you to back off seeing Charlotte to give her time to make up her mind about whether or not she wants to get back with me."

As far as Cal was concerned, Charlotte had made that clear. There'd be no reconciliation. And considering the way she'd kissed him, Cal believed her. Heck, maybe Noah believed her, too, but he might not be able to fully grasp yet that he'd lost her.

Cal's phone dinged, and he saw the message from Charlotte. Noah must have seen her name, too, because he said something that got another dirty look from Derek. Then Noah headed off the porch toward his truck.

Just an FYI, Charlotte had messaged. Dr. Kentrell has arrived with Harper.

So it'd happened. Cal had thought that maybe at the last minute Harper would refuse to come to Port in a Storm. Apparently not.

"You think we can talk later?" Cal asked his dad.

His dad gave him a flat look similar to the one that

Cal had given Noah just minutes earlier. "Blue told you about the PI report on my son."

"He did," Cal verified.

"And you think I should back off and wait for my son to contact me." There was plenty of surliness in his dad's tone, but then he sighed and dropped it down a couple of notches. "I'm tired of waiting. It helps to find out everything I can about him. It's like actually getting to know him."

Cal couldn't quite wrap his head around that, but then he wasn't in his father's shoes. And that's why he, too, dialed down his concern. "Just don't try to contact him," Cal urged. "That might put him off if he's still trying to make up his mind about talking to us."

His dad shook his head, not in disagreement but rather frustration. Cal could tell he saw the logic in waiting. "All right," his father finally said. "Now, you go ahead to Charlotte." He paused a beat. "What's going on between you two, anyway? Did the fake stuff turn into something not so fake?"

"It's not fake," Cal could say with certainty.

But as for what was going on, that was still in the to-be-determined category. Maybe a fling. Maybe just a temporary attraction. Maybe that dreaded rebound reaction on Charlotte's part.

And maybe something much more serious that could stir up things six ways to Sunday.

He told his dad goodbye and went to his truck to start the drive to Charlotte's. Thankfully, it was short so he didn't have the time to delve into a whole bunch of bad *what-if* scenarios. A few still sped through his head, though. It was possible that Harper would pitch a fit when she saw him. The only contact he'd had with her had been that *just give the hell up* text.

As usual, there were a lot of other vehicles at the ranch. The tasks of the day seemed to be painting the exteriors of the house and barn while the landscape crews were tackling the yards and trails. He spotted Becker in his wheelchair seemingly testing out one of those trails while Jack trotted along behind him.

Cal also spotted the medical-transport van in the mix of the other vehicles. It appeared to be empty, and neither Harper nor Dr. Kentrell were anywhere in sight. Gathering his breath and trying to tamp down his nerves, Cal went inside the house and didn't have to look long before he found them. They were in the downstairs suite that Charlotte had set up for Harper. Someone had already brought in Harper's suitcases, and there was a woman in purple scrubs placing some bottles of medication on the nightstand next to the bed.

All of the women shifted their attention to him, but the one in purple—probably the home health worker—quickly returned to her duties. The other three, however, pinned him with their gazes. There was concern in Charlotte's eyes. A breath-held look in the doctor's. And Harper, well, she was more in look-what-the-cat-dragged-in mode.

He'd tried to steel himself for what he might see, but there wasn't enough mettle in the universe for this. For just an instant, he got a flash of the last time he'd seen Harper. About three months ago after a NATO flying competition that he'd won. Harper hadn't been all smiles about losing, but she had posed for photos with him. She'd been healthy, strong and fierce.

Nothing like she was now.

His first thought was that she looked like a survivor of a nearly fatal car crash. Which she was. A crash that had clearly taken its toll. Her head had been shaved, no doubt to perform the surgery that had left a scar that was nowhere close to being healed. It was still angry-looking and red, and her hair hadn't grown back in enough to cover it.

There were yet other scars on her throat and her hands from what appeared to be multiple surgeries, and her right leg was in some kind of brace. Since she had no scrapes or bruises that he could see, Cal supposed those had healed by now, but there was also very little color in her face, and she was thin. Way too thin. He was guessing that she had lost at least twenty-five pounds, which meant she no longer had that athletic build.

She didn't attempt to speak. No surprise there since he'd already known her vocal cords were damaged. However, she could certainly see, because she was giving him one hard look. She was able to move, too, because she used her stiff and crooked right index finger to turn her motorized wheelchair in his direction. It was similar to Becker's, but this one had a small tablet anchored onto the left arm of the chair. The right arm had the controls.

"Harper," he managed to say despite the fact that his throat had clamped shut. "It's good to see you."

She could apparently react, too, because the corner of her mouth lifted in a purely sarcastic "Yeah, right" smile. Cal didn't let that pass.

"It is good to see you," he reiterated. "I'm glad you're alive, and I'm very sorry this happened."

He figured that would earn him another snarl or hard look. It didn't. Harper continued to stare at him for several seconds and then she typed out something on the tablet. The device was obviously set to convert text to speech because the computerlike voice said what she'd typed.

"Halo."

Just that, just his call sign. Cal thought it was probably a dig on his heavenly reputation, but she could have chosen a whole lot worse to address him.

Harper didn't add more. Well, not words. She pressed something on the tablet and music blared out. NSYNC's "Bye Bye Bye."

"That's a little loud, Harper," the doctor commented, and judging from her frustrated sigh, this wasn't the first time she'd dealt with something like this. "Harper downloaded some songs that she uses instead of responses. 'Bye Bye Bye' is one of her favorites, along with 'Blah Blah Blah' and 'Take This Job and Shove It.'"

Harper turned her wheelchair back toward Charlotte and the doctor, and she typed something else that the computer read aloud. "I have eclectic taste that gets the message across." She finished that by hitting "Bye Bye Bye" again.

The doctor glanced around as if she might be looking for some reason to stay. Harper put a stop to that by wheeling farther into the room and making a shooing motion for them to leave. They did. All three walked out and then just lingered there in the hall.

"Sonora's there if Harper needs anything," Charlotte said as if to reassure the doctor and herself.

"Yes. Sonora's résumé and job experience are amazing," the doctor finally said, and she looked at Cal to fill him in. "Sonora Billings, the LVN who'll be looking after Harper and some of the other residents. Charlotte not only hired her but also offered her one of the rooms on the third floor so that Sonora won't have to drive back and forth to San Antonio."

Charlotte picked up the explanation from there. "Sonora will stay a week, and then another LVN will come in and take her place. They'll trade off like that as long as necessary. Added to that, a counselor will come in twice a week, and Harper will get PT every other day."

Charlotte gave him a wary glance as if trying to figure out if he was okay with all of this. With Harper being here. And with him seeing her.

Dr. Kentrell was doing some wary glancing, too, at the door. "By the way, Harper can walk. Not easily, but she's mobile when she wants to be. She'd be a lot more mobile if she'd done the exercises the physical therapist prescribed."

Cal had to shake his head. "Does it hurt her to walk? Is that why she uses the chair?"

"She still has pain, but she has some limited mobility. It's easier for her to use her voice tablet from the chair than it is when she's standing or attempting to walk. I also want her to work on that during her physical therapy." She gathered her breath. "I can't promise you Harper won't lash out and then demand to leave. If she does, call me, and I'll see what I can do to help.

I just hope she gives this place a chance," she added with concern.

"And so say all of us," Charlotte replied.

The doctor left, but Charlotte and Cal stayed put. Maybe because they were both expecting the door to fly open with the lashing out that Kentrell had suggested might happen. But there were no sounds of outburst, no computer-voice gripes that Harper had typed out. Just silence, and after a few moments, Sonora came out.

"Harper wants a nap so I helped her into bed," the worker said, and she held up the monitor she was holding. "I'll keep an eye on her while I maybe fix her a snack plate that'll be by her bedside when she wakes up. You said it was okay if I used the kitchen?" she said to Charlotte.

"More than okay," Charlotte assured her. "Use whatever part of the house that isn't being painted or repaired. If you need something you can't find, and I'm not around, you've got my number so just give me a call."

Sonora headed to the kitchen, and Charlotte and Cal walked back toward the front of the house where he was certain Charlotte would be questioning him about how he was doing. But the queries would apparently have to be put on hold when they saw the man standing in the foyer.

Paul.

Cal didn't groan, but Charlotte wasn't quite able to suppress all of hers. The sound spluttered out before she tried to cover it with a greeting. "Mr. Johansen. How are you?"

Paul must have decided to skip the small talk. "Gossip is that my daughter is here."

Charlotte didn't jump to answer that.

"You can tell me if she is," Paul insisted. "She put my name on her medical forms so I could be told about what's going on with her."

Cal glanced at Charlotte to see if she had any idea if that was true. Evidently it was, because Charlotte nodded. And Cal wondered if that kind of consent had been voluntary on Harper's part or if Paul had pressured her into it.

"Harper's here," Charlotte said, but she stepped in front of Paul when he started to move, presumably to head down the hall. "But she's sleeping. It's been an exhausting day for her, as I'm sure you can understand."

Judging from the way Paul's jaw set, he wasn't as understanding as Charlotte hoped. "How'd she take coming here?" he finally asked.

"Everything's going well enough," Charlotte said, and Cal knew she'd carefully chosen her words.

Paul made a snorting sound to indicate he wasn't quite buying that. "Hard to believe, especially if she saw Cal. Seeing him would set her off because she blames him for everything. I told her if she wants somebody to blame, all she's gotta do is look straight in the mirror." He stopped, shook his head. "Stupid. She threw it all away because she couldn't handle a little competition."

Cal's first instinct was to punch the man. Not the way to go, though, since a fistfight wouldn't help Harper. So he tried something more diplomatic.

"Harper will get the help she needs here," he said.

"What she needs is her head examined," Paul grumbled. "Is she getting that?" He waved that off, indicating he didn't care for a response. His gaze came back to Cal. "Your daddy's ticker might be bad these days, but he raised his kids all with spines. He didn't raise losers."

Charlotte perhaps anticipated Cal's desire to use his fist, because she stepped in between Paul and him. "Harper's not a loser. She just needs to find her way again, and we can all help with that. With therapy, yes, and by giving her a quiet, nurturing place to heal. Quiet and nurturing," she emphasized in a tone that managed to sound cheerful instead of insulting.

Paul must not have known how to respond to that, because he stared at her for a while and then checked his watch. "So does this place have visiting hours or something?"

"Yes," she was quick to say, though she'd never mentioned a word about such things before. "I'll be asking visitors to come early afternoons, provided the clients don't have already-scheduled appointments." She groaned, but it sounded darn fake to Cal. "Which Harper does. She'll have PT this afternoon. I suspect she'll be very sore and tired afterward, so maybe it's best if you come back tomorrow or later in the week."

That added more tightness to Paul's jaw. "Tomorrow. I'll be back at one, so make sure my daughter doesn't have any other scheduled appointments." He spoke those last two words as if they were a waste of time.

In his mind, they probably were.

He seemed to have already written off Harper, and that made Cal wonder why Paul even wanted to see her. Was it because he loved her but wasn't able to express that? Or was this more about wanting to have some control over her? Cal hoped it was option number one, but he was betting it was the second. If so, he wanted to be in the vicinity in case Paul's visit turned ugly.

"So," Charlotte said, looking at him, "would a good, long French kiss level you out and make you feel better?"

Cal certainly hadn't been prepared for that offer. He'd thought she would go with a simple *I'm sorry* or maybe some other soothing words. He hadn't expected her to jump to kissing.

Of course he was interested in that. And it would indeed make him feel better. Or at least it'd get his mind off his troubles for a while.

"You're going to turn me down," she said, probably interpreting his expression. "You're worried about me, about how I could be led on by kissing. Because you're not in a place to be able to commit to anything."

True. So very true. But Cal didn't get a chance to voice that.

"You could also be troubled about your visit with Noah," she went on, taking him by the hand and leading him up the stairs. "How did I know about the visit, you ask? Well, the gossip mill is on speed dial. One of your ranch hands who's prepping the space for the rescue horses saw Noah arrive at Saddlebrook as he was heading out. He figured Noah was there to have it out with you." She put that last part in air quotes. "And the hand mentioned that to one of the painters, who then in turn mentioned it to me."

She looked back over her shoulder and was clearly waiting for an answer as to how the meeting had played out.

"Noah didn't have it out with me," Cal assured her. "In fact, we didn't have much to say to each other."

Charlotte sighed. "And that hurts. Believe me, I know. I don't miss Noah as a part-time, off-and-on boyfriend. But I miss the friend part. Those times when we used to be able to talk about anything. That's gone forever."

Yes, it was, and Cal missed that as well. Maybe years down the road all of this would be water under the bridge, but it was much too recent for things to be dismissed.

"Noah hasn't given up on getting you back," Cal went on as they walked. And, yeah, despite this conversation about nonkissing, nonsex things, his body was already starting to rev up.

"And I haven't given up on making him give up," she was quick to say. "No way, no how, am I getting back together with him." Still no trace of a rebound.

But was he being foolish to think it wasn't there?

Probably, but the thought of kissing Charlotte was once again overshadowing common sense.

"Oh, and Alden gets here tomorrow," Charlotte said, and this time there was some genuine glee in her tone. "Of course, that means Noah will visit him. I'll deal with that, though. I'm hoping that Noah does the noble thing and doesn't try to use his visits with his brother to wheedle some time with me."

Cal figured Noah wouldn't be able to stop himself from doing just that. Desperate people did desperate things, and there was no mistaking that his former best friend was in that particular mindset.

They kept walking up the stairs, and the moment they reached her room, she pulled him inside. Then she pulled him into the kiss she'd promised. It was indeed French. It was long. It was good. So good that it pushed aside some of the stuff he was feeling. So long that all of the crap feelings vanished, and the only thing he could think about and feel was Charlotte. The only thing he wanted was her.

That's why he cursed when she abruptly backed away.

Her breath was heaving, and she was clearly aroused. Clearly. But she held up her hands in a "stay put" gesture when he moved in for more.

"I want you to imagine me kissing you again. Really kissing, I mean. The kind you feel all the way to your toes."

"I *was* feeling that last one in my toes." That was the truth. But he was feeling it more in other parts of him. Specifically, one part. "Why do I have to imagine the next one instead of it being the real deal?"

"Because we're alone in my room with tensions running high. We're very attracted to each other. Very," she emphasized. "And that means another kiss will quickly escalate to the point where we end up naked and having sex."

Yeah, his body was interested, all right. "I see absolutely nothing wrong with that." Of course, that was the lust talking. There were probably plenty of things wrong with it, but at the moment he couldn't think of any.

"Getting naked and having sex is a problem," she went on. "Well, it is unless you tell me you have a condom with you."

Oh, this was going to hurt to say this. "I don't."

She nodded. "And I didn't think of it until we were already on our way up here. If I had, I might have suggested kissing in the foyer. That would have tamped down the escalation."

"Maybe," he admitted. "Or we might have just ducked into a nearby closet."

She laughed as Cal had hoped she would. He needed the laughter to try to cool down some of the heat in his body. A heat that was quickly turning into a throbbing ache. Man, when had he started needing Charlotte this much?

The answer was, apparently, *right now*.

"I don't have a condom, either," she said, "and since we don't have an unplanned pregnancy on our bucket lists, then we'd better do this the safe way. Certainly you have a sex bucket list."

Cal shook his head. He didn't, but with Charlotte so close, he thought it might be time to come up with one that included her.

"I'm a guy," he finally said. "The sex itself is the bucket list."

Her smile took on a naughty, heated edge. "All right. Then I'll tell you mine. Sex on the hood of a car at night in the rain with no one else around. I saw that in a movie once."

That gave him an instant hard-on. Instant. Even though that had nowhere near been in his notion of a fantasy. Or at least it hadn't been until Charlotte had brought it up. Now it seemed like an amazing, stellar idea.

"Can you imagine that?" she continued, and she moved farther away from him to sit on the sill of the window. Facing him with her back pressed against the glass.

She certainly made a picture there with the sunlight streaming through the window. Like him, she hadn't settled for paint-splattered clothing today but instead was wearing jeans and a top that was the same color blue as her eyes. He'd always known that Charlotte was beautiful, but he'd never allowed himself to dwell on that.

He did now, however.

Along with dwelling on that fantasy of hers. The rain, the hood of a car, the night. Just the two of them.

"Of course, we'd kiss before the sex," she said. "You probably don't have to think too hard to imagine that, since we just did that."

Cal made a sound of agreement, kept his eyes on her. Yes, that memory was indeed very fresh.

"The kissing would quickly get out of hand," Charlotte continued, "because, hey, lots of pent-up lust here. Then the touching would begin. Oh, so very much touching. I'm thinking I'd love to get my hands on your abs. And your butt. You've got an amazing butt, Cal."

That made him laugh, but there were some strained nerves behind it. This was sweet torture, and he made a mental note to buy condoms. Lots and lots of them.

"So I'd squeeze your butt cheeks and dally with your abs," she said, the heat rising in her voice.

"Dally?" he questioned.

"That's the only way to deal with your abs. Light touches, fingertips barely trailing over them, brushing against every inch of them." Her gaze dropped to the front of his jeans. "You never know where dallying will lead you."

Hell. That notched things up even more. "And what about me? Do I get to touch you?"

"Oh, I certainly hope so," she was quick to say. She touched her right breast and circled her nipple with her finger. It was erotic as hell, and he had no trouble imagining himself touching her there. Or imagining her stark naked, either.

And that's why he was staying put.

He cursed the condom-makers for not having products that could be delivered with the snap of a finger.

"But I have one very sensitive spot that I want you to imagine touching," Charlotte murmured.

Cal glanced between her legs, causing her to laugh.

"Yes, that is indeed sensitive, but we're still doing foreplay so I was thinking here." She touched the inside of her thigh. So very close to the center of all that heat. "There's a little spot that'd enjoy a kiss or two."

He groaned because he ached to kiss her there. To kiss her everywhere.

"With or without your panties on?" he asked.

"On, for starters, but then that would really skyrocket the foreplay and send us into now, now, now. Want to know what happens when we're in that mode?"

"Sex," he was quick to say.

She nodded, smiled. "Got it in one. First, though, there'd be clothing removal. Not pretty, either. This wouldn't be a slow striptease to finish awakening every nerve in our bodies, because all those little suckers would already be awake and revved."

Hell. Now he wanted her to do a striptease for him. But she was right. That first time would be a frantic race to find first the pleasure, then the release.

"So clothes come off, all willy-nilly. It goes with the dallying," she added when he raised an eyebrow. "And since we're outdoors on the hood of that car, my bare butt would be on the hood, and you'd be standing between my legs."

She stopped, frowned. Eyed him from head to toe.

"Would that work?" she asked. "I mean, would the height be right?"

"We'd make it right," he assured her.

Charlotte smiled again. "Yes, we would. And since this is a fantasy, everything is perfect. No bugs. No lightning. Just a gentle, warm rain sliding down our bodies while you put on a condom. We couldn't forget that. And you'd push into me."

He felt it. Damn it, he felt it. And he wanted it more than air, more than common sense. More than a condom, which wasn't exactly a safe thought to have.

"Lots of thrusting would happen next," Charlotte spelled out. "I'm in favor of the hard and deep ones that are just on the edge of being out of control. How about it? Would that work for you?"

Since he wasn't sure he could speak, Cal just nodded. He was reasonably sure that any form of thrust would work with Charlotte.

"Good. So, hard, deep and frantic. Lots of need. Oh, so much need. And pleasure. Let's not forget that. It's all about the pleasure, pushing us. Driving us to find just the right spots to make the world explode." She paused, leveling her gaze on him. "You'd find the right spot," she said with absolute confidence.

"I would." Cal's confidence matched hers.

She smiled again, and every bit of it was naughty,

bordering on raunchy. "I'd find your spot, too, which wouldn't exactly be difficult because yours is a lot bigger than mine. A lot bigger," she murmured, her gaze sliding over his erection again. "So, more thrusts. Maybe some whispered nonsense, because the only thing that would make sense right then would be finishing it. Finding that click." She snapped her fingers. "Getting to that moment when the now, now, now is the yes, yes, yes…yes!"

Charlotte stopped again. Smiled again. And locked gazes with him. "Was it good for you, Cal?"

He smiled. Really smiled. Because it was.

CHAPTER THIRTEEN

CHARLOTTE STILL HAD the nice floating feeling that came with a sexual buzz. A nice bonus, since Cal and she hadn't actually had sex the day before when they'd been in her room. It gave her lots of hope that the real deal would produce something even better than the aftermath that she was feeling now.

Of course, there were no guarantees that Cal would go through with the real deal, but even that wasn't putting a damper on her buzz. It was possible, however, that Cal would do a whole bunch of thinking and decide that sex was carrying things too far. He didn't want to hurt her, she was positive about that, and he might believe he couldn't offer her anything but a one-off.

And maybe he couldn't.

Ever.

All right, that dampened the buzz a little, but it needed to be taken down a notch since she didn't want to be floating when Alden arrived. Which—she checked the time—should be any minute now. Taggert had texted her that he'd picked up Alden and was driving there with him.

Charlotte hated to linger around, staring out the living room window, but she also didn't want to be in another part of the house when Alden got there. She wanted to be able to run out and greet him. And she was hoping that would be an awesome greeting, since his room was ready for him. Much of the downstairs was, too, and there were wonderful smells coming out of the kitchen, where Maybell was cooking a pot roast and some apple pies.

Watching out the window and soaking up the scents of the house, however, meant she wasn't working. There was still plenty of that to do, but it did give her the bonus advantage of observing Cal do some manual labor. He was repairing a portion of the fence. Hammer swinging, muscles reacting and the movement straining the fabric of his jeans over his butt.

It was indeed superior.

And she had an internal debate about where said butt would rank on a list of his best features. His face had to be at the top of that list. His smile, too. And his eyes. Yes, those dreamy eyes. But the butt was definitely in the top five.

She stopped daydreaming at a whirring sound and turned to see Harper making her way toward her. Charlotte made sure she gave her a bright smile and had no expectation of Harper giving her one in return, which she didn't.

"Did you sleep well last night?" Charlotte asked.

Harper shrugged, which could have meant anything, and she stopped her chair next to Charlotte in front of the large bay window. When she spotted Cal, she made a grunting sound and then typed something on her keyboard.

"Admiring the scenery?" the computer voice asked.

Charlotte couldn't tell if it was snark or attempted

humor, but she went with it. "Actually, I was admiring his butt. It's impressive."

Harper's mouth tightened, and she typed out a response. "I've seen better."

"I wish I could say I'd actually seen his so I could dispute that," Charlotte muttered. She winced. "Sorry. TMI."

Harper stared at her before doing some more typing. "So, it's really over between you and Noah?"

"It is," Charlotte verified.

Maybe soon she'd be able to convince Noah, and Cal, of that. Her mother, too. Then again, Izzie wasn't responding to her texts and calls, so there weren't many opportunities for convincing. Charlotte had made multiple mental notes to pay her mother a visit, but so far she hadn't carried through on them since she'd been so busy.

"And you're heating up things with Cal?" Harper typed.

"Attempting to do that," Charlotte muttered, and she hoped all this chatter about Cal wasn't irking Harper. Or rather irking her more, since Harper seemed to be in a constant state of agitation.

Charlotte decided to change the subject. It probably wouldn't do squat to soothe Harper, but it was something important that she needed to pass along to the woman.

"Your dad was here yesterday, and he said he'll be back today at one," Charlotte said, and she carefully watched Harper's face for a reaction.

Harper kept her attention pinned to Cal while she typed. "Okay." That was it. All the verbal response she intended.

But Charlotte pushed a little. "Harper, if you don't want to see your father, I can talk to him and explain you need some time to get settled in." That might work. Might. But it was just as likely that Paul would demand to see his daughter.

Harper's forehead bunched up enough to let Charlotte know she was considering that, but then she shook her head and typed. "He's my dad. He gets to see me."

Charlotte sighed. "Harper," she said, and would have launched into a plea for Harper not to let Paul belittle or browbeat her, but the sound of the approaching van stopped it. It was another NEMT, a nonemergency medical transportation like the one that had brought Harper the day before. Today, it was Taggert who stepped out, and when the side door of the van opened, Charlotte saw Alden. Two EMTs stepped out as well, but they stayed back, maybe waiting for a signal if Alden would need their help.

"Alden looks worse than I do," Harper's keyboard voiced for her.

Charlotte couldn't disagree more. Yes, Alden had scars on nearly every visible part of his body, but he wasn't in a wheelchair. Instead, he was using a cane, and his mood was a lot better than Harper's. He was smiling, and that light in his eyes told her that he was indeed very glad to be here.

Charlotte welcomed the smile, returned it and hurried out to greet him. Since his balance looked a little precarious, she was careful when she pulled him into a hug.

"It's so good to see you," she gushed, and she meant it.

Taggert was plenty happy, too, and he gave his son a kiss on the cheek before he went to the back of the van to haul out a suitcase. He'd already brought over some of Alden's things, but this was obviously more.

"I'll take these to your room," Taggert offered, going ahead of them while Charlotte and Alden made their way up the ramp together.

"You did it," Alden said, glancing around. "You got your dream."

"I did. With a lot of help from a lot of people." She paused to gather her breath. "How are you? Was the trip here okay?"

"Good, and yes," he said. "How are you?" he echoed. "And are you with Cal now, like Noah said?"

"Good, and potentially," she answered, causing Alden to chuckle.

She was thankful for the laugh. It meant he wasn't all torn up about her and Noah parting ways. She wanted Alden to be able to focus on healing his body and mind and didn't want her relationship with Noah playing into this.

When she stepped into the foyer ahead of Alden, Charlotte glanced around, but there was no sign of Harper. Apparently she'd wanted to skip the meet-and-greet, which was probably a good thing. Though, Charlotte was hoping Harper would eventually have more interaction with the staff and fellow residents. She was also hoping that Harper would have less interaction with Paul.

"Something smells good," Alden remarked the moment he was inside.

"You're in for some culinary treats. Maybell is doing the cooking this week, and next week, her niece, Frannie, will start working here full-time. It seems Maybell has passed along all of her best recipes to Frannie."

"Frannie," he murmured, "I remember her."

And there was something in his voice that made Charlotte think he remembered her fondly. She hadn't heard any gossip about them over the years, but it was possible he and Frannie had once been an item since they were about the same age.

"Here's the quick rundown on the layout of the place," Charlotte explained. "The living room," she said, pointing to it as they went past it. "The library." She pointed to the left. "Dining room. The kitchen's there," she added, pointing to the archway in the dining room. "And your suite is down here."

She led him to the hall, tipping her head to the closed door. "Harper's staying there."

"Harper," he repeated, and there wasn't any wistfulness in his tone now. Only concern. "How's she doing?"

"Maybe you can ask her yourself since I'm sure you'll be seeing her," Charlotte settled on saying. She had no intention of talking to residents about other residents, even when one of them—Alden—was one of her favorite people. He was the little brother she'd always wanted but never had.

It occurred to her then that Alden's feelings toward her might change now that he would never be her brother-in-law. Then she looked at him and saw him smiling at her, and she knew her worries were all for nothing. Their fondness for each other wasn't tied to Noah.

She held her breath a little when they finally made it

to his suite, and she stepped back so Alden could walk into the room where his dad was already putting his things away.

"Wow," Alden said, glancing around. "It's perfect."

Her breath let out, and relieved that he liked it, she continued the tour. "I tried to match it to what you had in the facility you just left. And the bathroom was already modified. But if there's anything that needs adjusting—"

"It's perfect," he repeated, taking hold of her hand to give it a gentle squeeze. "Thank you, Charlotte."

Taggert was muttering his thanks as well when they all glanced toward the sound of approaching footsteps. A moment later, Cal appeared in the doorway. He smiled at her, an oh-so-dreamy smile that had her melting more than a little, before he went to Alden. He leaned in and hugged him.

The two exchanged warm greetings, and the embrace lingered on for a couple of seconds. "So you stole Noah's girl," Alden joked when they eased back and faced each other. Then he laughed. "Sorry, I couldn't resist. All this scar tissue has given me no filter when it comes to what I say. I'm picking up on vibes that Charlotte and you are worried about how I'll react to you two seeing each other. Well, I'm reacting just fine," he assured them.

"And so am I," Taggert piped up. "I just want Noah and you to be happy, and if that happiness doesn't happen together, then I still want you to find it elsewhere."

"Thank you," she said quietly. It was a huge deal for Taggert to say that, especially since she and Noah had been together for so long that everyone had just assumed it would be forever. *Forever* had been crossed out now, and both her and Noah's futures were up in the air.

Alden's phone rang, and he smiled again when he saw the screen. "It's a friend checking to make sure I got here all right."

Charlotte motioned for him to take the call, and she went back into the hall to give him some privacy. Cal followed her, but Taggert stayed behind, probably so he could continue getting Alden's things packed away.

"I was watching you from the window earlier when you were fixing the fence," she told him in a whisper. They walked back to the foyer. "Admiring your assets."

"You can admire them without the glass," he was quick to say.

That got her pulse hopping. The rest of her, too. "Sneak up to my room tonight. Or I'll sneak up to yours."

She saw the split second of surprise flash in his eyes. Then the smile came. So did other footsteps, and one of the painters came in through the front door. He nearly smacked them with a ladder before he noticed them.

"Sorry," he said, heading up the stairs just as one of the other painters called down for him to hurry.

"This is definitely not a private spot," she said, "so you'll have to imagine me kissing you right now."

"I'd rather have the real thing. The fantasy is good, but nothing beats an actual kiss." And then he stole her breath by touching his fingers to her mouth. "The next time I kiss you, I'll have a condom. I'll even keep one in my wallet."

No footsteps this time but a gasp. Cal and she whirled toward the door to find Izzie standing there. It was obvious from her expression, and the gasp, that she'd heard what Cal had said.

"I'll pretend I didn't hear or see that," Izzie remarked.

Her mother's tone was a lot milder than she'd expected, and Charlotte soon realized why. Izzie was glancing around the foyer because she'd likely heard that Alden and Taggert were here. No way would she want to come off with her surliness and demands as she had last time, when Taggert had ended up breaking off things with her.

Izzie's gaze, though, was a lot sharper than her tone, and she glanced at Cal the way someone looked at poop on their shoes. "Could you excuse me and Charlotte for a few moments?"

Cal didn't budge, not until he'd held gazes with Charlotte for a couple of seconds, and she nodded. Despite his earlier insistence that he wouldn't kiss her again until he had a condom, he kissed her anyway. Nothing hot and heavy, but it still packed a punch and caused Charlotte to smile and make a dreamy, sighing noise. Her mother probably thought that was for show, but it wasn't. This heat between her and Cal was the real deal.

Izzie didn't say anything until he had left, and then she stepped into the foyer, glancing down the hall. "Taggert's in Alden's room," Charlotte provided.

Her mother's shoulders pulled back a little. "I didn't ask."

"You didn't have to. I know you want to see him."

That shaved off some of her mother's defensiveness. "I do, but I was hoping he'd come to me so we can talk things out. He hasn't."

"I'm sorry," Charlotte said.

"You should be." Izzie's tone had changed in the blink of an eye. "If you got back with Noah—"

"No," Charlotte interrupted. "I've been into playing out fantasies lately, so let's you and I play a *what-if* scenario. What if I got back together with a man I don't love, a man I don't want, so that you can have your dream fairy-tale wedding? A wedding that probably wouldn't happen, since you aren't even together with Noah's dad."

Her mother continued her snappish tone. "Taggert and I could get back—"

"Play out the fantasy, Mom," Charlotte interrupted again. "You'd want to get back together with a man because it could create that fairy-tale wedding you're dreaming about. That's not a relationship. That's an arrangement."

"Well, maybe I want an arrangement," Izzie grumbled. She stopped, huffed and shook her head. "I want something more than what I have." Her voice was a lot softer now, and the anger was gone. Not the hurt, though. It was there big-time.

Charlotte wasn't immune to the tears that filled her mother's eyes. But she also wasn't a doormat. Not any longer. And those tears wouldn't send her running back to Noah.

"If you want more with Taggert, then work on that," Charlotte spelled out. "Or maybe someone else. Maybe you just work on making yourself a better person."

"You're lecturing me?" she snapped.

"Yes." And her quick, honest answer was enough to shock her mother into not giving one of her automatic, irked responses.

Charlotte didn't figure the reaction would last long,

but then there was some movement from the corner of her eyes, and she saw Taggert making his way toward them. Not quickly. It seemed to Charlotte he'd slowed considerably once he saw her mother.

"Izzie," he said.

"Taggert," she said back.

And that appeared to be the extent of what they intended to say to each other. Taggert finally shifted his attention to Charlotte.

"Alden wanted to go help Maybell in the kitchen," Taggert explained. "I think he was hoping to get samples of whatever she's cooking." He tipped his head toward the van that was still parked out front. "I wanted to tell the crew that it was okay to leave, that Alden's already settling in just fine."

"I'm glad to hear that. By the way, you're welcome to stay for lunch," Charlotte offered as Taggert started out.

The man hesitated, and it was obvious, too: Izzie clearly had no trouble picking up on it or the reason for it. "I won't be staying for lunch," Izzie said. "So you go ahead and enjoy the meal with your son."

Taggert muttered a *thanks* and walked out.

Izzie watched him for a few moments before she turned back to Charlotte. "I did have a reason to come here other than Taggert. I wanted to see if you were far enough along on the place to send out a photographer to get some pictures for the town's new website. It'll be good PR."

It would be, and the reno was indeed coming along, but the timing was bad. "Give Alden and Harper more time to get settled in. At least a week, maybe longer."

Maybe a lot longer, if Harper continued with her current attitude.

Charlotte walked out with her mom and saw Cal waiting in the yard. He was probably worried that her mother would try some strong-arm tactics on her again, so she smiled to let him know all was well. Or well-*ish*, anyway.

"You okay?" Cal asked, approaching Charlotte.

She nodded. Then she noticed there was something in Cal's eyes that had her worrying. "What's wrong?"

"Noah just texted to let me know he'd be visiting his brother in a little while." Cal went closer and held up his phone for her to see. "He said you'd blocked him so he couldn't tell you himself."

"I did block him, and that's part of the reason."

She motioned toward the stains on the end of the porch where the flowers had been before they'd finally gotten hauled to the new compost heap. The petals had caused some greasy-looking spots on the wood when people had stepped on them.

Cal didn't get a chance to voice his opinion about Noah's visit or the blocking because while he was still holding up his phone, it rang, and she saw Audrey's name on the screen.

"Oh," he muttered, and she saw the quick debate he had with himself about whether to answer or let it go to voicemail. He finally answered, and he was close enough to Charlotte that she had no trouble hearing the woman.

"Awesome news, Cal," Audrey said, the enthusiasm

practically bursting in her voice. "The best news ever. I finagled a dream job for you that'll keep you in uniform. No way you can turn this one down. *No possible way.*"

CHAPTER FOURTEEN

CAL HEARD EVERYTHING Audrey had just said. *Everything.* But since he'd had his attention on Charlotte through every word, he saw her reaction, too. Shock and maybe some sadness. She covered it up fast, however, and managed to plaster on a smile before she mouthed a goodbye and headed back into the house.

"Cal?" Audrey said. "Are you there?"

"I'm here," he acknowledged, but he kept his gaze on Charlotte until she was out of sight.

"Well, aren't you going to ask about this dream job?" Audrey prompted.

"Sure." He was well aware he sounded distracted. Because he was. But it was obvious Audrey had something to say, so it was best to hear it and then he could check on Charlotte. "What kind of job?"

"It's a joint forces special project where you'd provide air support services to rescue and evacuation teams." Definitely no shock or sadness in Audrey's tone, and it occurred to Cal that she rarely expressed this level of emotion. She seemed downright giddy. "You'd be making a real difference, Cal. Saving lives and helping people in hot zones all over the world."

That got his attention because he had indeed been

looking for something exactly like that. Or rather he had been before the crisis with Harper.

"If you think it sounds like a tailor-made job just for you, it's because it is," Audrey went on. "I brainstormed with a lot of brass on this, and we discussed how to best use your experience and skill set. And this was the outcome. A lot of people had to get on board with this, and yes, some strings were pulled. Favors were called in. But I just got the approval for it."

Cal took a moment. Had to. Because he had no idea what the heck he was feeling right now. Pulled strings and favors meant Audrey had put her neck, maybe even her career, on the line for this. He didn't need to process anything to know he didn't care for that, that he hadn't wanted her to take this kind of risk as it put pressure on both of them.

"Well?" she prompted again. "Are you going to snap this up?"

Hell. Cal mentally groaned. No way was Audrey going to care for what he had to say. "I'll give it some thought."

Silence. For a long time. "Thought?" she repeated. "What's there to think about? This is it, Cal, your dream job. You can save lives while your career continues to soar. You can have it all."

A month ago, it would have indeed been *all*, and he would have snapped it up. He just couldn't do that now because it would mean staying in uniform and going back in the cockpit.

Audrey's sigh came through loud and clear. "I know a stepmother shouldn't have favorites. But you're mine, Cal. You never gave me any trouble when you were growing up, and even though we don't have any DNA in common, I could see myself in you. You're the most like me."

He'd known part of that. Had always been able to sense that he was her favorite. And Audrey had certainly given him a lot of support in his career. He owed her so much. But part of what she just said was no longer true.

"I don't think I am like you," he admitted. "Not anymore. Audrey, I'm just not sure I can give this job the kind of focus and dedication it needs."

"Of course you can," she insisted. "Just dig down deep and do it. This is something that will still matter years from now. You can save people," Audrey emphasized. "You won't get many other opportunities to do that."

Cal glanced up at the house and found it ironic that saving lives and making a difference was exactly what Charlotte was doing. She'd created her own dream job.

"Don't you dare say *no*," Audrey added a moment later.

The sudden snap in Audrey's voice played havoc with his emotions, too. The lieutenant colonel nearly kicked in to respond to a superior officer. Heck, even the good stepson almost came out in a bid to please the woman who'd essentially raised him. Thankfully, though, Cal didn't give in to either of those. Or to the knee-jerk reaction to snap right back at her. A decision like this shouldn't be the result of any of those things. Or a collection of them.

"Like I said, I'll give it some thought," he assured her.

"Sleep on it, give it thought, et cetera." She stopped and huffed. "Because this is a once-in-a-lifetime opportunity, so don't just toss it away on a whim. Hell, don't toss it away at all."

Again Cal didn't give in to the plea, and he totally understood her anger. "Audrey, thank you for always going to bat for me," he said.

He waited for her to add something else or to restate her case. She didn't. She just ended the call.

Cal stared at his phone a moment before he slipped it back in his pocket. Of course, *giving it some thought* started right away. Or rather it would have, had Cal not tried to shut it down. He wasn't in the right frame of mind to evaluate anything right now. He wanted to see Charlotte and try to assure her... He stopped. He couldn't assure her of anything without all the thinking he needed to do, but he wanted to see her. In fact, he *needed* to see her.

He hurried inside, disappointed when he didn't find Charlotte in the foyer, and Cal was ready to head upstairs to her room when he heard her voice coming from the kitchen. He was still hurrying, practically running when he bolted into the room. All eyes turned toward him.

Maybell's, Alden's, Charlotte's and Becker's.

Cal wasn't sure when Becker had come in, but he was chowing down on some bread that probably hadn't been out of the oven that long. Steam was still rising from the chunk that had been slathered with butter.

"Just in time," Maybell said by way of greeting. "Bread's done, and I'm taking out the pot roast now." Her words trailed off when she glanced back at him, and even though she didn't come out and voice any concern, both Becker and Alden looked at him as if trying to figure out what was wrong.

Charlotte was looking at him, too, and she was still managing to tamp down her initial reaction. But she was studying him, no doubt waiting to hear how the rest of the conversation with Audrey had gone.

Since this wasn't something he could keep to himself, Cal just went with spilling it. "Audrey just called, and she wants me to take a joint command job."

No one jumped to congratulate him. Becker, probably because he didn't know enough about Cal's current situation. The others all seemed to understand the gravity of the offer.

"Audrey managed to get the job created," he went on. "It's air support for rescues and evacuations."

Charlotte was the one to break the silence. "It sounds very important." She cleared her throat, probably to ask if he was going to take it, but the sound of another voice cut her off.

"Well, that's just dandy," the computer relayed.

Cal turned to see Harper sitting in her wheelchair in the dining room that was adjacent to the kitchen. He hadn't needed to hear what she'd typed to know that she'd not only listened to what he'd said but that she also had a firm reaction to it.

Not a good one, either.

She was staring at Cal with what had to be contempt. And he couldn't blame her. Not really. It had to be hard for her to think of where she was now and then see him still on the so-called halo track. Seemingly on it, anyway.

"I didn't accept the job," he said, not to Harper but

to Charlotte. She was the one he wanted to hear it. And she was the one who needed to hear the rest. "But I did tell Audrey I'd think about it."

That brought on some more silence, even from Harper, who seemed riled, but Cal figured she would have that reaction no matter what he said. No anger from Charlotte, though. She went to him and pulled him into her arms for a hug.

"Congrats," Charlotte told him. "Audrey must have worked hard to put this together."

"She did. She obviously knows me well," he added quietly. Well enough that she knew not just any job offer could lure him back. But this one could. And he didn't want to keep that possibility from Charlotte. "I'll think about it," he said.

Charlotte nodded and smiled. This one wasn't so forced, and while there was still some disappointment in her eyes, Cal could tell that she would end up being happy for him if he accepted. After all, it wasn't often that someone got to tick off a major box on their bucket list.

"Well, your thinking about this job offer must have made Audrey mighty happy," Maybell said, breaking the third round of silence. "Egan will be pleased, too. Maybe your daddy and Blue as well. And all those people you'd help would be plenty thankful, no doubt about that." She pointed at him with a big fork that she'd just used to test the pot roast. "But here's the whopper question. Is this air support for rescues and evacuations what you actually want?"

It was indeed the big question. Cal didn't have a big answer. In fact, he didn't have an answer at all, which was why he shrugged. He really did need that thinking time, but not yet because someone else spoke.

"Audrey offered you a job?" Noah asked.

It seemed this was the day for people sneaking up on him, because Cal hadn't heard Noah come in, but there he was, standing right next to Harper. And Noah had a totally different expression than everyone else. There was hope in his eyes.

"I'm guessing since Audrey offered it, then it's a top-notch one," Noah added.

Cal nodded. "Joint command," he provided.

Noah smiled. "You'll make full-bird colonel before you know it."

Harper rolled her eyes and typed when she looked up at Noah. "You're only saying that because if Cal leaves, your competition is gone. Or is it?" The computer actually managed to make the question sound snarky.

Noah shrugged. "Cal's a superstar. I never once thought he'd give it all up." He shifted his attention to Charlotte now. "It'd be a disservice, literally, for him to walk away when he can still do so much good."

Cal wanted to believe Noah's remarks were genuine with no ulterior motive whatsoever. But that was—

"Bullshit," Cal heard, and for a moment he thought it'd flown out of his mouth. But it'd come from the computer.

Harper added an eye roll to what she'd typed. In fact, she typed a string of *bullshit*s before adding, "Look and see."

At first Noah just scowled at Harper, but the woman didn't give up: she pointed first at Charlotte, then at Cal.

Apparently, she thought there was something obvious that Noah hadn't already spotted.

Was there?

Becker had claimed to have seen a real relationship instead of the fake one they'd been trying to portray. Was Harper picking up on it, too? Maybe. Then again, he and Charlotte hadn't exactly been discreet with their long, lustful looks and kissing.

"I see a woman I've been involved with most of my life," Noah finally said, defiance coating each word. Coating his stare, too, that he now aimed at Cal. "Alden knows how much I care for Charlotte, don't you?"

Alden held up his hands in an "I'd rather stay out of this" gesture.

Harper didn't stay out of it because she began typing another string of *bullshit* that the computer in turn relayed.

Charlotte huffed, and she glanced around the room. "I'm sorry you're having to be part of such a private conversation when you're clearly just here for Maybell's good food. Well, since you've already heard more than you want to hear, then I'll burden you a little longer by filling in the rest." Her gaze shifted to Noah.

Just as Cal's phone rang.

Cal groaned and let it go to voicemail as it was probably Audrey calling back to remind him to think about the job. That could wait. For now, he wanted to hear what Charlotte had to say.

"Even if Cal goes," Charlotte stated, her stare still fixed on Noah, "you and I will not be getting back together." She spoke slowly, enunciating and pausing between each word.

"Told you," the computer said.

Maybell made a sound of agreement, and Becker kept eating bread and shooting annoyed glances at all but Maybell.

Charlotte seemed to tune them all out, and she turned to Cal. "I hope you heard that loud and clear. Even if you go, there'll be no kissing and making up with Noah. This thing going on between us? Well, it has nothing to do with him. This isn't a rebound deal."

Cal was glad to hear that. Well, maybe he was. If it wasn't a rebound, then it was the real thing, and that meant Charlotte could get hurt if he did leave.

"I don't expect you to stay," Charlotte added, clearly cluing in on what was going on in his head. "But I don't want you to think for one second that if you leave, I'll go running back to Noah. Because I won't." She looked at Noah and repeated that.

"Told you," Harper's computer repeated, causing Noah, Cal and Charlotte all to give Harper annoyed looks. The looks held.

And brought back a boatload of memories from their childhoods.

Harper had been the harbinger of snark, doom and gloom even back then. And Noah? Well, he'd always been so cocksure that he was and forever would be the top dog of the group. Charlotte had been the peacemaker. Cal, the do-gooder. Here they all were again.

Cal found himself smiling. Not exactly an appropriate response. But he thought he saw a smile tug at Harper's mouth, too. It was gone in a flash, and the doom and gloom returned.

No smiling for Noah. He looked as if he'd just been

slugged twice by every single person in the room. "It's really over," Noah mumbled, and his shoulders sank as low as they possibly could.

"It's really over," Charlotte verified.

Thankfully, Harper didn't interject another *Told you*. Like the rest of them, she just waited to hear what Noah had to say.

Noah nodded, attempted something that might pass as a smile in dim light. "All right. Then this is good-bye." He glanced at Harper, Charlotte and Cal, and Cal thought Noah, too, might be getting some flashes of the past. He shook his head as if trying to stave off the memories, and Noah looked at his brother. "Any chance we can go to your room and catch up before I head out?"

"Absolutely," Alden assured him.

He started walking, but he paused when he got level with Harper. He looked down at her, grinned, winked and tipped his head to her voice computer. "Gotta get me one of those. Obviously it's broadened your vocabulary."

Harper scowled, and it was an expression she was used to doling out when it came to Alden. Since Alden was six years younger than they were, he was often the pain-in-the-butt little brother. That was apparently going to continue. Cal had no idea if that was good or bad, but he hoped it didn't give Harper a reason to transfer out before she'd even given the place a chance.

Alden and Noah left, with Noah giving Charlotte one last glance over his shoulder, and once they were out of sight, Harper wheeled into the kitchen.

"Ready for lunch?" Maybell asked, and she started to dish up some pot roast before Harper even responded.

"I was hoping to take it to my room," Harper said using her keyboard. "Sonora's working on some paperwork, and I didn't want to wait for her."

"Oh, I can take it to your room for you," Maybell volunteered. "Or you can sit and eat in here."

"In my room," Harper insisted.

Since Cal figured he wasn't going to change Harper's mind about eating solo, he motioned for Charlotte to follow him so they could talk. Not only about what she'd just said to Noah but also Audrey's job offer. However, his phone issued a voicemail notification, and only then did he remember ignoring the call he'd gotten.

He took out his cell, expecting to see Audrey's name. But it wasn't a number he recognized. Since it could be someone from the base where he was stationed, he decided to listen.

"This is Rowan Cullen," a man said. "Guess I'll try to catch you later." That was it. The only message before Rowan ended the call.

CHAPTER FIFTEEN

HARPER CURSED WHEN her wheelchair bobbled over an uneven paver on the trail. Clearly, that needed some work, and if she didn't want to rattle her teeth, she should probably walk here next time.

Or just stay in her room.

But that hadn't felt like an option this morning. She hadn't thought she would get cabin fever after less than twenty-four hours, but she'd gotten that sick feeling of everything closing in, smothering her. Not enough to block out the memories, though.

Why the hell couldn't she have gotten amnesia? A fresh mental start. But no, she'd gotten broken bones, a fractured skull and a torn-up larynx. Which, of course, she had no one to blame for but herself.

There was a deep shame in that. So deep.

She cursed another rough spot on the trail but kept moving away from the house, away from the buzz of the workers. Heck, even away from the amazing smell of the cinnamon rolls that Maybell had made for breakfast. She wanted to find a place where there were no scents, no sounds, no people. Maybe then, she could clear her mind and decide what to do.

About everything.

God, her life and her body were a mess, and there

was no longer a career road map for her to follow. No goals. No ambition. Just the sickening horror over what she had done. Or had tried to do. Sometimes she regretted it. Other times she thought that regret was going to crush her until she was nothing.

Harper spotted the horses in the pasture ahead, and since the trail led to it and a cluster of thick oaks, she aimed for that. After more bobbling, she finally reached it.

And cursed again when she spotted Alden.

He was on a bench nestled under those trees, and he was chowing down on a cinnamon roll. Harper immediately frowned. He instantly smiled, and it caused the grafted skin on his face to shift and stretch at odd angles. It sort of looked as if he was wearing a thin mask that had been molded to his face. Not unpleasant or scary, just different.

"I think those two horses over there are either planning an escape or else they're gossiping about the stallion in the corral." He tipped his head first to a pair of roan mares and then to an Appaloosa stallion in an enclosure just off the barn. "You think mares do that, gossip about hot guys?"

She felt her frown deepen. "I wouldn't know," she typed out so the computer could relay it. And she started maneuvering the wheelchair so she could get the heck out of there—fast.

"Join me, Harper," Alden invited. He offered her the last bit of the roll.

Harper shook her head and continued to head off. The path was wide, but obviously not wide enough for her poor wheelchair skills, because she couldn't quite get the angles right. Probably because she was trying to hurry, and her hands were even more unsteady than usual.

"Want some help?" Alden asked.

"No," she was quick to type out. She hated help, and once again, she wished for the amnesia so she wouldn't have known that about herself.

She wouldn't have known a lot of things.

Since her fingers were starting to cramp on her right hand, Harper had no choice but to just stop as she could no longer manipulate the controls. However, her left hand seemed to delight in reminding her that it was functioning more than well enough to carry on a typed conversation. If that was what she wanted to do. She didn't. She didn't want company, small talk or Alden.

"Remember that time when I peed on you?" he asked. "Total accident, I swear. I was about four, which would have made you about ten, and you just happened to be walking past the open door of the bathroom. I turned and hosed you. A good stream reach for a little kid."

"I remember," she typed, and the flat computer voice matched her own tone. Harper figured her expression did, too. "You can't cure me with what you think are amusing blasts from the past."

Alden shrugged. "*Cure* is a word with a lot of expectations. Way too lofty a goal, if you ask me. I like *cope*. *Grapple* is a good one, too. Maybe *dillydally* works for some days. Or *lollygag*?"

Harper kept her flat look in place. "I don't want a counselor," she typed.

"Good," Alden was quick to say. "Because I'm clearly lollygagging today. Soaking it all in. Just chilling. I figure I'll do that for at least another week or so before I start up any PT or attempted head-shrinking."

She didn't want to smile, but it took a little effort to stop herself.

He smiled and looked at her. "So why did you come here? Not to the pasture, I mean, but to Port in a Storm?"

"I ask myself that same question at least every hour," Harper typed, but this time she didn't care for the computer flatness. It wasn't a snarky comeback.

It was genuine.

"Well, maybe the answer will come to you," Alden concluded. "So what's your status?" He glanced at the wheelchair. "Do you need that thing, or can you walk?"

She debated answering. Actually, she was debating a lot of things, including why she didn't just leave. But she stayed put and answered, "No. But I can't walk and talk at the same time." She motioned toward the voice tablet and then his cane. "If I'm using one of those, I can't type."

He nodded and examined both the wheelchair and the tablet. "Can you speak, too, without the computer?"

She opened her mouth and let the sound come. Nowhere near in the realm of speech or even a single word. It was basically air rasping out when she attempted to tell him *no*. She was pretty sure she could do better. A whole lot better.

But Harper didn't want better.

Alden grinned. "Well, I like that gravelly tone. And coupled with your expression, you got your point across."

Harper didn't grin; she scowled. "What was your call sign? *Sunbeam*? *Smiley*? *Overly Enthusiastic about Squat*?"

That didn't put him off. The grin continued. "KA-CEOTO," he said.

Rather than type anything, she raised an eyebrow.

"*Keep a Close Eye on That One*," Alden provided. "I don't think it was a compliment."

She laughed before she could stop herself. She instantly regretted it. Best not to break down any barriers between her and everyone else. But the laughter didn't last, anyway, because she heard someone call out.

"Harper, there the hell you are." It was her father, and she glanced over her shoulder to see him storming toward her. Then again, storming was his default when it came to most things.

"Dad," she typed in.

"*Dad,*" Paul said, his tone mocking. "You shouldn't be using that damn thing. You should be trying to talk on your own. You're not gonna get better if you don't push through the pain."

That had become practically a motto for him. Push through the pain. Push, push, push. Even now, with her a total physical and emotional wreck, her father thought she could come back from this. Harper wasn't sure if he was being way overly optimistic or delusional.

Alden got to his feet. Not easily, and to accomplish it, he had to put a whole lot of weight on his cane. "Harper and I were doing speech therapy," Alden said, his tone as light as the breeze. "We're in the raspy-breathing stage and making progress."

Clearly, her dad didn't know how to react to that. Not at first, anyway. His expression went from a bunched-up forehead to a glare in a handful of seconds.

"I didn't hear my daughter trying to get out one

sound other than with that dang computer." He stared down at her. "Let's take a walk and do some talking. Of course, that's a figure of speech since I'll be the one walking, and you'll poke along in that blasted wheelchair that we both know you don't need. If you're not up to that, then how about you just listen once Alden heads back to wherever he needs to be right now?"

"Well, actually, with raspy breathing checked off the list," Alden countered, "Harper and I were about to head to the barn to test out some of the exercise equipment."

He was giving her an out. Letting her know that she didn't have to go through this visit with her dad. But this visit was what she deserved. A penance of sorts. And that's why despite the cramp in her hand, she got the wheelchair turned around so she could go with her father. So he could lead her wherever the hell he wanted to go and say whatever the hell he wanted to say.

Yeah, full-blown amnesia would have been a nice bonus.

CAL STOOD AT the kitchen window at Saddlebrook and drank his third cup of coffee of the morning while he had a fierce debate with himself. And while he kept glancing down at his phone, willing it to ring. Something he'd been doing for a good chunk of the past twenty-four hours.

Seconds after he'd listened to Rowan's voicemail, he'd tried to phone him back. There'd been no answer.

So Cal had left a message about how sorry he was that he'd missed his call. He'd added some stuff that he wished he'd rehearsed because it had probably come out as ramblings. But the gist was he was glad Rowan had contacted him and he hoped they got a chance to talk soon. Hopefully, it hadn't come out as too overly enthusiastic. Cal didn't want anything he said to have put Rowan off.

"Watched pots don't boil, and watched phones don't ring," his grandmother muttered while she cooked breakfast. A chore she didn't have to do since Cal, his dad and brothers could make something for themselves. Still, she'd insisted on doing it while Maybell was pulling kitchen duty at Port in a Storm.

"Hard not to watch the phone," he replied.

She made a sound of agreement and assembled some plates and cutlery as sort of a buffet around the stove where she'd cooked sausage, scrambled eggs and some crispy skillet potatoes, and she assembled a plate of toast. Since his dad was eating healthier these days because of his heart, the sausage was turkey, the toast whole wheat, and there was a plate of cut-up fruit.

"The boy will call when he can, I'm sure," Effie said. "He's probably just as curious about us as we are about him."

Maybe, but he was betting his grandmother's feelings weren't as laid-back as she was making them out to be. After all, Rowan was her grandson, and she had to want to meet him.

Cal had had no choice but to tell Effie, Audrey and the rest of his family about the call, but it would have been easier on them if they hadn't known. Now they were all on pins and needles waiting and hoping that Rowan would call back.

Since he wasn't especially hungry, Cal set his coffee aside and put a sausage link in a folded piece of toast. He ate his makeshift sandwich while he continued to stare out the window. And glance at his phone. It was possible that Rowan had had a very narrow time frame in which he could make a call, and that such a window might not come up again for days. Or longer. After all, it'd been months since Rowan's initial contact with Blue, and it might take that long for him to get back to Cal.

But Rowan would get back to him.

Cal had to believe that, and he was certain his dad was hanging on to that hope as well.

"You're going over to Charlotte's again today, right?" Effie asked, dishing herself up a plate and taking it to the table.

On the surface, it seemed like an innocent question, but he figured that along with thinking about Rowan, Effie was doing plenty of thinking about Cal's situation. Specifically, his situation with Charlotte.

Whatever that was.

The fierce attraction was definitely drawing them closer and fanning flames that neither of them seemed to be trying to put out. Or at least Charlotte hadn't tried to do that before she'd heard about Audrey's job offer. Now Charlotte might attempt to put some distance between them. Not only to give him time and space to consider the job but also as a way of guarding her heart.

Cal hoped she did plenty of guarding.

He didn't want her hurt, especially since he had no idea what his future plans were. Twenty-four hours ago, he would have said with one hundred percent certainty that he was getting out of the military. Now he wasn't so sure. Audrey had managed to offer up the only thing that could have tempted him to stay in uniform. But being tempted wasn't an acceptance.

Audrey hadn't given him a deadline for the offer, but Cal knew it couldn't be unlimited time. His leave was running out fast, only eight days left, and he'd have to let her know before that. So a little over a week to make one of the biggest decisions of his life, all the while his feelings for Charlotte grew stronger and stronger...and while he waited for his half brother to call.

Cal definitely felt the pressure.

The pressure went up some when his dad came into the kitchen. He wasn't alone—Egan and Blue were right behind him—and all three immediately pinned their attention on Cal.

"Nothing yet from Rowan," Cal said, knowing it was going to put some serious disappointment in his father's eyes.

It did.

Hell. Cal didn't want to go overboard with this, but part of him wished he could tap into Audrey's connections or the info in the background report his father had had run on Rowan. Certainly, either the connections or the report would help him locate Rowan so he'd have another way to contact him other than just waiting for his call. But that would be overkill. This wasn't an emergency. No life-and-death situation. It was just an eager, impatient family wanting to hear from someone who might not be nearly as eager for the communication.

Of course Cal had played the voicemail for everyone here in the kitchen, and Marin and Alana had heard it as well. Not that there'd been much to hear.

This is Rowan Cullen. Guess I'll try to catch you later.

Rowan's tone had sounded neutral. But Cal figured Rowan had been feeling plenty when he'd left that message. Hard not to feel when the call was basically connecting him to a family he didn't know.

Cal had replayed the recording many, many times, and like everyone else, he had latched on to that one troubling word, *guess*. Without it, a follow-up call was more or less a promise. But the *guess* meant that Rowan might decide that that voicemail was it, that there'd be no more contact. No way was Cal going to say that aloud, however.

"I'll be at Charlotte's most of the day," Cal said, "but if Rowan calls, I'll let all of you know right away."

Unlike Cal, Egan and Blue were clearly hungry since they both were piling their plates with the breakfast. His dad settled for a half cup of coffee.

"And you'll let us know about the job offer," his dad said.

Of course Cal had told them all about that as well, and as expected, he'd gotten a mixed bag of reactions. Egan had been pleased that Cal had something that might lure him into not throwing away the stellar career Egan thought he had.

His dad was in the same camp as Egan. More or less, anyway. Cal liked to think that his dad was getting so used to him being around that he wouldn't see it as Cal throwing something away but rather moving on to something new.

Blue had been neutral, maybe because he hadn't had

much of a choice about having to give up his own military career. A knee injury had seen to that.

Effie and Maybell had fallen into the "do what's best for you" camp. Of course they had. They'd always given Cal blanket approval for whatever he'd done. Well, mostly. There were a couple of incidents as a kid when he'd earned their ire. But on this, they had left the decision-making ball firmly in Cal's court.

Cal assured them all that he would indeed fill them in on the job. Whenever that would be, he just didn't know.

Pushing that aside for now, he drove to Charlotte's and immediately saw the number of workers' trucks had thinned some. Progress. And despite the pushing aside he'd just done, he wondered how close the reno was to being finished. Would it happen before his last eight days of leave were up?

He inhaled, did more tamping down of feelings and parked. Cal had just stepped from his truck when he saw Mandy coming down the steps. She was carrying something that nearly had Cal taking a step back. He rattled off the f-word before he could stop himself.

Crap. It was one of those creepy dolls. This one had black tufts of hair spiking out of its head in what could have been mock fright or a tribute to the Statue of Liberty. There were also teeth. Big, gummy ones that were positioned in a smile. Perhaps a tribute to the Cheshire cat.

Or a cannibal.

The thick glasses perched on the nose magnified the blank doll eyes to the size of silver dollars. Overall, definitely not the image of a child's plaything.

"I found this under a creaky floorboard in one of

the second-floor bedrooms," Mandy announced. "I'm not sure if Becker's cousin was a closet psychopath or a creative genius."

"I'm leaning toward psychopath," Cal muttered.

"Same, but Izzie is leaning toward the creative genius."

"Izzie?" he said, confused.

Mandy nodded. "I took a picture of the first one. After I quit shrieking, that is, and I texted it to some people who ended up texting it to Izzie. She wants any and all dolls for a future local folk-art display at town hall or the library. She thinks it'll go viral and give the town lots of publicity."

It probably would, which meant Izzie would no doubt end up being interviewed by various press, which in turn would be publicity for her. Maybe that meant she had moved on from her breakup with Taggert and was focusing on her usual target.

"FYI, Paul came to see Harper this morning," Mandy said, glancing over her shoulder at the house.

Cal's gaze immediately followed hers, and he expected to see Paul there. "Is he still here? And did he cause any trouble?"

"Not still here. Trouble, yes. He'd managed to talk Harper into doing a workout in the gym, and he was badgering her to get out of her chair and onto the treadmill. Apparently, he thinks if Harper works hard enough, she can get back in the Air Force. She can't, can she?"

Cal had to give that some thought. It was possible Harper could recover enough from her injuries. Possible but not likely. And if she did, she almost certainly wouldn't be returning to the cockpit. She wouldn't just be able to step back into the old life she'd had, but then, he hadn't seen any signs that she wanted to do that.

He settled for a shrug in response. "What happened? Did someone stop Paul from pushing her?"

"Charlotte," she said on a sigh. "Alden, too. They kept it all civil by saying it was time for Harper's therapy session. Harper didn't admit she doesn't have any therapy sessions because she's refusing them, and Paul eventually left."

Good. But Cal knew that wasn't the end of it. Paul would keep coming back, keep pushing, and that meant he should have a talk with the man. That definitely wouldn't be any fun, but maybe he could make Paul understand that Harper needed some time and space to try to heal and work out what to do with her life.

"Where's Harper and Charlotte now?" he asked.

"In their rooms. Charlotte's doing paperwork and try-ing to pretend she's not upset that you might be leaving... Are you leaving?" Mandy tacked on.

Cal dragged in a long breath and admitted the truth. "I have no idea."

Mandy matched his inhalation with one of her own. "Well then, best to let Charlotte know."

She patted his arm and headed toward her car. But then turned back. "Oh, we also got a new visitor about a half hour ago. Resident," she qualified when he must have looked confused. "Jodi Seaver. Former Marine. And another is coming next week. Clearly, word is get-ting out about us."

"Clearly," he agreed. But then, he hadn't thought it

wouldn't. There were plenty of veterans out there who could use a place like this.

He watched as Mandy practically chucked the doll into the trunk of her car, and then he went inside to find Charlotte. Because Mandy was right: it was best to let Charlotte know there was a slim chance he might accept the job. *Slim* was still just that, but it was a big change from yesterday when there'd been zero possibility.

He passed a few workers on the trek up the flights of stairs, and he paused on the second floor when he saw the dark-haired woman standing at the window at the end of the hall. She glanced at him long enough for him to realize he didn't know her, but this was almost certainly Jodi Seaver. When she turned back to the window without uttering a word, he figured she wasn't in the mood for introductions.

He reached the attic level and found Charlotte's door open. She did indeed appear to be working on her laptop. Not at the desk in the corner but while seated in a chair that she'd moved next to the window. At the sound of his footsteps, she looked at him and smiled. It didn't look the least bit tentative or wary to suggest that she'd been worrying about the job question.

"I wasn't sure you'd come today," she said, getting to her feet and setting her laptop aside. "I'm glad you did."

So was he. He was especially glad when Charlotte went to him and kissed him. There was nothing tentative about it, either. It was a Charlotte kiss. One that packed plenty of heat and pleasure. One that drained so much of the tension he'd been carrying for the past twenty-four hours.

She was smiling when she eased back from the kiss, and her eyes met his. Studying him.

"You can ask me about the job and Rowan," he offered.

"Do you want me to ask you about them?" she countered.

He sighed. "No, but I owe you an answer, at least about the job."

Charlotte made a sound that was a mix of a tut-tut and a huff, and she closed the door. "Cal, you don't owe me anything. Well, except maybe a fun time in bed since we've been skirting around that for a couple of weeks now." She pulled something from her pocket.

A condom.

"What's your stance on morning sex?" Charlotte asked. "Yea or nay? Because my vote is for yea."

CHAPTER SIXTEEN

CHARLOTTE KNEW THIS was a risk. Even though she and Cal had indeed been lusting after each other for weeks, that didn't mean he was willing to risk complicating things by having sex with her.

And this stood a solid chance of doling out some complications.

Added to that, he might indeed not be a morning-sex person. Or a sex-with-her person.

"Yea," he said in the same moment he hooked his arm around her and hauled her to him.

She would have laughed with delight if he hadn't kissed her and therefore stopped her from voicing anything. That was all right. She liked having the kiss do the talking for them. And what a kiss. She hadn't thought that particular area could get any better between them, but she'd been wrong.

This was better.

It was even hotter, longer and deeper than usual. It was a slam of foreplay right from the start to let her know that this was going to be a quick escalation of all that skirted-around lust.

Without breaking the kiss or the hold he had on her, Cal somehow managed to reach behind him and lock the door. Good thing, too, because morning sex came with the potential of morning visitors, and they didn't need an audience for this. They just needed each other.

Really, really needed.

Cal raised that need tenfold when he dropped some kisses on her neck. He clearly had already figured out that was a hot spot for her, and her moans of pleasure likely gave him some encouragement in that area.

It would have been so easy for her just to stand there and let him make her mindless. Well, maybe not stand, because her legs were all wobbly now. But she could have just savored the moment by letting him savor her. Charlotte wanted to get in on that aspect of it, though.

She wanted Cal to moan.

To need.

To go a little wobbly.

So she touched him while he kissed her. All in all, she quickly learned she had the advantage. His mouth couldn't move nearly as fast as her hands could and couldn't cover nearly as much area. She tucked the condom back in her pocket, slid her palm underneath his shirt and touched and touched and touched.

She added some body bumps because that was a form of touching, too, and she maneuvered herself so that her center was against his. Clearly, he had a good reaction to that because he went hard as stone. And he cursed, which she was pretty sure was the male equivalent of a moan.

Cal didn't ditch the kissing, but he made adjustments. Frantic, needy ones that told her the escalation was speeding right along. He didn't just put his hand under her top, he peeled it off her, sent it flying and lowered his mouth to her breasts. First to the tops of them, and then to her right nipple when he shoved down her bra.

Her legs didn't just wobble, the bones dissolved from the intense heat, but Cal somehow managed to keep his arm hooked around her. Anchoring her against him while he taunted her with the possibility that she might indeed have an orgasm from just his mouth on her breasts. It certainly seemed possible. Everything was concentrating inside her. All hot and urgent. All now, now, now.

But she didn't want now.

Charlotte at least wanted the fantasy of seeing him naked so she turned the tide and went with a different escalation tactic. She lowered herself, sliding her body against his until her mouth was at the level of the zipper of his jeans. She kissed him there and made sure there was plenty of hot breath to it.

He cursed again, and Cal must have been battling his own potential orgasm because he grabbed on to her, scooping her up in his arms, and carried her to the bed. He dropped her there, the overly soft feather mattress puffing up around her. What he didn't do was join her, and she was about to protest that when she got a much-desired eyeful.

With his eyes locked with hers and with the air pulsing with heat, Cal pulled off his shirt, exposing all those amazing muscles. Not bulky or puffed up like the mattress. Just toned and perfect. She could have feasted on those for a while, but Cal gave her more.

So much more.

She levered herself up on her elbows and watched as he yanked off his boots. Then his belt. He lowered his zipper. Not in a slow, striptease kind of way, thank goodness. While she might have appreciated that and enjoyed the show, she was burning too much for slow. She needed the full monty.

And she got it.

Cal kept his gaze on her, and he whipped down his jeans and boxers in the same motion. Charlotte sacrificed the eye contact so she could look. Possibly drool. And positively want him more than, well, anything. In that moment, Cal ruled every square inch of her body.

Morning sex certainly had some advantages. Light. Lots of it. No darkness to obstruct this incredible view, and just seeing him was adding to the revving. To the heat. To the urgency.

Now he came to her, and she had an especially wonderful view when he leaned down and unbuttoned her jeans. First, he took out the condom from her pocket, and then he shimmied her jeans right off her. Panties, too. And he took his own moment and advantage of the light to look at her.

Normally, Charlotte wouldn't have enjoyed such scrutiny, but the heat had a way of canceling out modesty and worry over any extra pounds on her hips. Heat had a way of making that and everything else disappear.

Apparently, heat and need didn't hinder his multitasking skill set because he kissed her while he pulled on the condom. He paused the kissing, though, when he pushed inside her. Then again, everything paused in that moment. Breath, heart, thought. It only lasted a couple of seconds before the need clawed its way back to the surface, and the sex dance began.

He pushed, and she met the pushes. One by one.

Deeper and faster. Until she couldn't have held on to the pleasure for another second. Until Cal gave her no choice but to chase that orgasm after all.

She came in a flash, that avalanche of mindless pleasure where everything vanished. Everything but Cal. He was right there with her to achieve some mindless pleasure of his own.

CAL CAME OUT of the bathroom in Charlotte's suite, and he found her exactly as he'd left her a couple of minutes earlier. Naked and still on her bed. Still smiling. Still looking at him as if he were the master of the sex universe.

An incredible sight that was pure fuel for future sexual fantasies.

Despite having just had her, he felt that brainless part of him twitch as if gearing up for another round. Brainless, of course, thought it the best idea possible. It wasn't. Well, not unless Charlotte had more condoms. Or nothing else to do today. Which apparently she did because her phone dinged with a text.

That brought on a naked hunt through the discarded clothes on her floor, and after purposely bumping into each other, they were laughing when she finally located it. Although, the laughter stopped when she read what was on the screen.

"It's from Mandy," she relayed. "Noah's here, and he says he wants to talk to you."

Great. Talk about putting an immediate damper on a sex buzz. All right, not immediate since one glance at Charlotte and the buzz was still there, but Cal figured it would have to go on hold while he dealt with Noah.

Hopefully, this wouldn't turn into a rehash of *You're scum for going after Charlotte* and *I'm not giving up on getting her back.*

Cal had to concede that Noah did indeed have a right to think of him as scum since he had more or less gone after Charlotte. After some teeth-gnashing and worry he had, anyway. After countless mental lectures to leave her alone that had done absolutely no good. Lust could be a greedy piece of work.

So could feelings.

And while it would only cause more hair-pulling, Cal had to admit that what he felt for Charlotte had gone past the lust stage. No way would he tell her that, however, as she clearly had enough to deal with without adding his feelings to the mix.

Cal gathered up his clothes and started dressing. "I'll go see what Noah wants."

Sighing, she picked up her clothes, too. "And I don't want to be naked in case he wants to include me in on the conversation."

Good point, but Cal figured Noah would include the subject of Charlotte whether she was ready or not.

He finished dressing, kissed her and headed out before the kiss could turn scalding. Always a possibility when it came to Charlotte. Just as a conversation with Noah could turn out to be scalding in a different kind of way. One with lots and lots of temper. Of course, it hadn't always been that way, but Cal couldn't see it going back to the way things had been.

Cal made it down the attic and third-floor stairs, but then he stopped when he spotted Noah, not seething, pacing and waiting for a showdown but rather talking to the new resident, Jodi Seaver.

Noah turned to look at Cal. No angry expression, either, but Cal figured that was because Noah was in a conversation with someone that he clearly knew and was pleased to see.

"Cal," Noah said. Not a friendly greeting exactly so, yeah, there was a bit of fuming, but Noah probably didn't want to douse the place in it with Jodi right there. "Have you met Jodi?"

Cal shook his head, went closer and introduced himself. "Cal Donnelly."

Even though Cal thought the woman looked shocked, she still managed a polite nod. "Lieutenant Colonel Donnelly," she provided. "I watched you in a demo flight of an F-22."

Cal had done a few of those so he wasn't sure which one she meant. "I take it you already knew Noah?"

Jodi nodded, then swallowed hard. "I was special ops...but I took an early retirement."

Oh, yes. She was shocked. Maybe literally. He didn't see any visible scars, and she appeared to be able to stand and move of her own accord, but that didn't mean she hadn't experienced some kind of trauma.

"Jodi and I crossed paths a couple of times on the job," Noah provided. That made sense because Noah was also special ops, and sometimes there were joint operations.

"How'd you find out about this place?" Cal asked, hoping to shift the subject a little.

"From your brother Blue."

Cal looked at her with surprise.

"Blue and I see the same physical therapist at the base in San Antonio," she explained. "He told me about it, and I thought it might be a good place for me to get some downtime."

"It is," he assured her.

She obviously wanted that respite right at this moment, because she fluttered her fingers toward her room. "Sorry, but I need to go. I've got some things I need to do," she said, her voice barely a whisper, and she walked away.

Noah didn't say anything until she had closed the door behind her, and he didn't launch into any other info about Jodi. He set his focus on Cal and dragged in a deep breath.

"I'm leaving to go back to the base today, and I wanted to say goodbye," Noah said matter-of-factly. "I'd like to also say goodbye to Charlotte, but I don't think she wants to see or talk to me right now."

Cal shrugged. "I have no idea if that's true. It's possible Charlotte would be interested in a farewell."

Noah shrugged, too. "That's not the impression I got. She's washed her hands of me, and I only have myself to blame. I screwed up big-time and then came storming back in here, insisting she and I could make things work. I got so caught up in my own rhetoric that I forgot it hadn't worked between me and Charlotte in a long time. It was the reason I got involved with Elise. And the other women," he mumbled.

Since he had no idea what to say to that, Cal stayed quiet, but he was glad that Noah had seen the light.

Noah went quiet for a couple of moments, as well,

before his gaze came back to Cal's. "Don't hurt her, Cal. Please don't hurt Charlotte."

Noah had already said something similar, but it hadn't had the genuine pleading that it did now. And Cal felt the plea in the pit of his stomach. Felt it in his heart, too. Yeah, he was wrestling with these damn emotions and with his conscience. Unlike Noah, he couldn't have juggled the girl back home with the ones he met along the way, and that meant he either needed to commit to Charlotte or let her go.

That would be damn hard now that they'd landed in bed. He wasn't naive enough to believe that morning sex with her was stringless. Of course, Charlotte wouldn't put those strings on it. Nor would she put them on Cal. But that didn't mean strings didn't exist, simply because they'd come with the intimacy of what they'd done.

He cut off the rest of his thought when he heard the footsteps coming down the stairs and turned to see Charlotte. She didn't freeze when she saw Noah. Nor did she appear to be bracing herself for some kind of confrontation with him. However, there was alarm on her face.

"Cal," she said, holding up her phone, "I just got a call from Sonora."

It took him a moment to recall that was the nurse Charlotte had hired. "What happened? Did someone get hurt?" Of course, he had other worst-case scenarios already flying through his head.

"It's Harper," Charlotte said on a rise of breath.

Hell. The worst-case scenarios might be coming true. "What happened?" he repeated.

"Harper's not in her room, and Sonora can't find her." Charlotte's eyes were drowning in worry when she met his gaze. "She's missing, Cal. Harper's gone."

CHAPTER SEVENTEEN

CHARLOTTE TRIED TO tamp down her alarm over Harper being missing, and she hoped this wouldn't be a long search. After all, Harper was in a wheelchair and had no access to a car, so she couldn't leave the grounds. The house was huge, as was the barn, which meant there were many places to hide out, but Charlotte figured that with the search party she'd organized, they would soon find her.

Sonora, Cal and Noah were looking through the house. With the help of some of the workers, Alden had taken the barn along with doing checks inside the parked vehicles to make sure Harper hadn't ducked into one of those. Charlotte had opted for the grounds. It was also a huge space, but the trails weren't finished yet, which limited where Harper could go.

So they'd find her, Charlotte assured herself. Then she could find out why Harper had done this. Maybe it was something as simple as her needing space, but since it had only been a couple of months since she'd driven off that bridge, Charlotte and everyone else was concerned that Harper's need for space could turn out to be something a whole lot worse.

Unlike what was going on in the house and barn, Charlotte didn't call out Harper's name as she walked.

In fact, she tried to listen for the faint humming sound of the motorized wheelchair. She didn't hear it so she kept walking, sticking to the main trail that was finished. It led from the ramp on the house, through the yard and pastures and to a cluster of trees where there was a bench. Charlotte made it there in only a couple of minutes, but there was no sign of Harper.

The landscapers had purposely left many of the shrubs around this particular trail, and there were plans to add flowering plants that would brighten up the space. For now, though, without the floral additions, Charlotte rounded a corner and got a decent view of the rest of the trail. And where it ended.

Her heart skipped many beats.

Because Harper was right at the edge of the pond. There was a bench there, too, but Harper wasn't anywhere near it. She was right at the water's edge.

Charlotte tried not to panic or shout out because the alarm might cause Harper to drive her wheelchair right in. The water wasn't that deep, but the chair was heavy and would sink fast.

She sent off a quick text to Cal to let him know that she'd found Harper, and she told him the location. She also asked that he and the others hang back since it might make Harper do something reckless if all of them came rushing at her at once.

"Want some company?" Charlotte asked when she got closer. Her voice was a little shaky, but she'd managed to keep the fear out of it.

"No," Harper said using her computer. She typed it without even glancing back at her.

Charlotte didn't let that snarly reply put her off. She

kept approaching, and when she got close to Harper, she didn't grab for the wheelchair—which was what she wanted to do. Instead, she sank down on the bench and stared out at the water as Harper was doing.

From the corner of her eye, Charlotte saw Noah and Cal arrive on the trail, but as instructed, they thankfully stayed back. A few seconds later, Alden joined them, and all three men were wearing their concern in their expressions. Charlotte hoped she was keeping her own worried expression in check, but she clearly failed at that when Harper looked at her and huffed.

"I wasn't going into the pond," Harper assured her through the voice generator, and then she shot Charlotte a glare to go along with her huff.

That sounded like the truth, and Charlotte hoped beyond hope that it was. "Good. So what were you doing out here?" she asked. And then the image of the picture Harper had drawn flashed in her mind. "Were you reminiscing about the time Cal fell in the creek and nearly drowned?"

Charlotte wasn't sure what reaction she might get from Harper, but she hadn't expected tears. But they were there, pooling in Harper's eyes. And judging from the redness, these weren't her first tears of the morning.

"Yes," Harper whispered. And she didn't use the computer this time. It was her actual voice. Of course, it was filtered through those damaged vocal cords, but it was loud and clear enough to hear.

"Wow," Charlotte said. Apparently, Dr. Kentrell had been right about Harper being able to speak. "So how long have you been able to talk?"

Harper glared at her. "Since I was one or two." Her

gaze cut away. "I never fully lost it. I just put it away for a while. Might put it away again."

It was obvious Harper did have to strain to get out each and every word, and Charlotte didn't want her to overdo it, so she didn't fire off another question. She waited to see if Harper would continue. When she did, she went back to the computer to let it do her talking.

"That day at the creek, I knew the tree limb was cracked," the digital voice relayed. "I'd just been up there, and I knew it wasn't stable. We were taking turns, and I also knew Cal would be the next one to use it."

Charlotte turned her head to stare at Harper. "You…"

She'd been about to blurt out something along the lines of *You wanted Cal to get hurt.* No way could she say something like that without sounding angry or combative. Charlotte didn't want to feel either of those things, but Harper's confession had tapped into the fear she'd felt as a child when she thought he might die and what she felt for Cal now.

"Yes," Harper typed, even though Charlotte had bitten off the question. "I knew the branch would likely give way, and I didn't stop him."

"Why?" Charlotte had to know.

Harper took her time before she started typing. "He'd won the spelling bee, the math competition and even the blasted egg race at Easter. Even then he was better than me. Even then I knew he was the one I had to beat and couldn't."

Though the explanation hadn't been in her own voice, Charlotte could infer the hurt. Could see it on Harper's face. This had been a deep emotional cut, and it was still affecting her. That softened Charlotte's initial reaction.

"Now you know how horrible a person I am," Harper spoke, not going with the computer this time, and the tears rose in her eyes.

Charlotte could practically feel Harper's pain. "You were a child," she reminded her.

"A selfish, mean one," Harper argued verbally again.

"A child with a really crappy home life," Charlotte countered.

Harper rolled her teary eyes and went back to the computer for her response. "Pot calling the kettle black. You had a crappy home life, too. Don't deny it. Izzie can be demanding and unreasonable. And Cal, he also had a partially crap home life with his mom dying."

All of that was true, and Charlotte wasn't going to deny it.

"I used to wonder what was worse. Having my mom leave or having her die," Harper added a moment later.

Charlotte made a sound of agreement. "I had similar thoughts about my dad."

"Home life from hell," Harper concluded, "and yet it didn't turn you into a spiteful, sore-loser brat."

"No, but I had my uncle Rob. I could turn to him when Izzie was at her worst. And Cal had his dad. Audrey, too. She never became a mom to him, but she's been there for him over the years."

It occurred to Charlotte that Audrey could be pushy and demanding, but she was nowhere in the realm of Izzie. Or, worse, Paul. Audrey had helped Cal. Was still trying to help him.

And that brought her full circle back to the job.

A job that could fulfill Cal in so many ways. One for a real hero. And one that would take him away from her. Charlotte didn't want that to hurt, but it did. Mercy, it did. But she couldn't let Cal see that because it would give him the mother lode of guilt trips. She cared about him too much to put that on him.

"You're sighing and look like you're about to puke," Harper pointed out via the computer. "Are you finally wrapping your head around what I did that day at the creek?" She paused, studied Charlotte's face. "Or was the sigh about Cal?"

"Cal," she admitted. Since Harper was spilling stuff with her, then Charlotte wanted to do the same. "Things are complicated with him."

Harper made a snarky hmmph sound. "Of course it is," she typed. "You two always had a thing for each other, but you ignored it because of Noah. With Noah out of the picture, the thing took over. Now Cal will leave, and you'll be crushed into little bitty pieces."

Charlotte frowned. "I'll be sad. Hurt, even." *Really hurt.* "But not crushed. And I'll be happy for him since I know he'll be doing what he's always wanted to do."

Harper continued with the snark. "Goody-goodies to the core, both of you. The exact opposite of me. I'm rotten inside."

"No," Charlotte insisted, but Harper interrupted her before she could say more.

"I don't have amnesia, so I know what I was think-ing and feeling when I left Cal that note and drove off the bridge," Harper said herself. "Even that was selfish and bratty. *Rotten.* A way for me to give him a poke in the eye and say, *See? You caused this.*" She paused, her voice breaking on a sob. "But he didn't. Cal didn't do anything more, or less, than be himself."

Charlotte reached for her to pull her into a hug, but Harper pushed her hands away.

"No," Harper muttered. "No, no, no."

Charlotte eased back down onto the bench and tried to level out her own emotions so she could try and figure out what to say. But Harper didn't give her a chance to do that.

"I think it's time I talked to a counselor now," Harper said, and this time she didn't push Charlotte away when she pulled her into a hug.

Tears spilled down Harper's cheeks, and she buried her face against Charlotte's shoulder when she whispered, "I need help."

EVEN THOUGH CAL hadn't been close enough to hear Charlotte and Harper's conversation by the pond, he'd gotten the gist of it. Harper was miserable.

Broken.

And dealing with the intense emotions of what she'd done.

Definitely not a light and airy chat, but he had seen something hopeful, too, when Charlotte had pulled a crying Harper into her arms. It seemed to him that Harper had turned a very big corner in her life and that she might finally be able to heal. Cal wanted to help with that, and it was the reason he was now pulling to a stop in front of Harper's childhood home.

According to the sliver of info he'd gotten from Charlotte, Harper wanted to see the therapist. A huge step, and while he doubted therapy would be an instant cure, it was a start. A start he didn't want mucked up by Harper's father.

Although he'd left that note for Paul a couple of weeks earlier, it'd been nearly twenty years since Cal had actually gone inside the house. That visit had happened shortly after Harper's mother had left. There'd been plenty of gossip not only after her running off with Charlotte's dad but also talk that Paul had snapped and was maybe holding Harper captive or something. The gossip had been convincing enough to make Noah and Cal sneak here one night and tap on Harper's window and convince her to let them in.

What he and Noah had found had been both a relief and a worry.

There'd been no captive situation. Harper had insisted she was free to leave and go with her mother but she'd chosen to stay. She'd been plenty angry enough. All anger aimed at her mother, though.

And Harper had been convincing enough that she wasn't being held against her will, but later when Cal and Noah had compared notes about the conversation, they'd both thought Harper had been scared. Of course, they'd been sixteen and hadn't had a clue how to handle something like that, so instead of looking for a way to help her, they'd gone on with their lives, naively believing that Harper would do the same.

She had.

But that life had taken a dark turn.

And while he bore some of the responsibility for that, so did the man who came out onto the porch just as Cal stepped from his truck. Paul didn't greet him with a wave or smile. Nor had Cal expected that. Bitterness was Paul's default emotion now, and it was possible it extended to Cal even though Paul certainly hadn't directly blamed him for what had happened to Harper.

"Did Harper screw up again?" Paul was quick to ask.

Cal made sure his reply was equally fast. "No." In fact, just the opposite, but it wasn't his place to spill about Harper seeing a therapist. That info should come from Harper herself if she wanted her father to know.

"No?" Paul said. "So this is a social visit?" Though he sounded plenty skeptical about that actually being the reason Cal was there.

"I just thought we could talk," Cal settled on saying.

Paul continued to stare at him, and after muttering something Cal couldn't catch, he motioned for Cal to come in. Definitely not a warm welcome, but at least this would get his foot in the door.

Cal went in and immediately felt as if he'd stepped into a time capsule. As far as he could tell, nothing had changed in the past twenty years. The same furniture in the living room. Same rug on the floor. Cal didn't know what Paul's financial situation was, but the ranch itself hadn't grown, either.

"Wasn't expecting company," Paul grumbled, and he motioned for Cal to follow him, "so I can't offer you anything."

"That's okay. Like I said, I just came to talk."

"About Harper." That was a grumble, too, peppered with more of that skepticism. "You're sure she hasn't screwed up something?"

"I'm sure," Cal stated, making sure his tone was even; he used his lieutenant colonel's voice. Not intimidating but also a signal that he wasn't in the mood for any bullshit.

Paul led him into the living room, and Cal got a closer look at the mantel. Now here there'd been some changes. The family photos were still there, lined up in their pristine silver frames. Pictures of various stages of Harper's life from infancy all the way to high school.

Pictures that included her mother.

But someone, Paul probably, had just blacked out the woman's face and body. And not carefully. They were basically black blobs with permanent marker that he was betting had been done in fits of anger. The lesson was obvious. Screw up and you get erased.

Had Harper felt that way? Cal wondered.

Heck, had Charlotte?

After all, it was her father who'd left her to be with Harper's mom, and while Izzie hadn't scratched out photos—none that she'd put on display anyway—she'd become bitter about her ex, and she'd also done nothing to get him to reconnect with his daughter.

"Do you ever hear from her?" Cal asked before he could think the question through.

"Who? Oh," he snarled after he'd followed Cal's gaze to the photos. "Her. Doreen." Of course, he said her name like the vilest of profanity. "No, I haven't heard from her, and she'd better not try to contact me. Ever. I told her when she was packing to leave that once she walked out, she wouldn't be coming back, and that the only thing I ever wanted to see of her was her ass heading out the door."

Paul had built up both volume and intensity with each word, but when he stopped, he stayed quiet for a few moments. Cal found it refreshing that the man wasn't spewing venom and that he might be deep in some meaningful thoughts. But it didn't last.

"Some wife she turned out to be," he griped. "A crap mother, too. Harper was all crying and begging her to stay, and probably to shut her up, Doreen claimed that once she got settled that she'd send for Harper. *Send for her*," he repeated with a dry laugh. "As if I'd let that tramp get her claws in my daughter."

This was the first Cal was hearing of any of this. In fact, he hadn't heard Charlotte's account of when her dad had left, but there'd likely been a similar emotional upheaval. That, and the note Charlotte had told him about. The one where her father had blamed her for his leaving. That made him a piece of shit in Cal's eyes. Maybe that label applied to Harper's mom, too.

"Did Doreen ever try to send for Harper?" Cal wanted to know.

Paul spewed some more profanity. "She wrote letters, saying this, that and the other about meeting up with Harper so they could talk and figure things out. By then, Harper was within a year and a half of finishing high school. She didn't want to change schools and start all over again."

No, and by then, Paul had been the one to have his claws in her. Then again, the claws had probably already been there.

Paul's eyes narrowed when he shifted his attention from the photos back to Cal. "You didn't come here to bring up all this shit from the past. I hope you're here to tell me my daughter is doing everything possible to fix herself."

Again, Cal didn't want to mention the therapy, but he thought that was indeed the start of Harper getting better. "Harper's settling in, and I'm hopeful there'll be some healing."

"Hopeful?" Paul challenged. He barked out another dry laugh. "Hell, Cal, hope won't get her ass in gear. She needs to be pushed and pushed hard." He aimed his index finger at him. "And you can do that. Draw her back into competition. Give her a reason to start fighting again."

Cal had to fight the flashes of images he got. Of the note Harper had left for him. Of her scars. Of that lost, haunted look in her eyes. A look that she tried to mask with defiance.

"That's not going to work," Cal managed to say. "And even if it did, I wouldn't be the one to do it. I pushed her hard enough, and look what happened."

Paul flinched as if stunned. "Hell, that didn't happen because you pushed her. That happened because she lost her nerve."

Cal was stunned in turn. "She nearly lost her life."

"That was all bullshit, a cry for attention. Well, she got plenty of attention, and it's time to move on. She needs a challenge, and you're the one to give it to her."

It sickened Cal to hear the man spout this nonsense. "No," he stated as firmly and clearly as he could. "I'm not pushing her."

Paul's chin came up, and he looked at Cal as if he'd just dropped down a whole bunch of notches in his eyes. "All right. Don't push. But trust me, I will," he insisted. "One way or another, Harper is going to recover. No way in hell am I gonna put up with a loser for a kid."

"You need to back off from Harper," Cal said before he even knew the words were going to come out of his mouth.

"Excuse me?" Paul countered, both his tone and expression a challenge.

Cal met the man's fierce stare with one of his own. "You need to back off and give her some time to heal."

"Or what?" He didn't wait for a response. "You think you have some kind of pull with me? Well, you don't. Yeah, you're a hotshot hero, but that doesn't give you the right to tell me how to handle my daughter."

The anger sizzled through him like a pot that had just boiled over, and Cal was certain it came through loud and clear, because Paul actually moved back a step.

"Don't mistake me for a hotshot or a hero," Cal warned him. "Do anything else to harm Harper and I'll make you pay. Trust me on that. I will make you pay."

He stared the man down, and when he was certain he'd gotten his point across, Cal turned and walked out.

CHAPTER EIGHTEEN

CHARLOTTE LAUGHED WHEN she read the latest text from Cal.

Just moved three mares into a pasture so they can have sex with Ice Man. I feel a little like a matchmaker.

She was glad he was joking about the ranching chore. Heck, she was just glad to hear from him. Since Harper's breakthrough at the pond, Cal hadn't been around as much as she wanted. Then again, anything less than 24/7 wasn't enough, but there was no way for that to happen. Not only because he'd had ranch work to do but also because he was obviously still in need of time and space to think.

Charlotte missed him. Not just the sex. Though, she definitely missed that since their one actual time together had been amazing. But she missed Cal, too, and had to accept this absence might be his way of distancing himself from her so he could try to protect her heart. Of course, her heart was whining about that. Her body, too.

Six days.

That's when Cal's leave ran out, and there were times, like now, when Charlotte could hear those minutes ticking away. Cal was likely feeling the same time pressure since this was a huge decision. She only hoped it was the need for reflection that was keeping him away.

The visit with Paul had to also be bothering him, so that might be playing into this lack of connection she was feeling with him. Cal had told her about the conversation he'd had with the man, about Paul's idiotic notions when it came to Harper. But Charlotte figured Cal had left some things out, that he hadn't spilled all of what had been said. Whatever had gone on, though, Cal had asked that she call him immediately if Paul showed up to see Harper. So far, he hadn't.

And Charlotte hoped that continued.

Even if Harper wanted to see her father—and Charlotte wasn't at all sure she did—the man was just plain toxic. This time away from him might give Harper the chance to heal. She had certainly gotten a good start on that by beginning the therapy sessions and even doing some mild exercises on the equipment in the barn.

She answered Cal with the emoji of Shady-Looking Guy with Googly Eyes for his matchmaker comment and was debating if she should do a follow-up text to mention anything about his current ranching duties when she got a reply.

Horse sex already in progress. Minimal foreplay. And quick. One minute. Should I come over later and see if we can last longer?

Instant fire. Instant need. And she was laughing, and burning, when she answered him with a Yes. I can time you.

He didn't send a reply. Instead her phone rang with a call from him. "When's a good time?" he asked.

Charlotte would have said *now* if she hadn't heard a shriek, and she was pretty sure her mother had made the sound.

"Did Mandy find another doll?" Cal asked. He'd obviously heard the screech as well.

"Possibly, but if so, she must have shown it to my mother. Izzie's here." And she was apparently coming up the stairs since Charlotte could hear her muttering and her footsteps.

"Then I'll let you go. Text me and let me know when it's a good time for me to come over."

"Hopefully, the text will be in five minutes or less," she murmured, and she ended the call just as Izzie appeared in her doorway.

Her mother was out of breath and looking a little frazzled. Charlotte actually saw a couple of strands of hair out of place, and alarm shot through her when she realized there was something wrong with Izzie's eyes.

"What happened?" Charlotte asked, motioning to her own eyes.

"Oh, that. I put makeup on one and then forgot to do the other. I didn't notice until I got to work and then realized I didn't have my travel cosmetics bag in my purse."

All of that was completely out of the norm for her mother. "Is everything okay?"

"No, it is not," Izzie was quick to say. "When I got here, Mandy was coming out as I was going in, and she was holding out two of those dolls that the workers found. She was holding them away from her body, and I ran right into them."

That would have indeed been an unpleasant experience. "I thought you liked the dolls and wanted to display them."

Her mother huffed. "No, I don't like the dolls, but I was trying to placate some members of the garden guild and town council by agreeing that we should have more local arts-and-craft stuff on display."

Charlotte had no trouble hearing the frustration in her mother's voice, but part of her felt guilty for wanting to hurry Izzie along so she could fire off that invitation to Cal.

"Uh, did something else happen?" Charlotte asked. "I mean, you seem upset."

"I am upset," Izzie snapped, and then she groaned, muttered an apology and groaned some more. "I saw the latest poll results this morning, and I'm almost certainly going to lose reelection."

Another first. Charlotte had heard her mother mention dips and rises in polls, but she'd never seemed this down about it.

"It's my breakup with Taggert," Izzie went on. "People really like him, so being with him gave me a boost." Her sigh told Charlotte that the elevation in status hadn't been just in the job but her personal life, too. "But now that everyone's heard that it's off between us for good, voters are turning away from me."

Now it was Charlotte who sighed. She figured she knew where this was going, and the destination was the same as it usually was. "And it's my fault," she said before Izzie could.

Izzie stopped pacing and looked her straight in the eyes. "No, it's not."

Her mother said it with such conviction that it stunned Charlotte. This was another first.

"The breakup with Taggert is my fault," Izzie went on. Instead of pacing, she dropped onto the foot of Charlotte's bed. "I'm to blame for the drop in the polls, for people seeing the truth about me. Taggert saw it. He saw that I'm a mean, manipulative person."

"That's a bit harsh," Charlotte told her. "You wanted a fairy-tale wedding—"

"I wanted a husband that people respected," Izzie interrupted. "One who wouldn't run out on me for another woman."

"One that you loved?" Charlotte asked because she truly hoped that had been part of Izzie's relationship with Taggert.

"Yes, love," she muttered on another of those heavy sighs. "But he saw right through me."

Charlotte decided to try to cut off any more personal bashing. "No more *mean* and *manipulative* stuff. You have good qualities, or Taggert would have never gotten involved with you in the first place."

A burst of air left her mouth, a sort of laugh but definitely not a happy one. "He wanted fairy-tale, too, because he was so lonely, and for a while he was able to overlook my faults. Oh, God," she moaned, "I have so many faults."

Huffing, Charlotte went to her, caught her by the shoulders and was about to give her a lecture about whining and self-loathing. Izzie stopped her in her tracks.

"The note wasn't meant for you," Izzie blurted out.

Charlotte was confused for a couple of seconds, and then the meaning of that slowly started to sink in.

"You mean the note Dad left?" Charlotte asked.

Izzie nodded and kept their gazes locked. "He didn't leave it for you but for me."

Charlotte shook her head. "But it had my name on it," she pointed out.

"Because I wrote it on the outside of the paper." Izzie stopped, and tears began to slip down her cheeks. "I was going to say, *Charlotte, here's the note your dad left for me.* But then you came in, all upset and begging me to do something to stop him from leaving. You even said you wanted to go with him."

She had. A lot of that night was an emotional blur, but she recalled that well enough.

"And when I heard you say that, I snapped," Izzie went on. "I was so angry, not just at him but at you. Because you both wanted to leave me. So I gave you that note."

Charlotte eased her grip from her mother's shoulders and stepped back. "You did what?" was all she managed to ask.

Izzie stood, too. "I didn't want to lose you," she responded.

Charlotte's mind did a whirlwind recap of those moments. Of when her mother had indeed given her the note. The note she'd thought was for her.

I can't do this anymore. You've made it impossible for me to stay.

There it was. Those words that had tormented her for

nearly twenty years. Words that drowned her in guilt. Had made her feel like crap and unworthy of being loved. Had made her think that she owed her mother so very much because she'd driven him away.

But now those words took on a totally different meaning.

Charlotte attempted to say something. Anything. She even tried one of those shrieks usually reserved for creepy dolls. She couldn't even manage that. Thankfully, she could move, so she headed for the door and just kept on walking.

Izzie called out to her, but Charlotte ignored it and hurried down all the stairs. She didn't stop in the foyer. She went straight to her car and started driving. No uncertainty in where she was going.

She needed to see Cal.

He couldn't fix this. No one could. But she needed him to hold her and make her believe she wouldn't fall apart.

It wasn't a long drive to Saddlebrook, and she was equally thankful when she didn't spot Izzie trying to follow her. She still might, but Charlotte couldn't handle seeing her right now.

When she got to the ranch, it occurred to her that Cal might still be in one of the pastures with the horses, but then she saw him making his way from the barn toward the house. He saw her, too, and headed her way. Slowly at first. But after she stepped out of her car, he must have noticed her expression because he quickened his pace. She hurried to him, and once they met, she went straight into his arms. Charlotte held on, using him as the anchor that she very much needed.

"What happened?" he asked. "Is it Paul?"

She shook her head and eased back enough so they'd have eye contact. "It's my mother."

Apparently, his mind didn't go straight to an accident, probably because he knew Izzie. "What did she do now?"

"She lied," Charlotte managed to say. "A very big lie."

Cal muttered some profanity, but he didn't ask for more details. However, with his arm still around her, he got her into the house. No one was around when they stepped into the foyer, and they had the stairs to themselves as they made their way to the second floor.

And to his bedroom.

The moment he'd shut the door, he pulled her back to him, wrapping her in that hug she still craved. "All right," he muttered, brushing a kiss on her forehead. "Tell me what happened."

She did. While he held her, Charlotte poured out her heart to Cal.

CAL MENTALLY CURSED, calling Izzie every bad word he could recall that had been doled out to someone who'd done something lower than low.

And this was low.

He couldn't imagine anyone letting their teenage kid take the blame like that, but after Charlotte had told him what'd happened, he realized he wasn't that surprised. He'd always known Izzie could be selfish and a control freak. Not as bad as Paul but still there. Still just as damaging.

Thankfully, Charlotte was no longer crying. He'd

hated seeing those tears in her eyes, which had in turn only caused him to curse Izzie even more. But the tears had stopped, and now Charlotte was quiet and snuggled against him. Perhaps she was also silently doling out some curses at her mom. He hoped so anyway, because he figured anger was going to be a necessary step in getting over this particular hurdle.

Shortly after Charlotte had spilled all about what Izzie had done, those tears had started, and not long after that, Cal had moved her to sit on the foot of his bed. That'd lasted until back cramps had started to set in for both of them, and they'd moved to the top of the bed for some much needed support from the headboard.

"Some people drown their sorrows with eighty proof," Charlotte muttered. "The sugar solution tastes better."

Cal smiled, and he felt some of the tightness in his chest go away. They had indeed gone the sugar route. Charlotte had declined the shot of whiskey he'd offered her, but they were both sucking on some Jolly Rancher candy he kept on his desk in the corner. At the moment, the air was loaded with the scents of cherry—her choice—and green apple—for him.

Because Charlotte seemed to be shifting away from the pain and shock of what Izzie had done, he held back any questions, but one was front and center for him. Why had Izzie fessed up now? Had the breakup with Taggert sent Izzie spiraling over an emotional edge that had in turn made her confess? Possibly. The breakup must have rattled her. But then something else occurred to Cal. Something he'd heard his grandmother and Maybell talking about.

"Your mom's popularity is down in the polls," he muttered before he could stop himself. "She probably won't get reelected."

Charlotte lifted her head from his shoulder and nodded. "I think she was crying more about that than Taggert."

That made sense. Well, as much sense as something like this could make.

"Since my dad left, I think my mother has been on this quest to prove she's perfect," Charlotte said, articulating what Cal was also thinking. "Perfect hair, makeup, clothes, along with a perfect job…and daughter," she added. "Of course, it was never perfect, but now that the facade has crumbled, I think she has as well."

Bingo. And he wanted to believe this could be the start of Izzie dropping any and all charades and leading a *real* life. One where she didn't have such strict expectations for herself and Charlotte.

Would he be around to see that?

That was the question that flashed in his mind like a huge, tacky neon sign. Maybe. But *maybe* didn't feel like nearly enough to continue whatever it was he'd started with Charlotte. And that's why Cal loosened his grip on her, ready to put at least an inch or two of distance between them, since right now they were touching in a whole lot of places.

He moved, but Charlotte immediately took hold of him and pulled him back to her. She looked him straight in the eye. "You're trying to do the good-guy thing because you're not sure where things are going between us. You're not sure where you're going," she spelled out. "And I've just had this emotional punch from hell."

That was a darn good summary. "All of the above," he admitted.

She kept hold of his arm. Kept up the direct eye contact, too. "When I walked away from my mom, you were the first person I thought of. I wanted to come here. I wanted to see you."

He groaned because this was only confirming his fear that they were getting too close. But then, he realized something.

Charlotte and he were already close.

There was no getting to it.

"Hell," he muttered.

"Exactly," she said as if she knew exactly what he meant.

And she probably did. Because she had to know that just because they'd fallen for each other, it didn't mean everything was going to be as sweet as the Jolly Ranchers they were finishing up.

"What we do here in the next twenty minutes or so," Charlotte said, brushing a kiss on his mouth, "will not play into your decision about leaving."

He wasn't so sure about that at all, but that little touch of her mouth on his gave him a jolt of lust and no doubt dulled his mind. However, even the dullness wouldn't cloud the fact that it would play into his decision. Oh, he still might take the job, still might leave, but it would be with the sickening realization that he'd be leaving Charlotte behind. Which, in turn, meant neither of them would get out of this without dinged hearts.

"You're not going to question that twenty-minute remark?" she asked, giving him another of those light kisses. "I thought you might consider that to be an insult to your sexual prowess. It wasn't," she added. "I just figured we wouldn't be able to make out for long if we didn't have a condom."

And just like that, he got another debate with himself about whether or not to open his nightstand drawer. He lost that debate, opened it and took out one of the condoms he'd bought the day before.

"I even put one in my wallet," he admitted. "Just in case."

She smiled, a really big warm smile that quickly got covered up because he snapped her to him and kissed her. Cal didn't go with one of those lip brushes, either. Since this was probably a mistake of massive proportions, he made the kiss equally monumental. Easy to do since he'd been aching for Charlotte, and no amount of mental lectures and logic had been able to cool that ache.

The kiss did some cooling.

His body was practically cheering over it. But, of course, it then did the opposite of cooling and fired up that fierce need he had for her. Cal wasn't sure how he would ever be able to walk away from her, and at the moment he didn't even want to try to wrap his mind around it. He just wanted this kiss.

Just wanted Charlotte in his arms.

Charlotte was clearly on the same page as he was, and when the kiss deepened, the flavors of the remnants of the cherries and apples mixed together with Charlotte's own taste created an amazing sensation. If he'd had any resolve about not going through with this, that would have caused it to vanish.

"We've probably used up one of those twenty minutes," she whispered, her voice all silk and breath. It was damn hot, but then everything about her fell into that category. "It'll eat up another minute for me to get you undressed. Time me," she warned him a split second before she went after his shirt.

She didn't just take it off, however. She touched. And kissed, trailing her now damp mouth from his neck to his chest. By the time she reached his stomach, Cal figured any and all time had vanished from the known universe.

The kisses and touching didn't stop when she tackled his boots and belt. But they slowed just a little, and there was a naughty glint in her eye when she tongue-kissed his erection through the front of his jeans. Breath, mouth and heat. On his dick. A combination that caused him to snap.

Time returned to his universe but only because Cal decided he needed to break some speed records to get them both naked. Charlotte didn't help with that. She kept smiling, kept trying to torture him while Cal grappled to rid her of her top. No finesse whatsoever, but he hoped the prowess was there when he managed to pull her away from his dick and he took her right nipple into his mouth. It certainly caused her to moan in pleasure.

She moaned again when he slid his hand into her jeans, then her panties.

Cal savored the sound. Savored, too, that look on

her face as he touched her. It was a look he wanted to press into his memory so he could always hold on to it.

It didn't last, though, because touching like that was no doubt torture for her, too, and like him, she intended for them to finish off each other with the use of that condom. That meant more clothing coming off. Jeans and underwear. And the removal probably would have been much faster had they both not continued to grope and kiss. By the time they were naked, there was an extreme urgency—emphasis on *extreme*—for them to get down to business.

Cal managed to get the condom on, and there was a little more maneuvering and handling before Charlotte flipped him onto his back and straddled him. He suddenly became very aware of something.

This was the best idea ever.

No competition whatsoever.

The bright light streaming in from the windows and the position gave him an unobstructed view of her amazing, naked body. All of it. And all of her was amazing. Especially when she took him inside her.

Yeah, that was memorable, all right.

Memorable and so intense with pleasure that it flooded through him. He reacted on instinct. A primal urge to take and claim. But Charlotte must have been trying to sate those same urges because she moved into that equally primal rhythm that he knew would build the heat. Until it was hotter and hotter.

It did.

Until the thrusts were faster and deeper. Until Cal was pretty sure she was close to the finish. But then she met his gaze and slowed the pace. Drawing out the pleasure. Giving them these extra moments.

Of course, the slow pace only kicked up the pace of the taking and claiming, and even though Cal wanted to hang on and on, that didn't happen. Charlotte began to move fast again, and he watched her face as the climax pulsed through her. He'd store that image away, too. That was the last thought he had before Charlotte got back to the movements that finished him.

CHARLOTTE LAY IN Cal's bed while he was in the bathroom. Her body was still humming from the climax. It was a sweet fluttering sensation that perhaps was akin to a really good sugar high.

But she dismissed that.

Nope, no sugar high could come close to matching this.

She'd come here to Saddlebrook in the worst of moods, and while she knew she'd have to deal with what had caused that mood—her mother—she welcomed this short reprieve. Her body certainly welcomed it, too, because Cal had indeed managed to cool some of the fire. It would return, of course, but for now the humming and flutters were enough.

Charlotte amended that notion when a stark-naked Cal came out of the bathroom. He grinned at her and then joined her back on the bed, where he kissed her. She kissed him back and smiled when his mouth was still against hers.

"We failed," she muttered.

He practically snapped back from her, clearly questioning how sex had been a failure when it'd been so darn good.

"It lasted more in the range of twenty-five minutes, not twenty," Charlotte explained.

He laughed, and mercy, it was good to hear it. Good to see his face when he was happy—and perhaps experiencing some fluttering, too. She wanted to hang on to this moment. Just this. When there were no dream-job offers on the table, where any thoughts of Izzie and Paul were firmly on the back burner and where everything was right with the world.

Charlotte wasn't sure how much time passed, perhaps less than thirty seconds, when the hanging-on vanished. Cal's phone rang, and because he'd also apparently set it on Vibrate, the pocket of his jeans started to jitter around.

He cursed, and she could tell he was considering letting it go to voicemail, but then something occurred to her. "If Paul showed up, Mandy might be calling."

That sent Cal scrambling off the bed so he could snatch up his phone. He froze when he looked at the screen, and that sent her scrambling. Oh, no. Something bad had happened.

"It's not Mandy," he said. "It's, uh, Rowan." Another ring, more buzzing. "After his last call, I added his name to my contacts," he said quietly.

She was about to tell him to answer it, but Cal did it without her prompt. After he took a deep breath, that is.

"Rowan," he greeted. "Sorry that I missed your last call."

Charlotte could hear the faint murmur of Rowan's voice, but she couldn't make out what he was saying.

Whatever it was caused a serious mix of emotions of Cal's face. Happiness. Then not. Then something else she couldn't identify.

Cal cleared his throat. "I can make that happen," he said, but then paused. "I have a place in mind. Hold on a second, and let me see if it's all right." He muted his phone and looked at her. "Rowan's in Texas and wants to drive over so we can meet."

She practically bolted off the bed, ready to do a happy dance.

"He doesn't want anyone else from the family there," Cal specified. "And he doesn't want me to tell Audrey or Dad about his visit."

Charlotte didn't have to give that any thought to know it would be a challenge for Cal. He loved his family, and this would mean keeping a huge secret from them.

"I'm going to agree to that," Cal explained. "But I'd like to have the meeting at Port in a Storm. It's sort of neutral ground."

"Of course," she said as quickly as she could. Neutral ground, yes, but she was hoping she could also be there in case Cal ended up needing a shoulder after finally coming face-to-face with his half brother.

Cal took another breath and unmuted his phone. "I'll text you the address. It's not Saddlebrook," he was quick to add to Rowan. "It's a place for veterans, but there are rooms we can use to meet." Rowan responded, and Cal followed it up with, "See you then."

He ended the call but just stood there staring at his phone for a couple of seconds before he composed the text that was no doubt the address he'd promised Rowan.

"Uh, I need to shower and get dressed," Cal said. He checked the time. "Like, right now," he added.

"Right now?" she repeated, gathering up her own clothes.

Cal nodded. "Rowan's about twenty minutes out."

CHAPTER NINETEEN

WHAT THE HELL was he doing?

That was the main thought going through Cal's head as Charlotte drove him to Port in a Storm. He could have driven himself, of course, but when Charlotte had offered, he'd taken her up on it. He'd done that to give himself some time to think and not have to focus on the road. But so far, the focus had been seriously narrow.

Basically: What the hell was he doing?

He'd agreed to meet his half brother, and that was good. Cal had wanted to meet him since he'd first learned about him. But he had never once planned on keeping such an encounter from the rest of his family. He'd agreed to it, though, and now he was grappling with the big-assed worry that he might not be able to do it. It was possible his dad, Blue or Egan would take one look at him, realize he had a secret and figure it out. Then there'd be hell to pay as to why they hadn't been included in something this monumental.

"I'm a shitty liar," Cal muttered.

"You are," Charlotte agreed as she took the turn toward Port in a Storm. "Remember that time in fifth grade when you did Noah's homework for him, and Mrs. Gafford got suspicious and asked you point-blank if you'd done it? You said *no*, but your ears lit up like a Christmas tree."

"I remember," Cal assured her, but he kept his gaze fixed on the road ahead. Not that he could see the ranch yet, but he was looking for any signs of a vehicle he didn't recognize.

When Rowan had called, he'd said he was near Emerald Creek and had given him that twenty-minute ETA. But it could be sooner than that, depending on exactly where he had been.

"Your ears are the equivalent of Pinocchio's nose," Charlotte added.

He made a sound of agreement and leaned closer to the windshield when Port in a Storm finally came into view. Cal's gaze immediately swept around. No unfamiliar vehicles, which meant he'd actually have a little time to try to settle his nerves before Rowan arrived.

Charlotte parked, but she reached for his hand before he could get out. "How on edge are you?"

"Plenty," he admitted. There was no experience for him to fall back on here. No practice in meeting his father's grown love child.

"I thought as much," she readily agreed. "I can't believe I haven't made use of your lie-detector ears before but let's play a little game to tamp down all those edges." And she launched right into it before he could refuse. "Are my eyes your favorite part of my body?"

He wanted to scowl. What he didn't want to do was lower his gaze to her breasts. But damn it, he did. It was such a guy thing. "Yes," he lied.

And his ears began to flame up. He could feel it.

Charlotte chuckled. "And do you think we could aim

for forty-five next time, or is that too long for you to last?"

He didn't chuckle, but he did smile. "Aim high." No exacerbation of the red ears because it wasn't a lie. He would indeed like to test out the waters of going forty-five minutes or longer with Charlotte. "There'd have to be lots of foreplay."

"And what exactly is your favorite foreplay?" she asked. "Is it talking?"

"My whole head will ignite in flames if I say *yes*. It's this." And he leaned over and kissed her. That was true enough. The kissing was good, but it was tied with all the other stuff.

The kiss probably would have lasted a whole lot longer and possibly got a whole lot hotter if it hadn't been for the sound of an approaching vehicle. And just like that, Cal realized Charlotte had done the impossible.

She had indeed taken the edge off.

"Thanks," he told her, and he got out, turning in the direction of the Jeep that pulled to a stop behind Charlotte's car.

For a couple of seconds, the man in the vehicle didn't move. He sat there, staring out at Cal and muttering something. Since Cal was doing the same thing, he could relate. It wasn't exactly like looking in a mirror and seeing his own face, but there were plenty of similarities. The military-cut dark brown hair. The angles of his jaw. The set of his eyes.

"You can use whatever room you like, but my suite or the downstairs library will give you the most privacy," Charlotte offered as she got out of the car.

Cal nearly asked her to stay, to wait around for at

least an introduction, but Charlotte must have decided he wanted privacy from her as well because she headed into the house.

Rowan finally stepped out. He was wearing jeans and a black T-shirt covered by an unbuttoned gray cotton shirt. When he came closer, Cal saw they were nearly identical in height. Hell. Rowan must have gotten every possible Donnelly gene available.

"Rowan Cullen," he said, extending his hand for Cal to shake. It occurred to Cal that maybe he'd done that to eliminate the possibility of a brotherly hug. Not that Cal would have attempted one. Everything about Rowan's body language said *Give me some space here*.

"Cal," he greeted back, and since standing around with his look-alike could cause some gossip, he tipped his head to the house. "Let's go inside and talk."

Rowan followed him but was quick to add, "Like I said on the phone, I can't stay long."

"I understand. Are you asking yourself what the hell you're doing here?" Cal asked to try to break the ice a bit.

"Yeah," Rowan verified. Things remained awkward as he didn't add anything else until they were on the porch. "You said this place was for veterans?"

Cal nodded, opened the front door and led him down the hall toward what he hoped was the library. There were so many rooms in the house that he wasn't sure which one that was. "Charlotte Wilson, the founder, calls it a Care B and B."

"Charlotte," he repeated. "She's the woman who was in the car with you when I drove up?"

"Yes." He considered adding to that response with

something about her. But what? Girlfriend? Lover? A childhood friend who'd become a whole lot more? A partner in a complicated relationship with scalding-hot sex?

Cal opted for skipping any embellishments.

Thankfully, he'd been right about the room, and either it'd been preset for visitors or Charlotte had quickly put a tray containing bottles of water and a bowl of mixed nuts on the table nestled between two comfortable-looking chairs. Rowan took one of the chairs. Took one of the bottles, too, and he gulped down some as if his throat had turned to dust. Cal could relate.

"FYI, as you probably figured out, I got your phone number from the genealogy site," Rowan explained.

Cal nodded. "My brother Blue and I both added our numbers because we hoped you'd call at least one of us."

"Yeah, I picked yours because I'd heard your brother had had some medical problems. An injury."

Cal made a sound of agreement. "From a crash landing. But he's recovering." And Blue would have been damn glad to hear from Rowan. Anyone in his family would have wanted that.

"How much do you know about me?" Rowan asked. "Because I'm guessing that General Donnelly or your father did some kind of background check on me once they had my name." Not *Mom* and *Dad* or even *my birth parents*.

Cal remembered his ears, though he hadn't been planning on fudging this particular truth. "My dad did," he admitted as he took the chair across from Rowan. "Audrey did, too, but they didn't share much of the info with my brothers, sister or me."

"Your choice or theirs?" Rowan asked, but then he waved that off. "Doesn't matter. I did minimal background checks on all of you, and I realized your and my paths have crossed."

Cal had to shake his head. "I think I would have remembered your face."

"We were in gas masks. One of those NATO wargames exercises at a base in England about two years ago. You were there for an air show, and I was passing through."

Passing through. Vague wording.

"I've seen your sister a time or two," Rowan went on. He folded back the right side of his shirt so that Cal could see the special ops emblem there. An emblem he instantly recognized.

"You're an STO," Cal said, "and they often work with the CROs." This was one of those weird small-world situations.

Rowan nodded, drank more water. "I transferred from the Navy to the Air Force about three years ago. And don't read anything into that, like me sensing this genetic connection between General Donnelly and the rest of you. I had an opportunity for what I saw was a dream job, and I took it."

Cal nodded, too. "I know a little about offers of dream jobs." He paused. "If Remi ever recalled seeing you, I think she would have mentioned it to me."

"She wouldn't have known who I was, and I wish I could keep it that way. Since she knows my name, that's not possible, but I figured I could come here, meet with one of you and do some damage control."

Rowan hadn't said *one of you* with any kind of

venom, but certainly there hadn't been any affection in it.

"My parents never told me I was adopted," Rowan shared. "And they don't know I found out through that DNA test." Now there was a tinge of venom, and Cal figured he regretted ever taking that test. "They're not in the best of health, and I don't want to do anything to upset them. My job is already more than enough worry for them to handle."

Another similarity. "I understand. My dad had two heart attacks last year."

If Cal hadn't been watching Rowan so closely, he might have missed the reaction. It was a barely there flinch from surprise. So he hadn't known. Then again, that wasn't something they'd plastered all over social media. Cal volunteered another revelation.

"My dad and Audrey are separated, and that's adding some stress as well."

Rowan kept his gaze on Cal. "Separated because of me?"

Again, the ears could play into this. "Yes. My dad, uh, well, he's having a hard time forgiving her. I think she's having a hard time forgiving herself. Not always easy to figure out that stuff with Audrey." He left it at that, and Rowan didn't push for more info on the woman who'd given birth to him.

"Like I said, I don't want you to tell them about this meeting," Rowan went on. "Maybe down the road..." He stopped, shook his head. "I'm not sure if I can give any of you anything. It would feel as if I was betraying my parents. They love me, they've sacrificed for me, and I can't do anything that would make them feel less than my parents."

On the surface this didn't seem like yet another similarity, but it was. "My mom died when I was six," Cal said, "and my dad married Audrey four years later. I don't call her *Mom* and I've never thought of her that way. So trust me when I say I get it." He stopped, sighed. "I won't tell Audrey or my family about the meeting, but just know that won't be easy for me."

"I understand," Rowan was quick to say. "After all, I'm not telling my folks about this, either. Since you fly F-22s, you've got a Top Secret clearance, so you're obviously good at keeping things to yourself. And it'll probably be easier to do that when your leave is up and you go back to the base. When do you leave?"

Cal groaned and was about to give Rowan a thumbnail of his dilemma. Burnout versus dream job. Charlotte versus everything else. But the sound cut off anything he'd been about to say. Not a shriek for one of those stupid dolls. This was a shout, and Cal instantly recognized the shouter.

Paul.

"You're being brainwashed, and you're too stupid to see it," Paul yelled. "You're coming home with me now."

Cal immediately got to his feet and hurried to the library door. Rowan was right behind him, and they stepped out into the hall to see a cluster of people. Paul, of course. Harper in her wheelchair, Alden, Charlotte and even Maybell, who was holding a wooden rolling pin as if it were a weapon.

Paul had latched on to Harper's arm, and Alden was trying to maneuver both Harper and her wheelchair away from Paul's reach. Charlotte was trying to squeeze herself between Paul and Harper, which meant it was one very congested tangle.

"What's going on?" Cal asked, his question cutting through another tirade Paul had started.

Paul whirled in Cal's direction, and his initial stance was one prepped for a fight. Shoulders back, face tensed, fists clenched. The man seemed to back down a notch or two, though, when he saw Rowan. Maybe because he saw the resemblance to Cal or perhaps because Paul hadn't counted on taking on two able-bodied men in this particular fight. Judging from Maybell's, Charlotte's and Alden's expressions, though, they were more than ready to have it out with this asshole.

Cal didn't take down his own fighting stance even a smidge. In fact, he amped it up and walked closer to Paul. "Do you remember what I said to you?" He didn't wait for Paul to answer. "I said if you did anything else to harm Harper, I'd make you pay. Well, this looks to me like you're trying to do harm."

Harper made a sound like a breathy gasp, and her eyes were wide and pleading when she looked at Cal. Maybe she was asking him to back down, to not make this worse, but he couldn't let Paul get away with this.

"Let go of her," Cal demanded.

Paul did, yanking back his hand as if he'd just been scalded. But he did that while he kept his defiant glare on Cal. The thick silence hung in the air, and Paul must have realized this wasn't a fight he could win. Well, not against anyone but Harper.

He looked down at his daughter, his mouth tightened in a sneer. "I just wanted to talk to you, that's all. You owe me that."

Paul didn't spell out what he meant, but Cal figured the man was playing the I've-always-been-there-for-you card. It was the truth, in a sick kind of way, and Cal hoped Harper didn't fall for it.

But she did.

"We can talk in my room," Harper said using her computer to talk. She dodged everyone's gaze but Cal's. "It'll be fine. I want to talk to him."

Cal stepped closer to challenge that, but Harper met his stare head-on. "I want to talk to him," she rasped out with her own voice.

He still thought Harper was doing this to avoid a fight, but Cal didn't stop her when she wheeled away with a triumphant-looking Paul trailing her.

"I'll wait outside her door," Alden was quick to volunteer, already heading in that direction, "and I'll give a shout if there's any sign of trouble."

Cal nodded, muttered a thanks and was still trying to decide how he should feel about this. *Worried*, he decided, and he turned to Rowan.

"Sorry about that," Cal said, and he was about to expand that apology to tell Rowan that he needed to be the one who kept an ear out for any issues.

"It's okay," Rowan was quick to say. "I should be going, anyway. Thanks for seeing me on such short notice."

It was a polite, distant thing to say, and it in no way conveyed the emotional visit they'd just had. But Rowan's gaze skirted over Charlotte and Maybell, who was still holding the lethal-looking roller. Charlotte smiled, Maybell didn't. Her mouth had dropped open in surprise, and she no doubt had figured out who this was.

Neither Cal nor Rowan acknowledged the recognition in the woman's eyes. Just the opposite. Rowan turned to leave at the exact moment that someone came through the still-open front door.

His father.

Cal wasn't sure who was more surprised by the visit, but he thought he was actually the winner here. His father rarely went anywhere these days, and this was his first visit to Port in a Storm. Added to that, Derek seemed to look like a man on a mission, and his attention immediately zoomed in on Rowan. His dad sighed, a sound that was a thick mix of emotions.

"It's true," his dad said, keeping his attention pinned to Rowan.

Rowan was sending off his own mixture-of-emotions vibe. No sigh for him. A groan, followed by some profanity under his breath. He looked at Cal, the question clear in his eyes.

"I didn't tell him you were here," Cal assured him.

"He didn't," his dad verified, coming closer. "One of the ranch hands called me. He said he was driving home, and he saw somebody in a Jeep that had to be my kin since he looked so much like my boys. He said he was headed in this direction."

Rowan muttered more profanity, and he was no doubt wishing he'd steered way clear of Emerald Creek. Maybe he hadn't realized the resemblance he had to the Donnellys, who were well-known in these parts.

"You didn't let me know Rowan was coming," his dad said to him.

"I asked him not to," Rowan answered before Cal could respond. "In fact, I wouldn't have come if Cal hadn't agreed to keep this meeting from you and anyone else in your family."

A muscle tightened in his dad's jaw. "I understand."

"Uh, I think I'll stand watch with Alden," Charlotte said, obviously to give them some privacy. Cal wasn't sure it was needed, though. It seemed to him that Rowan was gearing up for as fast an exit as possible. "And Maybell will help," she added when the woman didn't budge.

"Derek didn't know about you," Maybell insisted, holding her ground and finally lowering that blasted rolling pin. "So he's not to blame for what happened to you."

Like his earlier profanity, Rowan's huff was barely audible, but it was there, all right. "What happened to me was I had, and still have, a very good life with great parents who love me."

That obviously caused Maybell to throttle back on some of her defensiveness. "Well, good," she murmured, and she turned to walk toward Harper's room. At least if Paul did anything reckless, there'd be plenty of witnesses.

Rowan shifted his attention back to Derek. "And I wouldn't trade the life or the parents I have for anything. *Anything*," he emphasized.

His father nodded, and Cal's heart broke for him. Cal could practically see the hope draining from his dad's eyes.

"If..." Derek started, but then he stopped and shook his head again. "Will Cal hear from you again?"

"No," Rowan was quick to say, but then he was the one who stopped and did some headshaking. "Probably not," he amended. He paused again. "Look, I don't know what went on between General Donnelly and you thirty-plus years ago, and I don't want to know. That's not meant to hurt you. It's just the way I need this to be."

"Of course," Derek muttered, and while Cal was still very concerned about how all this would affect his dad's health, there did seem to be a sliver of hope back in his expression.

If Rowan saw that hope, too, he didn't comment on it. He simply said goodbye and headed out. Both Cal and his dad turned to watch him leave, and they stood there in silence until Rowan's Jeep was out of sight.

Hell.

Cal really hoped this meeting hadn't been a huge mistake.

CHAPTER TWENTY

CHARLOTTE COULDN'T IMAGINE this ever feeling routine. Or anything other than simply amazing. Waking up in bed with Cal. Naked. And still sated and revving from the sex they'd had the night before.

This time hadn't been in a frantic hurry, and it hadn't started off as a need to comfort. There'd just been the need.

And a private place.

That had turned out to be her bed where they had ended up after the long, grueling day. A day that had been filled with emotion and upheaval, what with the ruckus Paul had caused and with Rowan's visit. Charlotte figured they hadn't seen the last of Paul, but she couldn't say that of Rowan. Cal's half brother hadn't left a very big gap in the proverbial door for any future visits.

Hence the emotion and upheaval.

That was probably twofold for Derek, and Cal had to be worried about the effect this would have on the man's health. So maybe the sex had been a little about comforting after all. If so, then she was glad Cal come to her because the comfort and sex had brought her here to this moment.

Naked, cuddling, satisfied. In a wonderful room in

an equally wonderful house that was quiet and settled. The morning breeze was even helping with the ambience. She'd opened the window the night before, and now the breeze was stirring the white gauzy curtains, shifting just a little to let slivers of sunlight slide in.

Definitely satisfying.

She tried to block out any unsatisfied thoughts that were pressing their way into her head, and while she was winning that particular battle for now, it wouldn't last. There were just way too many things up in the air for that. But now she blocked them out by snuggling even closer to Cal.

Charlotte aligned her body so it created the ultimate spooning with her back against his chest. Her butt against what felt to be the early stages of an erection.

"If you keep pressing against me like that," he muttered, "we'll need another condom."

Since there were several condoms in her nightstand, Charlotte smiled and kept wiggling. Cal didn't take the teasing torture for long. He slipped his arm around her, flipping her around to face him.

And he kissed her.

No, this would never, ever get old or feel routine. Cal always seemed to make each kiss feel as if it were that magical first time, but since her body knew what was to follow—a whole lot more pleasure—it instantly revved up.

Then instantly wound down when Cal's phone dinged. It wasn't the usual sound of a text, but it still made him groan and curse.

"It's a reminder on my calendar," he explained. "I'm supposed to call my commander this morning."

Well, that certainly didn't result in any sexual revving. But it did create a whole lot of questions, or rather one question, anyway. Why?

"Oh, is everything okay?" she asked.

He rolled over, located his phone and tapped something, no doubt so that it wouldn't ping again with a repeat notification. "Yes," he said. But then he paused. "I got an email from him yesterday, and he was asking about the job that Audrey offered me. He wants to know if I'm going to take it, or if I will be back from leave in five days."

Charlotte waited to see if Cal was going to add anything to that. He did after another long pause.

"I'm not sure what I'm going to say to him," Cal admitted. "That's why I didn't call him back yesterday right after I got his email. But I can't put off talking to him any longer, so I marked my calendar to call him at 0800."

She checked the time on the clock on the desk and saw that it was seven o'clock. So one hour from now. Of course, Cal likely intended to use an hour to shower, get dressed and go back to Saddlebrook, where he would be making that call. He didn't budge, though. He lay there, staring up at the ceiling.

"I'll need to carve out some time today to have a talk with my dad," he added a moment later. "I'm worried about him."

So was she. Charlotte couldn't imagine the shock of walking in and seeing your own grown son for the first time.

"Do you think your dad will tell Audrey or your siblings about Rowan's visit?" she asked.

"Not Audrey," he was quick to say. "He still hasn't

been able to forgive her, so he likely won't share any of it with her. But he might not be able to stop himself from spilling to Egan or Blue. I almost hope he does, and that way I won't have to keep the secret." He groaned softly. "It doesn't feel right to keep it from them."

"No," she agreed. "It wouldn't feel right. Maybe Rowan will relent and change his mind." However that it seem like a long shot after everything that Rowan had said.

Cal quit staring at the ceiling and turned to look at her and slid his gaze to her breasts. He smiled in a way that let her know he didn't think this would ever be routine or ordinary, either. This was something amazing that should be savored.

She hoped that savoring would require another condom. That's why she moved closer, taking his mouth in a long, deep kiss, a kiss that would've lasted a whole lot longer if her phone hadn't dinged. Her notification was for an actual text. Charlotte cursed when she saw it was from her mother. She cursed even more when she read the actual message.

"'I need to see you. It's important,'" Charlotte read aloud. "'I'm downstairs waiting, but I didn't want to just come up since Cal's truck is outside, and I figured he was with you.'"

Cal winced. "Sorry. I should have parked up the road and sneaked back here."

"No need," she assured him. "There's probably not one person within a one-mile radius who doesn't know we've been hooking up."

He looked at her again, his gaze locking with hers, and he seemed to be silently questioning the "hooking up" reference. Maybe he wondered if that was how she thought of them.

She didn't.

Charlotte didn't like to lie to herself, so she could admit with way too much certainty that she had fallen head over heels in love with Cal. So, in love *while* hooking up, which was probably what most people in love did. But since Cal wasn't in love with her, then she was going to keep that particular revelation to herself.

He finally tore his gaze from hers and got up to collect his clothes. That was always a task since the clothing items were always scattered. So perhaps there'd been some franticness to the night before after all.

Charlotte got up and dressed as well, and she considered a shower but nixed the idea. She'd do that after her mother left. And that brought her to the text itself. She'd been so annoyed with the interruption that she hadn't considered the actual content. This had better not be a visit to whine about poll rankings and such.

Cal kissed her after he finished dressing. "I'll call you later. Maybe we can go out to lunch or something. I mean, since everyone in a one-mile radius already knows what we're doing."

She smiled and returned the kiss. "I'd like that." In fact, she'd like anything that meant spending time with Cal.

Charlotte tried not to look all dreamy-eyed and in love when she said goodbye to him. Those kinds of reactions wouldn't send him ducking and running for cover. No, Cal would face any and everything head-on. But she certainly didn't want to add to his worries, and he would indeed have some of those. Especially if he ended up taking that job.

Since that particular thought ramped up her own worries, Charlotte went ahead and sent a response to her mother that it was all right for her to come up. She did. In fact, Izzie knocked on the door less than thirty seconds later, which told Charlotte she likely hadn't been waiting in the foyer but rather somewhere near her bedroom.

Charlotte opened the door, wondering if she was going to see a fretting, frazzled Izzie, the way she had been her last visit, or if her mom had gone back to her old self. On the surface, it was the old self with a perfectly tailored aquamarine-colored dress and heels, and every strand of hair in place. But Izzie certainly wasn't exuding her usual air of confidence and authority.

"I figure I'm the last person on earth you want to see," Izzie said in lieu of a greeting.

"No, there are a few people ahead of you," Charlotte remarked. Of course, she'd intended that to sound snarky, and it was, but then she instantly regretted it. She didn't want to snipe and snarl with her mother. With anyone for that matter, even the people ahead of Izzie on that list.

Her mother looked stumped for a couple of seconds. "Good. Well, I guess it's good." She was holding a folded piece of paper, and she thrust it out for Charlotte.

Charlotte opened it and saw the numbers written there. "What is this?" she asked.

"It's your father's phone number," Izzie answered without hesitation.

Charlotte certainly did some hesitating, along with nearly staggering back a step. She definitely hadn't seen this coming.

"I haven't personally tried to call it to see if he'll answer," Izzie went on, "but I have the assurance from a reputable PI that it's his correct phone number. Apparently, he's goes by the A. A. Wilson these days, and he's a financial adviser in Phoenix."

Charlotte shook her head to try to clear it. Nope, that didn't work, either. "What happened to Harper's mother?" No need for her to remind Izzie that he'd left town with her.

"Oh, they divorced about a year later. I wish I could say I felt sad about that, that he'd thrown away so much, only to have a year with the other woman." She put those last two words in quotes. "But I'll admit, I laughed like a loon. Twenty years isn't nearly long enough to let go of all the ill will that I feel for those two."

It seemed Paul felt the same way, but Charlotte... well, she wasn't sure what she felt. For those same twenty years, she'd thought her father's leaving was because of her, and look how that'd turned out.

Yes, look.

And she studied her mother now with what she was certain was some suspicion. "A PI?" Charlotte questioned, and she held up the number. "When exactly did you get this?"

Izzie's mouth tightened a little. "About four months ago when Taggert and I started dating. I just kept having this nightmare about your father showing up at Taggert's and my wedding. Not to try to win me back but to warn Taggert that he was marrying a cold, heartless bitch and that he should end things with me and run."

That caused Charlotte to sigh, and while she wouldn't put that particularly ugly label on her mom, Izzie could be demanding and self-centered. And could also with-hold critical info.

"Four months?" Charlotte prompted. "Did it occur to you to tell me?"

"Well, of course it did." Izzie groaned softly and squeezed her eyes shut a moment. "Of course it did," she repeated in a much calmer voice. "Around the time of the PI report, your father had just married wife number four—who's your age, by the way—and according to one of his social-media posts, he said he was very excited at the prospect of becoming a father."

The surprise of that came out like a huff of air from Charlotte's throat.

Izzie scowled. "I'm assuming he wasn't talking about being a father to his new bride because of their age difference. Sorry about the sarcasm," she added in a grumble. "Anyway, the *becoming* got to me since he was already a father and wasn't acknowledging it. Actually, it pissed me off, and I thought it'd just end up hurting you. That *he* would end up hurting you."

Charlotte tamped down some of the surprise from hearing all of this and stared at her mother. And stared. Because she was pretty sure Izzie was leaving some-thing out.

She was.

This time, Izzie scowled and huffed. "All right, that's true about me not wanting him to hurt you, but I also didn't want him back in my life. If he was to come back even for a visit, it would stir up the gossip. I'd be the center of Poor Pitiful Izzie talk. I'd be the wronged woman again and not just your mother, not just the mayor. I'd rather there be talk about my lousy poll numbers or, heck, even Taggert breaking up with me than the pity over my cheating ex-husband."

Charlotte didn't doubt a word of that. Her mother had been both selfish and selfless.

Some sadness crept into Izzie's eyes. "Things will never be the same between us, will it?" she said.

Charlotte considered her answer. "No. But maybe that's a good thing. We're on equal footing now. You can't play the dad guilt card anymore, and I…well, I don't have to feel pressure for anything fairy-tale."

Izzie stayed quiet, her gaze fixed to Charlotte's. "You're in love with Cal."

Crap.

Charlotte tried to deny it, but she only managed a splutter of sounds.

Izzie smiled. "Don't worry. Most people won't notice, but I know every inch of your face. I see it. You're in love with him. Does he know?" She paused a heartbeat. "No," she supplied while Charlotte just continued to hem and haw. "Oh, well. You should probably tell him."

No way. Charlotte didn't need actual words to convey that, either. She just gave her mother a flat stare that warned her that she'd better not be telling Cal herself.

Izzie smiled again, the touch of sadness sliding from her eyes. "Oh, well," she repeated. "You know best when it comes to Cal and you." She glanced at the note Charlotte was still holding. "Are you going to call your father?" Izzie asked.

Charlotte glanced at it, too. "Has he tried to call me in the past twenty years?"

Izzie's smile vanished. "No. And I'm sorry about that. As much as I despise him for walking out on me,

I despise him even more for walking out on you." With that, Izzie brushed a quick kiss on Charlotte's cheek and left.

Charlotte stood there, her thoughts freezing her in place. But not freezing in her head. She thought of her father. Of the sixteen years he'd been in her life. Of the day he'd packed a single suitcase and walked out, leaving most of his life and all of his immediate family behind.

At first, it was hard for Charlotte to filter those memories of a kid and teenager through her now-adult mind. He hadn't been a bad father like Paul. No bullying or abuse. However, he also hadn't been a present father, either. There'd been lots of business trips. Lots of late nights at work. And also lots of arguments with Izzie, and in some of those shouting matches, Izzie had accused him of cheating. Considering that he'd left because of another woman, that had probably been the case.

She tore up the paper with the number, but not in a hurt, tear-filled rage. She let the pieces fall into the trash can like confetti.

Charlotte smiled.

It wasn't every day that a woman could rid herself of some emotional baggage, but today looked to be her day.

CAL STOPPED AT the bottom of the stairs on the first floor and considered going right back up to Charlotte's room. Izzie wasn't Paul, but Cal was still concerned that Izzie's visit would upset Charlotte. She might need to vent to him after Izzie had delivered whatever news she'd come to deliver. So he lingered despite the fact the minutes were ticking away, and the countdown was coming fast for the call that he needed to make to his commander.

Of course, that call could happen anywhere, including his truck since it wouldn't be FaceTime, but Cal had figured if he was showered and not wearing yesterday's clothes, then he'd have a better mindset. Something he would need since he wasn't sure what he was going to say to his boss, but Cal was hoping the right frame of mind would lead to the right words.

He turned when he heard the whirring sound of a wheelchair and spotted Harper. She'd come from the direction of the kitchen, and judging from the immediate dread on her face, she hadn't expected or wanted to see him. Still, that didn't stop her from moving toward him instead of hightailing it to her room.

"How'd your visit go with your dad?" he asked right off, figuring that topic was causing some of the dread on Harper's face. Cal figured Harper would never look at him and not feel at least some of those overwhelming emotions that had caused her downward spiral.

"It went…" she said aloud. "It went," she finished. Which was probably about the best she could say for a meeting with Paul. "So was that guy a long-lost brother or something?" she asked, using the computer this time.

Cal figured there was now some unease in his expression as well. "Or something," he settled on.

She rolled her eyes. "A brother," Harper communicated through the computer. "He looks just as shiny as the rest of you Donnellys."

"Shiny?" Cal said. "Is that a compliment or an insult?"

She shrugged, and even though most people would have seen that as noncommittal, Cal looked at it as progress. Harper hadn't lashed out at him in her usual way.

"So did Charlotte tell you about the tree limb at the creek?" Harper's digital voice asked.

Cal was sure he looked confused. "Uh, no. What about it?"

Harper looked him straight in the eye while she typed. "I knew the limb was about to break, and I let you go up on it anyway."

He stared at her and realized this was truly bothering her. "I knew it was cracked, too," he said. "I heard it when you were up there."

Now she was the one to look confused. "And you went up anyway?" she asked, her own voice raspy but still conveying her shock.

"I was a kid and thought I was invincible. I figured it'd hold just one more time while I finished my turn. Obviously, I was wrong."

"Obviously," she repeated, and it had some of her snark to it. "It was a stupid thing to do."

"Hey, a kid," he emphasized, and then paused. "Have you been worrying about this all these years?"

She pulled back her shoulders, and it seemed to be an automatic defensive response. "Well, yes," she admitted. "I thought I'd set up an attempted murder because I was so jealous of you."

Shit. She was serious. "And you held on to it all this time," he muttered. "I'm sorry."

"You should be," she snapped, again in her own voice. She stared at him. "You really knew about the limb? You were really that stupid?"

"Yes, yes," he said, answering both questions. "Of course, if I'd known I was going to fall and hit my head, I would have rethought my decision. That life-pact with Noah has been a piss-off over the years."

Harper made a sound of agreement, with little snark, and that was enough to prompt him to try to go a little deeper with this conversation. Especially since he wasn't hearing any shouting coming from Charlotte's room.

"You want to talk about your dad?" Cal risked asking.

"No," she was quick to type out. "But I do want to talk to you about the job Audrey arranged for you."

Cal groaned and braced himself for some classic Harper attitude…which didn't happen.

"You should take it," Harper typed. "And, no, I'm not saying that because I want you gone." She switched to her own voice. "I'm saying it because if you win at it, then your winning could help people."

There it was. The best argument he'd gotten so far for accepting the job. It didn't give him an *aha!* moment, it just filled him with more dread over the decision he had to make.

It seemed almost selfish to turn it down, but it felt reckless to accept it. Like climbing onto a cracked limb and assuming it wouldn't fall. Because despite the progress Harper was making, she was still plenty broken.

And so was he.

But was he broken enough that he couldn't ever go back to the cockpit?

With that dismal thought racing through his head, he glanced one last time up the stairs. No Izzie or Charlotte appeared, so after he talked to his commander, he'd call Charlotte to make sure she was okay. He said a goodbye to Harper and headed out, hoping the short drive home would steady him some. It worked.

Until he saw the woman getting out of an SUV in front of the house.

Audrey.

Judging from the way her gaze went straight to his, she'd been waiting for him. She was in uniform and checked the time, which meant she was either annoyed that he hadn't been there when she arrived or else she was anxious to say whatever she'd come to say and leave. He didn't have to guess what the subject would be, and it was still plenty fresh because of the conversation he'd just had with Harper.

"I haven't made up my mind yet," Cal immediately said.

Audrey's expression was already tight, and that seemed to annoy her even more. "Too bad, because time is running out."

"Yeah, my leave is up in five days," he said, and motioned for her to follow him inside, but she stayed put.

"It's more than that. Now that I created the job, people are anxious for it to be filled. If not by you, then someone else. Major Jack Colby's name has been bandied about."

"A good choice," Cal said, and that caused even more tightening in Audrey's face.

"No, you're the good choice," she snapped. "I didn't go to all the work and trouble to create the job for him but for you."

He nodded. "I know, and I'm sorry I can't just jump

on it and accept. And I'm sorry you came all the way out here to get an answer I can't give you yet."

"I didn't come here just for that," Audrey informed him, that general's snap still in her voice. But her expression changed. Not so much annoyed-general but something else. "You met with Rowan," she threw out there. Not a question but a statement of fact. She clearly wasn't happy about that fact, either.

Cal didn't confirm the meeting, which was probably why she huffed.

"There are still people in this town who keep in touch with me. Gossip gets around." She glanced up at the second-floor window. His dad wasn't up there watching, but if Audrey had been parked out front for long, he had almost certainly gotten word of her arrival. "Did Derek see Rowan, too? Did you two go behind my back—"

"No." Cal cut off what seemed to be the beginning of a tirade. "No," he repeated to level out his tone of voice. "Rowan called and arranged the visit, but it was to tell me he doesn't want to be involved with any of us. Dad just happened to walk in as Rowan was leaving."

She studied his eyes as if checking to see if he was lying about any of that, and then she huffed. "Did Rowan ask about me?"

"No, but then he didn't really ask about any of us. He's got his own life, Audrey," Cal said, purposely using her given name. "And he doesn't want us to be part of that."

Audrey nodded. Swallowed hard. Then she closed her eyes a moment as if trying to block out whatever emotions were hitting her hard at the moment.

"All right," she said several moments later. She muttered those same two words under her breath and was making a visible effort to steady herself. "How did Derek handle seeing Rowan? Is he okay?"

Cal considered his answer and figured there was nothing he could say that was going to make this better. "It was a shock, of course. And painful. Just as it is for you. I believe it was painful for Rowan, too."

She nodded, paused again. "Did he seem happy?"

Now, this might make things better. "Yes." Cal was pretty sure it was true, so he left it at that.

Thankfully, that seemed to ease some of Audrey's tension, and she glanced back up at the window again. "No need for you to tell your dad about this conversation," she said. "He's got enough on his mind without adding anything about me to the mix. If he asks why I was here, you can just say it was because I was pressuring you to take the job. Which I am," she tacked on.

She was in the general mode again and already reaching for the door handle of the rental SUV. "I just hope the pressure works," she added.

"As you pointed out, someone else could do the job," Cal reminded her.

"Yes, but not as well as you could, and you know it." Audrey patted his arm, opened the door and got behind the wheel. "You're needed, Cal. Needed there more than here."

With that, she drove away with her words echoing in Cal's head. Echoing so loud that he actually listened.

CHAPTER TWENTY-ONE

HARPER WANTED TO turn her wheelchair around and go in the opposite direction when she spotted Charlotte coming her way on the trail. Avoiding people was her default and so much easier than dealing with them. Still, Charlotte was smiling and waving, and that meant she likely hadn't tracked her down for a lecture or a dumb-assed pep talk.

Plus, the trail was still too narrow here for a turn-around.

It was easier to be civil when there weren't many other options.

"I'm glad you're using the trail," Charlotte said. "How are you this morning?"

"Clearly, not as perky as you." And Harper might have had the computer add something about the perkiness being because Cal had stayed the night, but Charlotte beat her to it.

"Cal," Charlotte provided. "He's better than morning coffee."

Harper settled for a grunt and typed out, "Does your mother feel that way?"

Charlotte laughed. "Probably not. Izzie would prefer I provoke less gossip." She paused, and Harper figured saying that had taken a poke at a bad thought.

Like the thought that she might not have that "better than coffee" man around for long.

"Izzie was here earlier," Charlotte continued a moment later, and that caused Harper to rethink her conclusion about the reason Charlotte had paused. "She had a PI track down my father, and she gave me his phone number. The PI also found out he'd divorced your mother about a year after they left."

So that's what this visit was about.

"I'm not sure if your mother's still in the Phoenix area, but I thought you might want to know," Charlotte added.

"I already knew," Harper spoke aloud, causing the surprise to flash in Charlotte's eyes. Harper shrugged and went back to the computer. Using the keyboard seemed to remove some of the emotion of what she was saying. "I hired a PI years ago, shortly after I went into the Air Force. He found her, and I went to see her."

Charlotte's surprise went up a notch. "Uh, how did that go?"

Harper wished she'd prepped a snarky *Who the hell cares about my mother?* response, but with no prep, she went with the truth. "Badly." She voiced that but typed the rest. "She was quick to say I always took my dad's side and never hers. That I made her feel as if I was his daughter and not hers. Basically, she blamed me for cheating on her husband and walking out."

"What?" Charlotte blurted.

"Don't worry," Harper voiced, cutting off what would have almost certainly been Charlotte's *No way* protest. "It was bullshit." And because, hey, emotion, she went back to the keyboard to finish. "She was a weak woman, and by then your dad had long dumped her, so she was looking for someone else to blame."

"I'm sorry," Charlotte managed to interject before Harper could add to her account.

Harper shrugged. "FYI, she didn't know where your dad was. If she had…" She stopped, shrugged again. "I might have gotten around to telling you. That's about when I entered the phase of buying into my dad's hype that I could be the best if I tried hard enough."

Harper instantly regretted that confession when Charlotte patted her hand, and she quickly typed out, "Don't worry. I'm fine." Then she went with an equally quick question to shift the conversation. "What are you going to do with your dad's phone number?" she typed.

"I already trashed it," Charlotte announced, smiling again. She opened her mouth to say more, but the sound of shuffling footsteps stopped her.

Oh, joy, it was Alden. That was Harper's initial snark reaction, and she wished she could hang on to it. But her reaction was plenty lukewarm. Or even worse.

Shit.

She was actually glad to see him. Great day in the morning. What was this about? Better yet, could she stomp it to smithereens? She'd certainly try.

He was poking along toward them with a walker, one with tennis balls over the nonrolling feet. He'd hooked his cane over one of the side bars, and next to that, there was a duct-taped tablet with a purple plastic case.

"Sorry," he said. "Am I interrupting anything?"

"No," Charlotte assured him. "I need to go to my office in town and meet with a client."

Harper figured that was possibly the truth, but she

also detected that gleeful glint in Charlotte's eye, so it was possible she was heading out to give her and Alden some alone time. This could be either a lousy match-making attempt or Charlotte might be giving Alden a chance to test out his counseling skills.

"This is for you," Alden said once Charlotte was gone. He removed his cane from the bar, using it for support while he inched the walker toward her. "It'll help you get upright."

She scowled. "Maybe I don't want to get upright."

"It'll be easier for people to see your scowl if you're eye to eye with them."

That was probably the only thing he could have said that would have gotten her to consider using it. She used a firm grip on her chair to hoist herself up. Not easily. She wasn't sure there were usable bones or muscles in her legs so there was a colossal amount of wobbling in-volved. To his credit, Alden didn't try to take hold of her or attempt to steady her. He just held on to the walker with his free hand so it wouldn't slide away from her when she took hold of it.

The movement caused a rush to her head, making her dizzy and her stomach churn a little. She waited until that had passed, waited a little while longer until she tested out the scowl/eye-level theory. It worked. She scowled at Alden…and then practically dropped back down into the chair.

He grinned and pulled out a plastic bag that he'd tucked inside his shirt. "Four fresh snickerdoodles," he said. "Maybell just baked them, and I managed to snag us some before the workers got to them."

Even a snarly mood wouldn't have put her off one

of Maybell's cookies, so Harper accepted the one he handed her and bit into it. Maybell never disappointed.

"Why do you take shit from your dad?" Alden asked.

The question seemingly came out of the blue, but she figured he'd been wanting to throw it at her for a while. He was probably just waiting until she was in a better mood. Or experiencing a sugar high.

It wasn't the answer he likely wanted, but clamping the cookie between her teeth, putting the other on her wheelchair arm and standing, she scowled and then dropped back down, saying, "Because I'm clearly a glutton for punishment. Or maybe just a glutton," she answered using the voice of her tablet.

Alden chuckled and chowed down on his cookie. He didn't repeat his question, didn't do the raised eyebrow or dole out even a mild "I'm waiting for a response" huff. He wasn't pressuring her.

Which was probably why Harper answered through the tablet. "Because my dad was right about what he said. He stayed, and my mom didn't. Because he wanted me enough to stay, and she didn't."

He seemed to consider that a moment. "So, what... you think you owe him just for being a parent who lived with you?"

"Don't I?" Harper countered, but she no longer felt as if that question deserved a resounding *yes*. Heck, it might not even deserve a lukewarm *maybe*. Still, she wasn't so far removed from her connection to her dad that she couldn't understand what drove him. "He can't handle anything but the best from me," the computer voiced for her.

Again, he took a moment to consider that, then another moment to finish off the first cookie. "Is this the best you can do right now?"

She finished off her cookie as well and did her own considering. "This is pretty much it," she said. "Barely able to stand and only for a couple of seconds. Barely able to speak." She used her own voice to prove her point. "And so much shame and guilt that I'm not sure I deserve anything better."

Harper hated she'd added in that last bit, especially since it'd come through her damaged throat. It sounded wounded. Crushed.

Finished.

She steeled herself for the pitying look that Alden would almost certainly dole out. But he didn't. He smiled. "Then it's your best."

Harper blinked and was instantly wary this was some kind of trick. "Did you hear the part about drowning in shame and guilt?"

"I heard," Alden confirmed, adding a shrug. "But all of that is still your best for now." He plucked out another cookie, took a bite and then handed it to her. "Remember that the next time your father shows up."

CHARLOTTE WALKED INTO her law office and froze. The creatures, aka the dolls, were on seemingly every single inch of every single desk. One of them had either fallen or been tossed into the trash can, and its creepy eyes peered out over the rim.

"Sorry," Mandy was quick to say. She came up from behind Charlotte, who was still in the doorway, and Mandy was carrying yet another armful of the blasted dolls. Charlotte hadn't noticed her car when she'd driven up so she must have parked at the side of the building.

"Why are these here?" Charlotte demanded.

"Your mom ditched the whole notion of preserving local crafts and asked me to come and get them from the storage room in town hall. They were freaking out the cleaning staff. I was going to toss them, but then Frank Merkins heard about them and said he wanted them for the haunted house he sets up at the park every Halloween. He asked me to save them for him and said he'd be by later today to get them."

Charlotte couldn't dispute that they'd make a spooky addition to a haunted house, but she hoped Frank was quick about the pickup.

"Oh, and Velma Sue Parsons was here a couple of minutes ago," Mandy went on. "She took one look at the dolls and said she might sue you for nearly giving her a heart attack."

Charlotte sighed, not at the prospect of being sued: Velma Sue was true to her middle name and often made that threat. In fact, the reason the woman was coming in for an appointment was to talk to Charlotte about suing the US Postal Service for paper cuts she got from junk mail they'd delivered.

When Velma Sue had called to make the appointment a few days ago, Charlotte had told her up front that her chances of winning such a case were nil, but that hadn't put the woman off. Apparently, though, the dolls had. It almost made her want to keep a couple around to prevent future visits from the woman.

Almost.

"Velma Sue said she'd call you to reschedule once

these *ugly things* were gone and that she'd go up the street to Carson, Elder and Carson for the lawsuit against you," Mandy continued, dumping the latest armful of dolls onto the already cramped desk. Another of them toppled into the trash, landing next to the peeking one.

Charlotte wasn't bothered in the least about Velma Sue. The dolls, however, were a different matter. Apparently, there was some soft trash beneath them because the combined weight of the pair caused them to shift, sink and jiggle. Not at a jolting pace, either, but a slow slide lower into the trash.

"Now that Velma Sue has canceled, that means you don't have another appointment for an hour," Mandy explained. "Guess you can catch up on paperwork in your office."

It'd definitely have to be the office since Charlotte didn't want to work next to the dolls.

"Or you can stand at the window and drool," Mandy added a moment later.

Charlotte turned away from the dolls to see what had prompted Mandy to say that, and yes, it seemed drooling might ensue: Cal was walking toward the office. Cal, the cowboy in his Stetson, jeans, boots and shirt that fit just fine over his amazing muscles. He had a cardboard carrying tray with three to-go cups in one hand and a clear plastic bag in the other that revealed what she was certain was a stash of doughnuts from Desi's Diner.

"I'm not sure how you can think straight when you look at him," Mandy remarked. "I mean, look at him," she said on a sigh.

Charlotte wasn't at all sure she did think straight around Cal. Probably not good, especially considering how this could all end between them, but it was hard to have coherent thoughts with all the buzzing in her head, the fluttering in her stomach and her heart skipping beats and all.

Since both of his hands were full, Charlotte opened the door for him, and all those reactions jacked up even more. That's because she had more than a visual of him. There was his scent, clearly created to stir every sexual nerve in her body. It was especially potent today since it was mixed with the smell of sugar and caffeine.

"I was at the diner and saw your car," he said.

Now she had sound to add to the visual and scent. His voice—yes, it had her hormonal number.

"Velma Sue was in the diner, too," Cal explained, "and she was going on about canceling her appointment and suing you because of the dolls, so I thought you could use these." He held up the coffee and bag of doughnuts, and he only cringed a little when he looked at the dolls. "Desi knew what you usually order, so that's what he fixed."

"A coco-mocha choo choo?" Mandy asked, reaching for the cup with her name on it. Charlotte knew it was basically a triple chocolate latte.

"Yes," Cal verified, handing off the bag of doughnuts to Mandy. "I watched Desi make it. And I thought you might need this." He gave her a spoon he'd tucked on the tray and shifted his gaze to Charlotte. "Irish breakfast tea for you."

"Thanks," she muttered, and while Cal took out his own coffee—which she knew would be black—it occurred to her that he'd brought this over to soften some bad news.

Or rather bad news for her.

After all, he'd left her bed just a couple hours earlier because of the call he needed to make to his commander. It was possible that during that chat, he'd decided to accept Audrey's job offer. If so, then yes, bad for her but good for him. Good for all those people he'd end up helping, too.

He glanced around, perhaps looking for a place to sit. Or a place for a private chat, and Charlotte tipped her head to her office. "In here."

Mandy handed off the rest of the doughnuts to her. "I'm going to finish this and head over to the bookstore to pick up something. I'll be back before our next appointment, but I can lock up so that lookie-loos wanting a peek at the dolls won't just come strolling in." She added a smile to that.

Charlotte was reasonably sure there'd be no lookie-loos and the lockup was so she and Cal would have some privacy. Which was why she agreed to Mandy's plan. Privacy was the way to go if she was about to hear her fling with Cal would soon be over. A fling where she'd fallen in love.

Dang it, this was going to be bad.

Cal and she sipped their drinks and didn't say anything until Mandy had put the Closed sign on the door and left, doing the promised lockup.

"How'd your visit go with your mom?" he asked in the same moment she asked, "How'd your call go with your commander?"

So they apparently had more than one topic to discuss, and he motioned for her to go first. Charlotte put it in a nutshell since she was far more interested in what Cal had to say.

"My mother located my dad in Phoenix, but I decided I didn't want to reach out to him. And I'm in a good place, not only with that but also with my mom."

Cal raised an eyebrow. "A productive visit."

"It was. And your call? Was it productive?" she asked.

He didn't respond for several seconds. "My commander gave me his opinion of the job. He thinks I should take it. But he said that if I didn't, he'd be glad to hang on to me awhile longer until my next assignment." He paused again. "I told him I was thinking about this being the last assignment and that I was strongly considering getting out."

"And?" she prompted when she couldn't take the suspense of not knowing.

"And I also told him I was strongly considering staying in," Cal admitted.

There it was. All spelled out. Well, sort of. Cal still hadn't made up his mind, but just three and a half weeks ago, he'd been certain he would leave the military. Now that wasn't the case. While part of her, her blasted in-love heart, wanted to encourage him to stay, that might not be the right thing for Cal.

She needed to let him know he had an out with her if he wanted it.

"I do those pros-and-cons lists when I'm trying to make a decision," she said.

She motioned for him to follow her into her office, and she took out a pen and a notepad. Charlotte jotted down *Pros* for leaving the Air Force on one side of the page, and *Cons* on the other.

"Cons first," she started. "You don't get to save lives." She jotted that down.

His forehead bunched up, and he set his coffee aside, took the pen and under Cons, he scratched out her response and wrote *Someone else will get to save lives.* Under Pros, he made an addition. *Being near my family. And you.*

Oh, this was going to be hard, but she had to offer it. Had to. "You can have your family, me and the military. The family and I will be for just thirty days out of the year and the trips where we can travel to see you, but it's a way for you to have it all."

Cal immediately shook his head. "I can't ask you to do that. It's what you did for Noah."

Charlotte moved closer, slipped her arms around him and looked him straight in the eyes. She could say so many things. Like, what she felt for Noah had been a drop in the bucket compared to what she felt for Cal. Like, she could wait until he'd filled every spot on his bucket list as long as he came back to her in the end.

She could spell out that she would even go with him if it weren't for her obligations here. That would create a different kind of heart-crushing for her to leave Port in a Storm just when it'd gotten off the ground.

But Charlotte didn't say any of that.

Instead, she kissed him.

Yes, in some ways that was a cop-out, but it was an amazing one. Because this was Cal, and a kiss with him never felt wrong. Just the opposite. It couldn't have felt more right.

Or hotter.

That heat was instant, too. It came stampeding through her, and just like that the urgency followed it. Cal certainly felt the same way, because there was no resistance. He dove right into the kiss as if it were a *Goodbye* and a *Welcome home* all rolled into one.

Charlotte decided to go with that.

If this was goodbye sex, then she would make it count. She would make it memorable, which wouldn't be hard to do, because, hey. This was Cal. Memorable was the norm with him.

Unfortunately, even really amazing kisses didn't create finesse and good balance, because they stumbled and landed hard against her door. Charlotte was certain she would've seen stars from the pain that shot through her shoulder, but the heat had a way of taking care of such aches. The heat had a way of taking care of everything.

The finesse continued to take a hiatus. So did any slow, lingering foreplay. This was all fire, all speed. And yet the amazing factor was still there.

With the kisses raging on, she managed to get his shirt off. He managed to get hers off, and then his tongue kissing her neck caused the desperation to kick in. Need and desperation was a volatile mix, so she went for his zipper. He shoved up her skirt.

Somewhere in all the tongue kisses and franticness, they landed on her desk. Pens and paper clips bounced and pinged as they hit the floor. Charlotte ended up with her back on her closed laptop. Cal ended up on top of her. Again, no complaints from either of them, especially when Cal fumbled in his pocket and came out with a condom from his wallet. He'd kept his promise about keeping one there.

They put that condom to good use when he freed himself from his boxers and put it on. Then he pushed inside her. Coherent thoughts vanished, and Charlotte was all for that. All for the soaring pleasure. All for the way her body just accepted and gave. Until she and Cal could accept and give no more. Until they finished, the climaxes flashing through them and turning the incoherency into a beautiful, blissful haze.

Charlotte would have gladly stayed in that haze for at least a couple of minutes. Or at least until her breath stopped gusting, but there was an annoying sound cutting through her beauty and bliss. And it wasn't just one sound but two. Ringing and a vibrating rattle. It took her a moment to realize the sounds were coming from both her and Cal's phones.

That definitely couldn't be good.

Since he still had on his jeans, Cal was able to get to his phone first. "Alden," he relayed. And Charlotte was plenty close enough to Cal to hear what Alden said the moment Cal took the call.

"Cal, we've got trouble. Paul just showed up, and he's trying to take Harper."

CHAPTER TWENTY-TWO

CAL GOT OUT of the car before Charlotte had fully brought it to a stop because every second counted. They'd used her car to come to Port in a Storm since it would have eaten up precious time to hurry along the few blocks to his truck.

On the short drive, Cal hadn't been able to stop the worst-case scenarios from flying through his head. Paul was able-bodied; Harper wasn't. Neither was Alden, so unless one of the workers intervened, Cal knew it was possible that Paul had already taken Harper. But he might not have even had to do that with physical force since his bullying always worked just fine on her.

Cal cursed when he didn't see any workers' vehicles around. Cursed even more when he saw Izzie's car, since this definitely wasn't a good time for a visit. But at least Paul's truck was still parked out front, which meant he hadn't managed to leave with his daughter.

Charlotte was right on his heels when Cal bolted up the porch steps, ran through the open door and made a beeline toward Harper's room. He then had to come to a quick stop because of the crowd that had assembled.

No workers, but Becker was there, and he had positioned his wheelchair so that no one was getting in or out of this end of the hall. Maybell was at the other end, her rolling pin ready, and both she and Izzie were blocking that end. Harper was in the center of the barricades with Alden by her side and Paul right in her face. Literally. He had leaned down and was snarling at her. Cal couldn't hear exactly what the words were, but he was betting this wasn't some sort of praise.

"What's going on?" Cal asked.

Everyone except Paul and Harper had already looked in his and Charlotte's direction, and he was seeing a mixed bag of emotions. Becker and Maybell were pissed off and in a ready-to-rumble mode. Even Izzie had joined in and was staring Paul down. She was also holding up her phone, recording the incident. Alden was calm, but there was worry on every inch of his face.

"What's going on," Paul snarled, "is that I'm getting my daughter the hell out of here. She's being brainwashed, being turned against me, and I won't have it." He continued staring at Harper. "You know you've screwed up by coming here, don't you? You know I've always done what's best for you. Not these asswipes. Me." He jammed his thumb against his chest. "Me," he repeated.

Cal glanced around. "Has anyone called the cops?" he asked.

"No," Alden said on a sigh. "Harper told us not to."

"Every now and then, my daughter does something smart," Paul concluded. "No need to involve the law in this. It's a personal matter between me and Harper."

Beside him, Charlotte groaned, took out her phone and made a call to the sheriff's office. "You're on private property," she snarled. "So that personal matter doesn't just involve Harper and you but me and everyone else in this hall."

Everyone else grew by one because Jodi came down the stairs. She didn't have a weapon, but she looked more than ready to do whatever it took to bring this situation under control. Cal figured the control needed to start with Harper.

Cal threaded his way around Becker's wheelchair so he could get closer to Paul. "Harper?" Cal said. "Are you all right?"

He wanted to see her expression, wanted to see what was in her eyes. And it took a while for her to lift her head and meet his gaze.

Hell. She looked ready to cave. It was hard to undo thirty-six years of conditioning, and pretty much anything he said or did right now was a risk. Doing nothing, though, could be even worse. So he went with *something* and hoped for the best.

"Remember that competition in Germany last year?" Cal threw out there. "The one where you were leading the whole time, and I swooped in at the last minute to get to the simulated target just a breath ahead of you?"

Harper stared at him. And frowned. Cal considered that was a better expression than the kowtowing she'd been doing.

"The same thing happened in California two years ago," Cal went on. "Down to the wire. It could have gone either way."

"It didn't," Harper said, rasping out the words. "You won." She stopped. "Are you trying to piss me off?"

"Maybe," he admitted, "but I'm also trying to make you remember that we were the best of the best. Me and you. Yeah, I won, but so did you. You beat everyone else in the competition, and you did that over and over again."

"She lost every single competition," Paul interrupted, and he kept his attention fixed on Harper. "You're a loser, and if you don't want to stay one, then you need to come with me. I won't sugarcoat things. I won't tell you that being number two is something to brag about. I'll get your ass back in shape so you can be a winner."

"She is a winner," Alden insisted. "Harper's recovered far beyond even her own expectations."

Paul whipped around to face Alden. "And how the hell would you know that, when you've got *loser* written all over you? You're not some hero because you were stupid enough to step on some explosives that messed up your—"

He stopped when Harper latched on to his hand. It probably wasn't a hard grip, but it obviously managed to get Paul's attention.

"Don't," Harper warned him, and Cal was glad to see a tiny spark of fire in her eyes. He hadn't been able to light that fire with reminders of her being a damn good pilot. But Paul had lit it with his criticism of Alden.

"Don't?" Paul repeated. "What the hell do you mean by that?"

"I mean, hush and listen." Harper drilled her gaze into his. "You can say whatever you want about me, but you leave everybody else here out of it."

She paused a heartbeat, and her jaw tightened. It was obvious that speaking was painful, but she continued anyway.

"On second thought," she said, "I don't want you to

say anything else about me. I'll say it. I lost all those competitions. Cal has bested me my entire life. He did his best. But so did I."

Cal wanted to cheer. Apparently, so did Charlotte because she actually let out a loud whoop that earned her a scowl from Paul before he turned back to his daughter.

"Your best," Paul said, and he repeated it until he'd maxed out his mocking tone.

"Yes, my best," Harper asserted equally. It didn't cause Paul to back down any, though. Just the opposite: his face reddened with anger.

"I suppose you're gonna say it was my fault you're a loser," he snarled.

"No. It was mine for allowing you to push me the way you did," Harper said, and she looked at Cal. "I'm sorry for the tree-limb thing at the creek. And I'm sorry for blaming you in that note."

Cal had known that note was still weighing him down, but he hadn't known exactly how much until he felt some of that heaviness lift from his shoulders. He looked at Harper, and even though he didn't say a thank-you aloud, he was pretty sure she got the message because she nodded. Then she turned back to her father.

"This is the best I can do," Harper said, and even though her voice was hardly more than a whisper, it still packed an emotional punch. Well, it did for everyone except Paul, but Alden was certainly smiling.

The smile didn't last, though. Because Paul started up again. Apparently, the man wasn't giving up.

"Listen to you," Paul taunted, aiming that lethal glare at Harper. "This is your best? In a wheelchair, barely able to talk and with your head practically bald. If you wanted proof you're being brainwashed, then there it is. This isn't your best. I'm the only one who'll say it to your face. The only one, and there's nothing you can do about it, *loser*."

"No, but there's something I can do about it," Becker insisted, and his grouchy snarl matched Paul's. "I can ram this chair into your sorry ass."

Smirking, Paul turned toward Becker as if ready to take him on.

"And I can whack you on your numbskull head," Maybell piped in, testing out her rolling pin against her palm.

"I'm thinking a kick to the balls will do it," Izzie contributed. "If he actually has balls, that is. I doubt he does."

Of all the threats, Izzie's was the one that drew Paul's ire, and this time, he wasn't able to contain it. Especially because Izzie continued to bait him.

"No balls," she spewed. It seemed she had been storing up this particular tirade for a while. "I'm so tired of chickenshit men with a warped sense of self-importance. I was married to one of those, so I have no trouble recognizing one when I see him. No wonder your wife left."

Hell.

Paul started to move toward her. Cursing, Cal moved toward Paul, but he knew he wouldn't get there in time if Paul punched or rammed into Izzie, and since he was much larger than she was, he could hurt her.

Cal was still a couple of feet away when Paul lunged at Izzie. Even in heels, Izzie was fast, and she'd either had some kind of self-defense classes or she got lucky, because she landed a knee in Paul's crotch. The sound Paul made was like a deflating balloon, and he dropped to his knees, clutching his balls. Paul tried to curse her, but it came out as a wheeze.

Outside, there was the sound of approaching sirens, and Cal knew it wouldn't be long before Paul was arrested. And he would be. Even if Harper didn't file charges against him, Charlotte certainly would. Paul might try filing charges, too, but at least there were a lot of witnesses to say that Paul had gone after Izzie first and that she had merely defended herself.

Of course, that didn't tie up everything in a nice little bow.

This had to be eating away at Harper. Added to that, there were no guarantees that Paul wouldn't keep trying to bully her into doing his will.

"Anyone here got a permanent marker or a pen?" Harper asked.

The question surprised, well, everyone since Harper could use her tablet if she wanted to speak. Still, Izzie reached into her crossbody purse and came out with a pen. It was a promotional one with her campaign slogan on it. *The Best Choice for Emerald Creek. Vote for Izzie Wilson.*

When Izzie handed the pen to Harper, Cal moved closer. He didn't want Harper trying to stab her dad. With Paul temporarily incapacitated, Harper could almost certainly be charged with assault.

"See this?" Harper said, holding up the pen in front of Paul's glazed eyes. He was still trying to speak but was basically just making guttural sounds. "I want you to use it to block me out in the photos. Scribble me out the way you did my mother."

Cal thought of all the pictures he'd seen when he had visited Paul. And he smiled. Because this was indeed a good step for Harper.

It got even better.

Leaning forward, she slipped the pen into Paul's shirt pocket. "Use it to erase me from your sight. And your life." Harper leaned in even closer. "And when you're done erasing me, then I want you to shove this pen right up your ass."

CHAPTER TWENTY-THREE

CHARLOTTE SILENTLY GROANED when she glanced out into the reception area of her law office and saw yet someone else waiting. Velma Sue. The groan wasn't for Velma Sue per se, even though the woman did often elicit that response from Charlotte. No, she was reacting that way because this was her sixth visitor on a day when she only had two appointments scheduled.

Apparently, her legal services were in high demand.

She could thank her mother's rise in popularity over that. Izzie had posted her recorded encounter with Paul, and now she was basking in some hometown glory. Too bad that glory had spread to Charlotte and had spurred people to come in with some legal issues that were in some cases downright willy-nilly, all so they could get a firsthand account of Izzie's heroics and the incident that'd gone down at Port in a Storm three days ago.

Charlotte was proud of what her mother had done, and Izzie was thrilled because of her soaring popularity, which would likely get her reelected. But Charlotte was even prouder of Harper for finally standing up to her dad. So she'd accommodated her visitors and provided a firsthand account or two, but she had been far more interested in dealing with their legal concerns and sending them on their way.

That dismissal was what she'd been doing to Rose
Gonzales, who'd wanted Charlotte to go through her
mail to make sure she hadn't missed anything important in it. Rose hadn't. Well, unless coupons for grocer-
ies totaling over ten bucks was important. Even so, she
hadn't charged Rose and had thought with the woman's
exit she might finally get a chance to close up shop and
get out of there.

But there Velma Sue sat.

Charlotte gave another silent groan but had to admit
she would have had that reaction had she seen anyone but
Cal hanging around. Then she wouldn't have groaned,
but she might have been wary. After all, there were less
than forty-eight hours until his leave was up, and she was
expecting a goodbye from him anytime now.

"I explained to Velma Sue that you were busy today,"
Mandy said. She was at her desk, and there thankfully
wasn't a doll in sight. Izzie's fame might have helped
with that, too, since there'd been plenty of volunteers
who'd stepped up to transport the dolls to Frank.

"And I told Mandy I wouldn't be taking up much
of your time," Velma Sue was quick to counter. "I just
wanted to talk to you about these paper cuts."

This time, Charlotte wasn't able to bite off the sound,
and the groan happened aloud. Still, she would have
brought the woman into her office and heard her out if
it weren't for two things.

First, Charlotte got a text. From Cal. You busy?

Once she'd settled down the fluttering in her stomach and heart and had fired off the outright lie of No,
she spotted Harper.

Harper wasn't in her wheelchair but using a walker,

the one that Alden had rigged with the tennis balls for her. Alden and Jodi were with her, and they were heading into Desi's Diner.

Charlotte smiled. Progress. And she still intended to call it that, even though Harper was scowling some and Jodi looked ready to bolt. Still, they were going inside a diner, so that was a huge step.

"Heard Harper's daddy is disowning her," Velma Sue remarked, obviously noticing what had gotten a portion of Charlotte's attention. Another portion of her attention was waiting for a response from Cal.

Yes, that was true. In fact, one of her unscheduled clients was a phone call from Paul.

"All right, then," Velma Sue said when Charlotte didn't confirm or deny the disowning. "Are you ready for us to talk about the lawsuit for these paper cuts?"

The woman held up her right hand, and while there were some old marks and age spots, there didn't appear to be any recent scarring. Charlotte was about to remark on that when her phone dinged again, and she nearly smacked herself in the head when in her haste she hobbled it so she could read the text.

It was from Cal.

Good. Glad you're not busy. Want to meet me at the swimming hole at the creek where I fell out of the tree?

Charlotte had a split second to wonder why that spot, but she sent off another quick reply, a *yes*, and added Be there soon. Only then did she tamp down all the heat and glee that was rushing through her.

This could be it.

The dreaded "Goodbye, but I hope we can still be friends" conversation. She'd been steeling herself against it for days, and yet this still felt like a punch of surprise. There was also a lot of dread in the mix.

"I have to go," Charlotte said, glancing first at Velma Sue and Mandy. "Could you schedule an appointment for Velma Sue?"

"But I'm here now," the woman protested.

Charlotte didn't even pause at the protest, and she wished that putting the woman off like this would stop her from coming back. Sadly, it wouldn't.

Charlotte hurried to her car and started driving. With a good five miles to go, however, her split second of wonder returned and lingered. Since that particular spot by the creek was on Donnelly land, it was private, and it was possible Cal wanted that privacy to give her the crushing news. Of course, she wouldn't let him see her reaction. She'd plaster on a smile and would then give in to her emotions when he wasn't around. If this was indeed a *Goodbye* or a *Farewell for now*, she didn't want his parting memories to be of her breaking into a million little pieces.

Of course, she had no one to blame but herself for the potential breakdown. She'd known what she was getting into when she'd started this fling with Cal. Still, it felt as if at some point the decision to be with him had been taken out of her hands. Her heart and certain parts of her body had definitely been calling some of those shots.

She drove onto Saddlebrook, following the dirt road that led to the creek. This was sort of the dividing line for the ranch with fenced pastures with Angus cattle on one side and a pasture of Andalusian horses on the other. Not all the horses were pastured, however, since Ice Man was moseying by the creek helping himself to the spring grass there.

It was a beautiful scene worthy of a postcard, but there was an even more incredible scene.

A naked Cal.

Well, almost naked, anyway. He'd stripped down to his boxers so she had a great view of his body. All the toned and tanned parts of him. Of his incredible face, too.

He dived into the creek just as she came to a stop. He stayed under for a couple of seconds before his head surfaced. The water sheeted down his face.

And onto his smile.

That smile eased a lot of the knots in her stomach. Eased some of the pressure in her chest, too. But just because he was glad to see her didn't mean the next few minutes were going to have a happy ending.

"Why meet here?" she asked when she stepped from her car. She even managed a smile though she was certain hers was a lot more tentative than his. "Returning to the scene of the crime?"

"Something like that. This was the site of a big turning point for me. Almost dying. Doing that life-pact with Noah."

He didn't mention the part about Harper knowing the limb was unsteady, but that had played into it, too.

"I'm glad you were able to come," he added a moment later while he treaded water. "I heard you were awfully busy at work."

Of course he'd heard about that. Most of the people who'd come in to see her today were also big gossips.

Charlotte nodded. "I even had a call from Paul. When he asked me to do the paperwork to disown Harper, I declined. But I told him I was doing my own paperwork to adopt her."

Cal laughed. "Good one. Harper will get a kick out of that."

She agreed and thought Harper just might. So far, Harper had shown zero signs of taking back anything she'd said—or given—to Paul.

Charlotte walked closer to the water, slipped off her shoes and stuck in a toe to test the temperature. It was only slightly cooler than a swimming pool.

"Thinking about coming in?" he asked in that sexy drawl that caused some heat to start swirling inside her.

It was so tempting to give right into that heat, especially since this part of the creek offered a boatload of privacy because of the trees, but if there was going to be skinny-dipping, followed by sex, then she needed to get something out of the way first.

"I figured you'd asked me here to talk," she threw out there.

"Oh, I did," he was quick to assure her. He tipped his head to his clothes that he'd left in a pile by one of the large boulders. "And I wanted you to see those."

Since she doubted he was talking about his Levi's, she went closer and saw the pictures. There were six of them, all group shots of Cal winning various competitions. In these, Cal hadn't erased himself with a pen or marker. Instead, there were circles drawn around him. Highlighting him. And in each one of them he was smiling. He was celebrating.

He was happy.

No doubt about that, and her heart felt as if someone had clamped a fist around it. "I get it," she said. "You want that level of happiness again."

His smile dropped. His forehead rose. "Uh, not quite. In all of those pictures, I had just done my best. And gotten lucky," he quickly added. "I wasn't thinking about quitting but moving on to the next competition. Then, Harper nearly died, and that changed everything."

And just like that, her emotions flipped, and her heart ached not for herself but for him. Sometimes it was easy to forget the impact this had all had on him.

"Those pictures made me see I've been looking at this all wrong," he went on. "I was asking myself if I was too broken to go back to the cockpit. What I should have been asking myself is why I thought I was the only one who could do a job that's important...but not one I want."

Charlotte mentally repeated that and was processing it when Cal hoisted himself up out of the creek, walked to her and completely clouded her thought process by kissing her. He was all wet. And wonderful. So was the kiss, even though it wasn't a particularly long one. Still, it was a magic kiss because, unless she was totally off base with her interpretation, Cal wasn't taking the job.

"I don't expect Audrey to ever understand or approve, but that's on her, not me," Cal went on. And he kissed her again.

Charlotte was torn between just giving in to the heat and getting that creek sex or getting this all clarified. The kiss was quickly moving her to choose option number one, but then Cal stopped again, and he pointed to the tree. Yes, the very one he'd fallen out of when they were eight.

"I was thinking of climbing that," he said. "If I fall and bash my head on a rock, will you rescue me?"

"Of course, but don't fall out of it," she quickly added. "In fact, don't even climb it. We're not eight years old anymore."

He grinned at her, went to the tree and started the climb. Whatever point he was trying to make, she didn't approve.

Or so she thought.

But the moment he reached a tree limb that had grown big and strong just above the old broken one, Cal maneuvered out onto it. And then dropped into the water. Nowhere near the rocks but in the center of the creek. Water splashed up, dousing her and causing her to gasp.

Then causing her to laugh when Cal took off his boxers and threw them at her feet. "I think I need rescuing now," he said.

Charlotte stripped off her top and skirt, tossing them on the rock next to his stuff, and then she jumped in. Since this was a narrow spot, she made it to him in one leaping stroke. He caught onto her, pulling her to him, a moment before he dropped down under the water.

He resurfaced with her bra. The man certainly had fast hands.

"Now that you've saved me," he said, "I'd like to make a life-pact. I owe you, and you can ask me for anything, and I'll have to do it."

"Anything?" she asked.

"Anything," he verified.

"It's a biggie." And what she was about to say was a huge risk. "Don't run if I tell you I'm in love with you. Just accept it and understand you don't have to do anything about it. And you most certainly don't have to love me back."

She might have continued to ramble on. Blasted nerves. But he kissed her and made all those nerves go away.

"Don't run if I tell you I'm in love with you," he said. "Just accept it and understand that you don't have to do anything about—"

"I want you to do something about it," she interrupted, and she was reasonably sure her smile couldn't get any wider and her heart couldn't get any fuller.

She'd taken the risk and heard exactly what she'd wanted.

Cal was in love with her.

"What do you want me to do about it?" Cal asked in that tempting drawl that only he and Lucifer could have managed.

"Everything," Charlotte said, and she pulled him back to her to get started on doing just that.

* * * * *

If you missed the first two books in USA TODAY *bestselling author Delores Fossen's miniseries,*
Cowboy Brothers in Arms,
you'll find Heart Like a Cowboy *and*
Always a Maverick *wherever Canary Street Press books are sold!*